PEMBERLEY TO WATERLOO

Georgiana Darcy's Diary, Volume 2

THE *PRIDE AND PREJUDICE* CHRONICLES

Georgiana Darcy's Diary
Pemberley to Waterloo
Kitty Bennet's Diary

PEMBERLEY TO WATERLOO

Georgiana Darcy's Diary, Volume 2

ANNA ELLIOTT

with illustrations by Laura Masselos

a WILTON PRESS book

PEMBERLEY TO WATERLOO
Georgiana Darcy's Diary, Volume 2

This book is a work of fiction. Names, characters, places, and incidents either are products of the author's (or Jane Austen's) imagination or are used fictitiously. Any resemblance to actual events or locales or persons, living or dead, is entirely coincidental.

The cover incorporates a portrait of Rosamund Hester Elizabeth Croker painted in 1827 by Thomas Lawrence and the *Duchess of Richmond's Ball* painted in 1868 by Henry O'Neil as well as a letter in Jane Austen's own hand. The title font is *Exmouth* from PrimaFont Software, and the date entries and Georgiana's signature are set in Pia Frauss's *Jane Austen* font.

All sketches are by Laura Masselos and are used with permission.

Anna Elliott can be contacted at ae@AnnaElliottBooks.com. She would love to hear your comments.

ISBN-13: 978-0615636498
ISBN-10:   0615636497

 WILTON PRESS

for Jane Austen fans everywhere

AUTHOR'S NOTE

Pemberley to Waterloo is the sequel to *Georgiana Darcy's Diary*, the first book in the *Pride and Prejudice Chronicles* series. Thank you so much to all the readers out there who wrote to me, asking for more of Georgiana and Edward's story!

Pemberley to Waterloo can be read alone, but it does build on the events of *Georgiana Darcy's Diary*. For new readers, I will explain that these books were born of my love of all things *Pride and Prejudice*, and the character of Georgiana Darcy in particular. After (many, many, many) readings of *Pride and Prejudice*, Georgiana was the character whose fate I wondered about the most. And I always felt that she and Colonel Fitzwilliam belonged together. As I explained in the author's note to Volume 1, the modern reader may be surprised, since Georgiana and Colonel Fitzwilliam are cousins. But in Jane Austen's day, marriages between cousins were common—even to be encouraged. In fact, Jane Austen herself wrote about such romance in *Mansfield Park*: Fanny Price and Edmund Bertram are first cousins.

Georgiana Darcy's Diary, Volume 1 is the story of Edward Fitzwilliam and Georgiana discovering their love for each other. But—as you will see in *Pemberley to Waterloo*—they still have a long journey and a great many obstacles to overcome, including the threat of renewed war with France.

In writing Georgiana's experiences in Brussels during the Battle of Waterloo, I drew heavily on the period accounts of Charlotte A. Eaton, Magdalene De Lancey, and Juana Smith—three fascinating women, all of whom actually experienced the terror of being a few short miles away from the field of battle, just as Georgiana does.

Nick Foulkes' *Dancing into Battle: A Social History of the Battle of Waterloo* was also an invaluable resource.

It was an incredible privilege and a delight to live in my imagination inside the world of Jane Austen's *Pride and Prejudice*. And—as with Volume 1—*Pemberley to Waterloo* is meant as an entertainment only, written for readers who love Jane Austen's story as much as I do. I certainly would never compare my books or my writing style to the immortal Jane Austen's.

I am especially excited in *Pemberley to Waterloo* to be able to write that my incredibly talented friend Laura Masselos has provided all original drawings for the illustrations. Thank you, Laura! You truly brought Georgiana's love of drawing to life.

PEMBERLEY TO WATERLOO

Wednesday 21 June 1815

I'm writing this on the inside cover of my diary. Which means that the rest of my entry may be entirely illegible. There's barely space for a tenth of what I wish I could write—and besides, the cover was dampened by seawater on the journey here, so that it's still slightly bent and smells of old seaweed.

There's no other paper to be had. Half the shops in Brussels are still closed, since the shopkeepers fled to Antwerp or further with everyone else, and are only now beginning to trickle back. I've no other blank writing books with me—and we've used up all the writing paper in our house to take down letters for the wounded men in our care. They're all desperate to send word to their families back in England. Assurances that they are alive and expected to recover and return home. Or in the saddest cases, bidding their loved ones good-bye.

I wrote one of those letters just this morning. For an Irish rifleman who was shot in the stomach and has been slowly dying of the wound for the last three days. He's so young—younger than I am, and I'm nineteen. Or rather, he *was* so young. He died this morning, just after dictating his words to me, addressed to the girl he'd been engaged to marry. His face was stark, livid with pain, and his lips were so dry they were cracking because the surgeon said that with a wound like his, he mustn't be allowed to drink.

But he whispered his message to me, telling his betrothed how much he loved her—and that his last wish was that she go on living without him, make a life for herself, marry another man. Be happy. He said she was too young to be lonely for the rest of her life.

And then he died.

That's really why I'm writing this—hoping that it will help me put the memory of it somewhere I can bear to keep it. Just now, I feel as though I could cry for days—except that if I once let myself start, I would not be able to stop.

This entry will make quite a prologue to the first proper entries in this diary, which, flipping through, I can see are mostly an account of our Christmas at Pemberley.

That seems so far removed and unreal now that even glancing at what I wrote all those months ago is like reading a novel, or looking through a window into another life. And poor Kitty—I'm so sorry for everything I wrote about her now.

I feel as though we've been trapped in Brussels for an eternity, feeling the noise from the city outside beat on the walls of the Forsters' house like a physical force. First the artillery fire from the fighting at *Quatre Bras*. Then the thunder and rain on the night before the battle at Waterloo. The cries and alarms from the street during the following endless day and night, when every moment it seemed brought another report that all was lost, that Wellington's troops had been defeated and the French armies would be pillaging the city by dawn.

Now even the wild celebrations of our army's victory have died down. But still the city is not quiet; it is filled with the rumble of carts carrying the dead and dying. The groans of the wounded. There are so many wounded soldiers that hundreds of them are lying in the streets on whatever beds of straw can be thrown down for them.

Even the Duke of Wellington—who was in the thick of fighting throughout the battle, but by miracle came through it without even the slightest wound—is sad and downcast, so they say. Napoleon has been defeated, finally and completely—but at what heavy a cost.

And I have had no word of Edward. No word of whether he is alive . . . or prisoner . . . or—

Edward would have been in the thick of the battle, too. I know him well enough to be certain of it. And he was one of Wellington's aides-de-camp.

The last report we had was that before the French turned tail and fled, they killed all the British officers they had taken prisoner.

I keep thinking that if Edward were killed, some part of me would *know*. I have turned the ring on my finger round and round a thousand times, feeling as though the emerald would have split—or *something*—if he had been killed. That I would—must—feel something myself. But would I?

I have said prayers for Edward's safety every moment of every day. *Please, please let him be alive, let him come back home to me, and I'll—*

But then I always stop short. Any clergyman would probably tell me it is bordering on the heretical to try to bargain with God. But I would—I'd do it in a heartbeat, if only I could think of anything to offer up against Edward's life.

But what do I have to bargain with? What exactly does one offer an omnipotent Divinity?

And besides, other women have said those same prayers. I have nothing, really—no possible assurance or guarantee that in the midst of so much death, my love should have been one of the few to survive.

BOOK I

Sunday 18 December 1814

If I hear the word 'beau' one single time more, I am perfectly convinced that I am going to scream.

To think that a mere three weeks ago, I did not even know the meaning of the term. Of course, anyone who has spent any time in London has heard of the famous Beau Brummell, the ultimate arbiter of men's fashion—or so it's said in all the circles of high society that Mr. Brummell still frequents, despite his quarrel with the Prince Regent. But I had never heard the word used as a simple descriptor. As for example: *There were a vast number of smart beaux at the party last night.*

Or, *Oh, if only Mr. Norton were not engaged to that horrid, freckled Miss Price, I think he would be quite a beau.*

Or, *Mr. Osborne tried to kiss me under the mistletoe last night, wasn't it shocking? But he is such a beau that I gave him my hand to kiss to show we were still friends.*

Or any of the other several dozen uses of the term I have heard from Kitty this morning alone.

Kitty of course is Kitty Bennet, Elizabeth's younger sister, who has come to stay with us here at Pemberley for the Christmas holiday.

This year our Christmas celebrations will be very quiet, since Elizabeth is so close to her confinement and naturally cannot travel or go out very much. But our neighbours, Mr. and Mrs. Herron have their granddaughter Maria here on a visit. The Herrons are an older couple, Mrs. Herron plump and comfortable, Mr. Herron devoted to sport and still wearing an old-fashioned powdered wig. But they are both very kind and love to have young faces about them. This last fortnight, they have been organising almost nightly supper parties and dances for Miss Maria's amusement—and Kitty has been to them all.

And I am probably being unkind writing of her this way. As well as Kitty, we also have Thomas and Jack Gardiner here for the holiday. They are Elizabeth's nephews, the children of her Aunt and Uncle Gardiner. Thomas is five and Jack is nearly seven. And they've come to Pemberley because Mr. Gardiner's mother has been very ill, and has come to stay with the Gardiners for a time. She is, it seems, in need of complete quiet and rest. And, as Mrs. Gardiner wrote Elizabeth, 'complete quiet,' is more or less an impossible dream with four children under the age of ten in the house.

Thomas and Jack also have two older sisters, Anna and Charlotte; they've gone to stay with Elizabeth's sister Jane.

Part of the reason Kitty came here was to help with looking after the boys, because Elizabeth *is* so near her time. She thinks the baby will be born by the end of the month, so just two weeks at the most, and really it could be any day now at all. And of course Thomas and Jack scarcely know me. They've only come to Pemberley with their parents once, and I was on a duty-visit then to stay with Aunt de Bourgh.

Elizabeth thought a familiar face would help—and Kitty is very, very good with them. Poor boys, they were so homesick right at first for their mother and father, and wishing they could be in their own home for Christmas. Kitty plays spillikins and hide-the-slipper with them all day long, and she's been working tirelessly on Christmas preparations for them: cutting up paper stars and angels for decorations, speaking to Mrs. Reynolds our housekeeper about having bullet pudding and snapdragons and all the other traditional children's Christmas games. Of course I have helped, but it has all been Kitty's ideas first and foremost.

It's just that for all her endless talk of 'beaux' and dancing and parties, Kitty is already engaged to a perfectly nice young man of her own. Her betrothed, John Ayres, is a captain in Edward's regiment. I've never met Captain Ayres, but Edward speaks of him as a good soldier and a good man, sober and responsible and kindhearted, as well. And Elizabeth has met him once and says that she liked him very much indeed.

Elizabeth is worried about Kitty. Or rather, what she said to me this morning was, "I'm not entirely sure whether to hope Captain Ayres never hears of Kitty's behaviour—or to hope he does."

No fewer than seven notes had just arrived for Kitty by the first post, and she'd read them all one after the other, giggled, made a show of putting them away in her reticule . . . looked hopefully at me and Elizabeth as though wishing we would ask her what was in them . . . and then left, still giggling, to take Thomas and Jack outside to play.

Elizabeth and I were left alone in the morning room. I was painting a rendition of a pirate ship's flag that I'd promised to Jack for one of their games, and Elizabeth was lying on the couch looking cross. Or rather, as cross as it's possible for Elizabeth to look, which is not very.

Elizabeth is so active and vivacious that she's not used to having to be quiet so much of the time, having to lie on the sofa and rest in the afternoons or stop to catch her breath climbing stairs. The other day I asked how she was feeling—and she made a face at me and said, "Like an over-stuffed goose in a *much* too small oven." But then she smiled and put her hand over the swelling mound of her stomach, and I saw the fabric of her dress move as the baby kicked hard in response.

We both laughed, then, and Elizabeth said that the baby must be as anxious to be born as she was to have it *be* born.

This morning, though, she was frowning as she looked through the window to where we could see Kitty and the two boys playing chase up and down the paths in the winter-frozen garden. Kitty has dark hair like Elizabeth's, but where Elizabeth's hair curls, Kitty's is perfectly straight—unless she tortures it into ringlets with the curling iron—and her eyes are hazel instead of Elizabeth's brown. But I can see the resemblance between them; their faces are the same shape, and they both have the same creamy-pale skin. Kitty isn't as lovely as Elizabeth, perhaps, but she's very pretty even still, and so high-spirited and ready to laugh that I can see why the young men flock round her so.

I watched her make a jump at Jack from behind a mulberry bush, sending him shrieking with laughter off down another path, then said to Elizabeth, "Do you mean you hope that Captain Ayres may break off the engagement if he hears of Kitty flirting with other men?"

Elizabeth sighed and shifted and rubbed her lower back as though it ached. "It is a horrible thing to say about my own sister, isn't it? But maybe I do, a little. It's just that Captain Ayres is . . . good. Good and earnest and a little shy. When I met him, I thought he was an unlikely choice for Kitty to have made—I would never have expected her to find him anything but dull, much less accept a proposal from him. But I thought it showed that perhaps she had more good sense than—" Elizabeth stopped, her mouth twisting into a small, wry smile. "More good sense than I'd given her credit for, though that is more or less a horrible thing to say about my own sister, too. But I thought Captain Ayres might . . . might be a steadying influence on her. That maybe his earnest good-sense was exactly what she needed." Elizabeth looked out into the garden and sighed again. "And maybe it still is. The trouble is that Kitty doesn't seem to think it so. If Captain Ayres hears of how Kitty has been behaving, he'll be hurt—maybe heartbroken. He truly does love her, I think. But even still, that might be better than if he actually marries her, and finds he has absolutely nothing in common with his wife."

Elizabeth's eyes went distant and pensive, and I knew she was thinking of her and Kitty's own parents. I have met them, of course, and Elizabeth has spoken of them enough to me that I know theirs has not been the happiest of marriages. Mr. Bennet is a rather reserved, scholarly man, with a dry sense of humour and a sometimes sarcastic tongue. And Mrs. Bennet is . . . well, when she was young, she may well have been very much like Kitty. Though from what Elizabeth has said, I think without Kitty's genuinely affectionate heart.

"Have you tried speaking to Kitty about it?" I asked.

Elizabeth nodded, her eyes on the garden. "All she does is roll her eyes at me and say that she's engaged, not dead and buried. And that she means to keep on enjoying herself as much as she possibly can for as long as she can, before she has to resign herself to all the dull duties of being someone's wife." Elizabeth let out her breath. "And if I scold her too much—or refuse to let her go out to the Herrons' parties—she's likely to leave Pemberley altogether. She'll either go back to our parents, or she'll go to Lydia, which will be even worse." Elizabeth rubbed her back again. "Every time I debate the question with myself, I come to the conclusion that letting her stay is the only way of preventing her from getting into even worse trouble than she's likely to get into here. If only it weren't for—" she stopped abruptly.

However she feels, Elizabeth looks just as lovely as ever. Her face fairly glows. And her dark eyes have always been bright with laughter, but all these last months there has been a kind of deep, quiet happiness to them, as well, even when the baby has made her uncomfortable or ill.

This morning she was wearing a morning dress of peach- and white-striped percale, with a lace cap perched on her dark curls. But she looked tired, I realised all at once, with faint bruise-like shadows under her eyes. And when she fell silent, she looked, not back at Kitty and the boys out in the garden, but down at her own two hands, resting in her lap.

I hesitated another moment—and added a few more streaks of white paint to the skull-and-crossbones design I was painting onto the black background of the boys' flag—then asked her, "Elizabeth, is there something . . . something wrong? Besides Kitty, I mean?"

I thought perhaps that she'd be worrying about the birth. Because women do die in child-bed.

I hate writing that—I hate even thinking that. But that is how my own mother died. And the baby—the baby that would have been my younger brother—died, as well.

I can't imagine Pemberley without Elizabeth here, for all she has only been married to my brother these two years.

I thought Elizabeth might have been about to say something—to ask me something, perhaps—because she looked over at me and drew in her breath. But then she seemed to change her mind. She shook her head and said, instead, "Nothing—except perhaps that I'm beginning to feel as though this child has decided never to be born at all." She smiled. There was just a faint edge of strain in the smile, I thought. And then she said, "I had a letter from Darcy this morning. I know he's to arrive this afternoon with Edward—but he must have posted the letter when he was still in town. He wrote that he happened to run across Caroline while in London. And since she was at a loose end for the holiday season, he's invited her here."

"Caroline? Caroline *Bingley*?" I looked at Elizabeth in disbelief. Because after what happened last spring, I should have thought Pemberley the last place on earth Caroline would wish to be.

Elizabeth got awkwardly to her feet, and seemed very focused on rearranging a vase of flowers as she nodded. "Yes. She's not coming with Darcy and Edward. Apparently she had some engagements in town. But Darcy says she'll be here in a few days' time."

And then she came over to the table I was working on and hugged me and said, "And you are now officially released from listening to my moaning—you can go and sit by the window and watch the approach to the house for signs of Edward's arrival—as I know you must have been longing to do all morning long."

Later . . .

I only have a moment to write this; the gong for dinner will be rung soon, and then I'll have to go downstairs. But Edward has finally arrived. And everything is all right, it really is.

I hadn't even realised I was going to write that until I saw the words forming on the page; it doesn't at first glance seem to make any sense. But as silly as it sounds,

I was nervous of meeting Edward again.

I've known Edward all my life, of course. But somehow now that we are engaged to be married, it seems as though he is someone else entirely to me. Which in a way he is, really: a lover, not just a friend.

I should be grateful, I know, that Napoleon was defeated last year and exiled to the Isle of Elba—which means that the seemingly endless war between our two nations is finally, finally at an end.

But Edward is still a colonel in the army, and his regiment has been posted to Ireland these last months. Which I should be grateful for, too—grateful that Edward is with the cavalry and not the infantry. Because so many regiments of the infantry have now been sent off to fight the war against the American colonies.

Still, Edward being posted to Ireland makes his travelling to Pemberley almost as difficult as it would be from France—and that in turn is why I've only seen him twice before this in the last half year.

We've written letters, of course—at least it is permissible for us to correspond, now that we are betrothed. But it's not the same as being with him. And each time we've been apart and it turns into weeks and then months since I have last seen him, I have started to feel as though . . . as though I must surely have just imagined his falling in love with me.

Edward is ten years older than I am, which makes him nine-and-twenty this year. And I've been in love with him since I was six years old. Hopelessly in love, I always thought—because it seemed to me I stood a greater chance of being struck by lightning than ever hearing Edward say that he loved me in return.

And then, too, it occurred to me that our whole relationship has changed. And to worry that perhaps I wouldn't have anything to say to Edward-the-lover. I scarcely ever have my old childhood attacks of freezing shyness anymore. But waiting for Edward's arrival this morning, thinking about seeing him again at last, I could feel one coming on. I kept thinking how awful it would be if he came and we were stiff and awkward with each other, instead of easy and friendly as we've always been.

I kept playing horrible scenarios over and over in my mind in which we talked to each other like over-polite strangers at a dinner table.

Terribly cold weather we're having, isn't it?

Yes, but if it stays so, we may have a white Christmas after all.

But everything is all right. Better than all right.

Edward rode up to the house just before dinner time. My brother was with him. I suppose I should have explained before that Edward wrote a few weeks ago to say that he had business in London, and then would travel from there on to Pemberley for Christmas. And since Fitzwilliam also had business to conduct in regards our family's London property, he rode out a week ago with the plan of meeting Edward in town, settling their business, and then travelling back together.

When they arrived, Elizabeth had finished her conversation with Mrs. Reynolds and come to sit with me, so we went out to meet them together. It was then I realised fully how nervous I was of seeing Edward, because my heart was pounding, and I didn't even mind keeping to Elizabeth's slower pace as we walked out to the drive, where some of the stablehands had come out to take Edward's and Fitzwilliam's horses.

The air was thickening with the shadows of twilight, the sun sets so early in the winter time. Despite the cold, it hasn't snowed yet, and the landscape looked frozen and barren, drained of all colour in the gathering dusk. Even the Pemberley woods looked a little desolate, stark, treeless branches reaching towards an iron-grey sky.

Edward was just swinging himself down from the saddle when Elizabeth and I came out. He was wearing riding breeches and boots and a dark-green greatcoat instead of his army uniform. And for a brief instant I did feel . . . not that he was a stranger, not exactly. Edward could never be a stranger to me, and I know his face so well I could draw it from memory: the lean hard-cut lines of his nose and jaw, dark-brown eyes set deep under straight dark brows. The white line of a scar running down one cheek, a relic of the fighting he saw last year in France.

But just for an instant, it did seem suddenly unreal. Too much to believe that seven months ago Edward really *did* tell me he loves me. That we'll be married by the end of this coming summer, just a few short months away.

But then Edward saw me, and his whole face changed. Edward has always been one of those who can talk to anyone—and make practically anyone into a friend, even on just a few hours' acquaintance. He's so very relaxed and easy in company and so self-assured, without being in the least egotistical or vain. But when he saw me today, he smiled and his eyes lighted up—that sounds like a novelist's figure of speech, but they really did. And yet if I hadn't believed I would never write the words *shy* and *Edward* together in a single sentence, I should have said that that was how he looked. Suddenly uncertain, almost shy.

His hair is a little longer than when last I saw him, and he looks a little tired, I suppose from the travel.

And even at a distance, I could see the love and longing in his lean face. But he went still a moment, his hands on his horse's reins—and that was when I realised he must have been nervous of this meeting, too.

The gong has just rung, which means I do have to go down. But I'll write this last part, because it's so clear in my memory now and I want to capture it here so that I can remember it always.

I heard myself say, "Edward!" And then I felt laughter bubble up inside me, where the clenched knot of worry had been before. I'm not sure who moved first, but all at once his arms were around me and he was swinging me up and off the ground, the muscles of his chest and shoulder solid and strong under my cheek. His voice had gone husky and he whispered into my hair, "God, it's good—it's so good to see you again."

Monday 19 December 1814

Did I say everything was all right? I only wish it were.

Last night was . . . perfect. So perfect that it hurts in a way to remember it now. Still, I'll write it all down—if only to remind myself of how things *can* be between Edward and me. At least I hope they can. Even if at the moment I don't see how.

Edward and I were seated next to each other at dinner. I could scarcely eat anything, though. I kept looking sideways at Edward and feeling . . . feeling as though I'd stepped through a door from winter into a summer's day.

That also sounds like a novelist's exaggeration, I suppose. But even if the fighting in France has ended, there's still a part of me that's been afraid all the time Edward has been away. There can be trouble anywhere—

and in Ireland especially, where there's constantly the threat of another uprising like the one just over fifteen years ago. And wherever there's trouble, the army can be called in to fight, just as they have been in the past.

Finally Edward looked at me and smiled, his dark eyes crinkling at the corners. "You know, keep looking at me that way, and I'm going to start thinking that you're glad to see me again."

I laughed. "Oh, well, that won't do at all. Give me a moment to shift my chair and I'll turn my back so that I can ignore you properly. Then you can try to persuade me into marrying you all over again."

After dinner, Kitty went upstairs to the nursery to help with putting Jack and Thomas to bed. Fitzwilliam said he had some letters to write, and so went to his study. And Elizabeth looked exhausted and said she was going up to lie down herself. Though she laughed and kissed my cheek as she went out and said that at least the baby saved her the trouble of *pretending* to be too tired to stay downstairs with Edward and me.

So Edward and I were left alone in the parlour. We spoke of—

Come to think of it, I have no idea what we spoke of. Though I suppose I must have asked him about his journey from London. We were standing together in front of the warm glow of the hearth. The firelight was casting a patchwork of shadows over Edward's lean face—and every part of me wanted to reach out towards him and touch his cheek, run my fingers through his hair. But I was feeling . . . if not quite shy, at least still a little unfamiliar with the Edward standing before me— the Edward who isn't just my guardian any longer, but the man who'll be my husband in a few months' time.

But then—I can't even remember whether Edward

said anything, or whether he only reached out and took my hand. I felt the warmth of the touch run through me like the glow of the fire. Though all Edward really did was pull me down with him to sit on the hearthrug, wrapping his arms around me so that I was sitting facing the fire and leaning against his chest, the back of my head resting against his collarbone. He'd taken off his dinner jacket, and I could feel the steady beat of his heart, the rise and fall of his chest as he breathed.

I have no idea how long we sat like that, either. That was something else I'd worried over—that Edward and I wouldn't be able to sit and just be *quiet* together as we always had before, neither of us feeling as though we had to say a word if we didn't want to.

I could have stayed there all night. But then Edward let out a long breath and said, "I'm sorry, I'm not being very good company—I must be boring you to tears."

I was so astonished I pulled away to look up at him. "*Boring* me? This is—" All of a sudden I felt a lump come into my throat. Because none of the things I'd been afraid of for Edward had happened. He was really, truly here, alive and safe.

I did reach out and touch Edward's cheek then, tracing the line of the old scar. "I'd be happy to go and sit outside in a mud puddle in the middle of a thunderstorm if it meant I got to be with you like this again."

Edward is always so easy-mannered and self-assured that it's not often I've seen him look utterly caught off-guard. But complete and total surprise flashed across his features then. It made him look all at once a little vulnerable, and younger, for all the battle scars and the fine network of lines about the corners of his eyes.

But then he grinned and said, "You do realise you're setting a low standard if I'm supposed to be persuading you into marrying me all over again?"

I laughed. "Well, I suppose you could try kissing me. Just to prove to me that you haven't entirely forgotten how."

Edward was still smiling, but the smile changed somehow. "Oh, could I?" One of his hands slid slowly up my arm, and his fingers brushed along my neck. Just the lightest touch, but it still felt as though flames were spreading outwards, kindling every nerve. Edward bent his head and touched his lips to mine—and I felt as though time had frozen, as though the whole world had narrowed to the warmth of Edward's kiss, the salt smell of his skin, the blood racing through my veins, the sound of his voice, husky again, as he said my name and pulled me into his arms.

When we finally drew apart, I felt as though all the air had gone from my lungs. But I managed to catch my breath enough to smile up at him and say, "Do you know, I don't think I'm entirely persuaded yet. You'll just have to try again."

I suppose I can't exactly be surprised that writing all that down has made the thought of recounting what happened this morning hurt even more.

Today *began* well. When I came down to breakfast this morning, Mrs. Reynolds took one look at me, shook her head, and said it was tempting Providence to look so pleased with life. But then she patted my cheek and said, "Ah, well, I was young once, too, child. And it's good to see Mr. Edward himself again, and not so thin and worn-looking as he was when he came back from fighting that nasty Frenchman last year."

Edward has spent the last ten years serving in Sir

Arthur Wellesley—now the Duke of Wellington's—army. He fought in the campaigns in Portugal and Spain. And this past spring, he was wounded at the Battle of Toulouse. I suppose no man can live for ten years amidst all the blood and death of the battlefield and not return home changed. Not that Edward has ever spoken to me very much of the things he saw and did while at war. Only bits and pieces. But even the scraps he's sometimes let slip are enough for me to guess at the whole.

Last spring, when he came home from France, Edward was suffering from nightmares. And he couldn't be in crowds or hear loud noises without it bringing back his memories of battle. I still remember the way his muscles would tense as he tried to stop his hands from shaking, even at a casual after-dinner dance.

Still, part of me would very much love to see the former Emperor Napoleon's face if he could ever hear himself being described as 'that nasty Frenchman' in Mrs. Reynolds's broad country tones.

But I haven't yet said what happened today. Which began when I came down this morning, and found Edward and Fitzwilliam had already breakfasted early and gone out to make a tour of the estate and the tenant farms. My brother always likes to do that after he's been away, even for a short time. And then of course there are the charity gifts to the poor for Christmas to be delivered this year—to spare Elizabeth the worry and bustle of having crowds of people coming up to the house. Elizabeth was still upstairs in bed—she often feels ill in the mornings, even still—and Kitty had taken the boys out for a walk. All of which meant that I was alone when Mr. Folliet called.

To be proper, I should call Mr. Folliet the Earl of

Cantrell, for he succeeded to the title earlier this year. But he was Mr. Folliet when I met him last spring, and I suppose that's how I think of him, still.

He'd sent no word, so we'd not expected to see him at all; I should have expected him to be at his estate, which is in Hertfordshire, or in London for the Season. So it was an utter surprise when Thompson, our butler, came into the music room where I was playing the pianoforte and announced that Lord Cantrell had come to call, and was waiting in the morning room.

"Lord Cantrell, what a nice surprise," I said when I came into the room. And it truly was. Despite Lord Cantrell's having been one of the suitors my Aunt de Bourgh tried to fling at my head last year, I've always liked him very much indeed.

He rose to greet me and took the hand I'd offered.

Lord Cantrell is the type of young man Kitty would certainly describe as a beau. He's very handsome—really, one of the handsomest men I've ever seen, with classically portioned features, dark eyes, and waving dark hair. And he dresses very well without being in the least foppish—snowy-white cravats, well-tailored coats, gleamingly polished Hessian boots.

It's quite lucky for him that Kitty wasn't home when he came to call. Though I'm one of the very few people who knows how pointless her trying to flirt with him would be.

This morning I thought he looked thinner, and more sober than he had when last I saw him. But he bowed and then gave me the ghost of his old, flashing grin. "Do you think you could possibly manage *Hugh*? *Lord Cantrell* always starts me looking over my shoulder for my grandfather. And I've spent the last six months almost exclusively on the estate, where everyone *my*

Lord's me every other word. It's been so long since anyone's called me by my Christian name that I can scarcely remember how it sounds."

It's strictly speaking an utterly improper request, asking me to call an unmarried gentleman by his Christian name. But he was my only confidant last year when I was so in love with Edward but *believed* him engaged to another girl. And I am one of the very few people to know that Kitty would never get anywhere by flirting with Lord Cantrell. Not because she's frivolous and silly. But simply because she's a girl.

So I smiled in return and nodded. "All right. Hugh, then." And then I sobered. "I heard about your grandfather. I am so very sorry."

Hugh nodded and bowed his head. "Thank you." His grandfather, who raised him from a boy, was an old man, and ailing for some time. But it was just this past August that I heard he had finally died. Hugh lifted his head. "That's why I've come. To deliver something that my grandfather wished to be given to you."

"To me?" I was completely startled for an instant. But then I remembered what I'd told Hugh six months before: The old earl's final wish had been to see his grandson happily married, or at least engaged. Not knowing how utterly unlikely that wish was to be fulfilled.

What Hugh actually said when he spoke to me of it last spring was that he'd meant to tell his grandfather the truth. But then the old earl's health began to fail. And after that, Hugh didn't dare tell him. The shock might have been enough to kill him outright. And besides that, dying as he was, the earl would never have had time to grow accustomed to the news—to accept it, if he could. He'd only have died angry and bitterly disappointed in the boy he'd raised almost as a son.

And yet he so much wished, before he died, to know that his grandson would marry and have a family of his own. So seven months ago, I told Hugh that he had my free and full permission to tell his grandfather that he was engaged to me.

"Here." Hugh dug in the pocket of his waistcoat and came out with a small, paper-wrapped parcel. "It was my grandmother's. My grandfather said"—he stopped and cleared his throat—"that it would have given her great happiness to know it would one day be worn by my bride."

There were no strings tying the parcel, so when he handed it across to me the paper fell open to reveal a necklace, made of diamonds, set in a pattern of silver filigree to form the tiny leaves and flowers of some delicate climbing vine.

I drew in my breath and started to shake my head. "I can't possibly accept—"

Hugh stopped me. We had sat down on chairs opposite one another, and he leaned a little towards me, his hands loosely clasped between his bent knees and his dark eyes intent on mine. "Please. Take it. You gave the old man . . . you gave him very great happiness, letting him think we were engaged. He had known your mother, when she was a small girl. He and your mother's father were old friends. My grandfather was . . . his wits wandered a good deal, towards the end. And for the last two months he was entirely confined to his bed. But he would sometimes be aware enough to recognise me. And he told me several times that I'd done well to"—Hugh pushed a hand through his hair and had to clear his throat again—"to win your hand. He wanted you to have the necklace. As do I."

For a moment, he looked so sad that my chest ached for him, wondering what it must be like to have to keep part of yourself always hidden, even from those you love best in the world. On impulse, I reached forwards and touched Hugh's hand. "I'm so truly sorry," I said again.

Hugh squeezed my hand in return. But then he looked up and said with a gleam of his old smile, "And just at the very end, my grandfather was himself enough to say that he wished he might have met you—but that he promised to come back and haunt me if I ever let you down. So you see, you really have no choice but to take the necklace. You don't want to be responsible for my grandfather's uneasy spirit rising from the grave."

I laughed at that. "Well, in that case, thank you. I'll wear it and think of him—and of you."

It was at that precise moment that—apparently sent by the god of social awkwardness, if there is such a one—Edward walked into the room.

I felt myself jump—and Edward stopped dead just inside the door, his straight dark brows shooting halfway up to his hairline.

Not that I could in all fairness entirely blame him. He had only arrived the night before. And this morning, the first he sees me, I'm alone with a handsome man, holding his hand and accepting an obviously very expensive gift of jewellery.

"Edward," I said quickly. "You remember Lord Cantrell. You met him here at Pemberley last spring." I got up and crossed to Edward and took hold of his arm. It was like holding onto a marble statue, his muscles were so tensed, and I tightened my grip, afraid—

I'm not sure *what* I was afraid of exactly. It's not as though I truly believed that Edward might take one look at Hugh and challenge him to a duel with pistols on the spot. But I suppose I was afraid that Edward might lose his temper.

He didn't, though. The muscles under my hand were still tight and hard as stone. But he didn't move or try to pull away, only nodded and greeted Hugh with painstaking courtesy. I'm not sure anyone who didn't know Edward well would even have been able to tell he was angry.

Hugh had risen to his feet, as well, and returned Edward's greeting. A little warily, I thought. Though I couldn't in all fairness blame Hugh, either, since the last time the two of them met, Edward—mistaking him for someone else—had punched him in the face.

And then Hugh said that he must go, he was expected at a house party near York, and must journey on directly if he was to arrive in time.

Since I do know Edward, and I *could* tell that he was angry, I didn't argue or press Hugh to stay, only said that I would see him to the door. I half expected Edward to move or make some protest when I let go of his arm, but he didn't, only stayed stock-still where he'd been.

Hugh was silent, too, as we walked together back into the entrance hall and to the front door where Thompson was waiting with Hugh's hat and greatcoat. Then Hugh bowed, though he didn't take my hand. "Thank you again. With all my heart." He looked up at me, dark eyes once more earnest and intent. "And please if there is any way I may be of service to you, you have only to ask."

When I went back to the drawing room, Edward had crossed to where the diamond necklace had slipped down to lie on the cushions of the chair I'd been sitting in. He was motionless again, standing and looking down at the jewels with an expression I couldn't read at all on his face.

"Edward." My heart was beating quickly, but only because I wanted to have the explanations over with as quickly as possible—and because I was sorry I'd caused Edward even a moment's unease. "The necklace—it's not from Lord Cantrell. He was only delivering it. It's a gift—a bequest, rather—from his late grandfather."

Edward looked up. "A bequest from his grandfather," he repeated. His brows had risen again, but that was the only show of expression on his face, and his voice was curiously flat. He looked at me, his eyes, too, still unreadable. And then he said, "Why?"

"Because—" and then I stopped dead. It was only then that I realised I *couldn't* explain. Not without Hugh's permission. He scarcely knows Edward. And besides that, according to the law, men like Hugh are criminals, and treated as such—jailed, even sometimes hanged. "I . . . I can't tell you," I finally said. "Not because I don't want to, but because it involves a story that isn't mine to tell."

"You can't tell me." Edward's voice was still flat, deadly calm, and his expression was so completely impassive and controlled—so utterly unlike his usual one—that I felt suddenly afraid. And suddenly angry, as well—because I couldn't even tell whether he believed me or no.

"No, I can't," I said. "But I told you last spring when you asked that I have never been in the least in love with Lord Cantrell, nor he with me. Do you think I lied to you? Do you honestly know me so little that you think there might be something improper between Lord Cantrell and me now?"

Edward closed his eyes briefly, raising one hand to

brace his fingers against the space between his eyes. It was only then that I saw the fine tremor running through his arm, making his hand shake slightly, and the slight tick of a muscle in his jaw. Something I'd not seen since last spring, when he first came back from the fighting in France, and his nerves were so much damaged by all the death and destruction he'd seen.

And all at once, all the little signs from the night before seemed to fall into place. The shadows under his eyes—even Edward's behaviour, his not wanting to talk. I was too happy to realise it before, but he was unlike himself.

A part of me wanted to run across to him and slide my arms about him. But the spark of anger still felt like a glowing coal, burning a hole under my ribcage. I narrowed my eyes at him instead. "Something is wrong. Something apart from Lord Cantrell's visit, I mean. Something has happened. Was it in London? Or in Ireland?"

Edward didn't look at me. But neither did he deny it, just shook his head. "It's nothing." The muscles of his jaw were still tight. "And besides, that's not the point. I—"

"That's exactly the point!" The glow of anger in my chest kindled to a sudden blaze, as though the coal had been touched to dry wood. "You're angry because I can't share a secret that isn't even mine. And yet you won't even share your own with me. You could have told me last night whatever it is that was troubling you—that's troubling you still. You could *still* tell me, now. But you didn't—and you haven't. Because you're still shutting me out. Treating me as though I were a child who couldn't possibly understand your worries or cares."

Because that's why Edward and I aren't married yet—the year-long engagement was his idea, not mine. He wanted time, he said, to put the scars of battle behind him. Which I could understand. I could even accept that he doesn't wish to speak of whatever memories still haunt him. But they obviously haunt him still, and yet he won't let me even try to share them.

"How—" Edward's chest rose and fell, and he spoke through gritted teeth. "How did we suddenly get from this"—he gestured towards the necklace on the chair—"to whether or not I'm talking to you enough?"

"Because the answer is the same in either case." All of a sudden I felt tears stinging my eyes, and my throat tighten so that I could barely speak the words. "All you had to do was trust me."

Edward stood very still, the line of his mouth grim and tight, his muscles still tensed—this time I thought because he was trying to keep his hands from shaking again. And then he took a step backwards. First one, then another. And then, without another word, he turned and went out the door.

Tuesday 20 December 1814

I'm supposed to be dressing for dinner again. But I wanted to write this down, since I'm still so utterly surprised by what I learned today.

Nothing about Edward. Last night he agreed to accompany Kitty to the latest of Mr. and Mrs. Herron's endless Christmas parties. And this morning when I came down, he and Fitzwilliam had already ridden out early—more business on the estate, Elizabeth said. So in fact I haven't seen Edward since he walked out of the drawing room yesterday morning.

And maybe the best thing about this morning's discovery is that it's distracted me from thinking of Edward more than half a dozen times. Every hour.

It really *was* an astonishing discovery to make, though. After breakfast this morning I went up to the nursery, since I'd promised Thomas and Jack that I'd come and play pirate ships with them again. When I arrived, they were already playing at knights, though, beating at each other with wooden swords.

Kitty was there, too, kneeling next to an open trunk of old clothes that we use for a dressing-up box now. She had what looked like a folded-up piece of paper in her hands, and she looked up when I came in and said, "Georgiana, come here! You must see this!"

I had barely slept the night before; all the angry words Edward and I had spoken to each other had kept echoing through my mind like hammer strikes. But I crossed to take the paper from Kitty, thinking that if it was a letter from one of her 'beaux'—or worse yet if she was planning to tell me about the party she and Edward had gone to the night before—I really *was* going to scream.

But then my eye fell on the first line of the letter Kitty had handed me—for it was a letter, the ink slightly faded and the paper a little curled at the edges, as though it were several years old.

My dearest Ruth, it began. *I've begun this letter half a dozen times, but everything I try to write seems to go flat and lifeless on the page.*

Maybe I should go out into the garden and try looking at flowers and butterflies until I can think of better rhymes than 'moon' and 'June.' Your young charge once informed me gravely that all young ladies like to have poetry written for them. But since I'm trying to tell you my feelings, not

send you into fits of laughter, I'll merely say that you have
my heart, now and for always. With every breath I take, I'll
be thinking of you until I can see you again.

Yours ever,

The letter was signed only with initials: *G. T.*

I looked from it up to Kitty. "Where did you find
this?"

Kitty gestured to the trunk of old dressing-up clothes.
"In there. It had slipped down behind the lining, and I
felt it when I was rummaging around looking for pirate
costumes for the boys. So I fished it out. Isn't it perfectly
thrilling? A love letter! Not a very long one, to be sure."
She wrinkled her nose slightly. "I think he *should* have
written her poetry; it would have made it much more
romantic. But still, that last part is quite nice. I wonder
who 'Ruth' was?"

I was looking down at the letter in my hand, reading
it through a second time, still feeling utterly surprised.
"I know who she was. Ruth Granger. She was my governess until I went away to school in London."

"Oh." Kitty looked disappointed. "That makes it
much less exciting. I thought perhaps Ruth was one
of your ancestors, and the letter had been lying here
forgotten for a hundred years. If she was only some old
dried-up stick of a governess, that makes it much less
romantic."

She moved off to settle the boys before they smashed
any windows with their wooden swords, but I stayed
where I was, still staring down at the written words.
G. T., whoever he had been, had had nice handwriting, I
thought: not overly careful, maybe, but bold and strong.

I folded up the letter abruptly and looked up at
Thomas and Jack. "What do you think of taking a walk
into Lambton, boys? We can always play pirates later

this afternoon. And we could call at Mr. Todd's confectionary shop."

Miss Granger was my governess from the time I was ten until I turned thirteen and was sent to school, just as I told Kitty. But she wasn't at all a dried-up stick. In fact, Miss Granger was quite young when she had charge of me—just twenty when she came to Pemberley. So she's only twenty-nine now.

In the ordinary way she would of course have taken a post with another family after leaving us. But just before I was to leave for school, she fell terribly ill with scarlet fever. And it left her with a weakened heart. She couldn't work to support herself, clearly, and so my brother gave her a pension and a small cottage on the outskirts of Lambton.

She lived very quietly there for two or three years, her health making her still very nearly an invalid—and then quite by chance, an uncle of hers in the East Indies died and left all his fortune to her. Not a vast fortune, but enough for her to live on, and to buy the cottage outright. My brother tried to tell her it was already hers, of course. But Miss Granger is quite as proud as he is, in her way, and she insisted on paying him the full amount. So now she owns her own cottage free and clear.

And she lives there still: a small, stone-built house with a thatched roof, standing back from the main road in the midst of a grove of birch trees.

I expected Kitty to at the least notice the name was the same as the one on the letter when I told her I wished to call at Miss Granger's on our way into Lambton. But then the letter was addressed to 'Ruth' only; I was the one who supplied the 'Granger' and Kitty probably scarcely heard me, or at least not to remember the name later on.

And besides, between keeping a watch to be sure the boys didn't run under the wheels of any carriages or farm waggons, and telling me all about the gown she planned on wearing to the ball we're to have at Twelfth Night, Kitty didn't even ask me why I wanted to make the call.

When we arrived, she looked at the tiny cottage with its neatly swept front step and white curtains in the windows. Everything clean and spare and not in the least fussy, but very neat. Kitty said, "Oh good heavens, the boys will be like bulls in a china shop in there. Why don't we wait outside for you? There's a field over there." She gestured across the lane. "Thomas and Jack can play at running races until you've finished your call."

It was very nice of her—and so I told her, and asked if she was sure she didn't mind. To which Kitty made a face and said, "Mind? I can tell just by looking at the place that I'd as soon find a horse in the middle of the ocean as anyone worth talking to in there." By which of course, she meant any young men. She waved her hand at me to go. "You go on and enjoy your stuffy visit, I'll be much happier out here."

So it turned out that I was alone when I knocked at Miss Granger's front door.

Miss Granger's—Ruth, she insists I call her now that I'm no longer her pupil—health has improved very much in the last few years. She still grows tired on a long walk and can't lift anything terribly heavy. But she's well enough that she can take in a few day-pupils from the town for French and music lessons—not that she needs the income, but she says she likes the diversion teaching provides. And she doesn't look an invalid anymore at all.

She was frowning a little when she opened the door, but the look cleared when she saw me. "Why, Georgiana! What a nice surprise! I thought you might be old Mrs. Prouty from up the road, come to tell me my dog had been digging in her flower beds again." The dog she'd spoken of—a big, shaggy-coated sheep dog she calls Pilot—was behind her, pressing against her skirts and whining trying to see who was at the door. "But this is much nicer. Come in, please."

Ruth's cottage has only the two rooms downstairs: a kind of kitchen/dining room at the back, and the sitting room/parlour at the front. And everything inside is the same as out—simple and clean and as unadorned as a place can be without feeling stark or barren. The only incongruous note is Pilot, who sprawls untidily on the hearth and sheds hair on the furniture. Though I know Ruth doesn't mind; she loves all dogs. I am sure she would keep more, if her cottage weren't so small.

She offered me tea, but I only shook my head, knowing that I was staring at her, and yet not being quite able to help myself. I was thinking how you can know someone for years—and yet suddenly discover that obviously you haven't really known them at all.

Ruth is tall and slender, with curly, russet-red hair and grey eyes. She's quite lovely, really—though she looks a good deal like her cottage: very plain and sensible and unadorned. Today, for example, she was wearing a gown of dark-brown muslin with a high collar and long, straight sleeves, and her only jewellery was a small silver locket at her throat.

She asked after Elizabeth, and I told her the news— or rather, lack of it—that the baby hadn't come yet, but was expected any day. And then I reached into the lining of my muff, where I'd put the folded-up letter. "I have to confess that this isn't entirely a social call. I came to return something of yours. Something we found this morning in the nursery. And I thought . . . I thought you might like to have it back."

Ruth's eyebrows lifted in surprise. But then she caught sight of the letter in my hand—and just like that, the colour drained from her face, leaving her almost chalk-white to the lips.

I started to get up, afraid I'd brought on an attack of illness—and Pilot, as though sensing something was wrong, came and thrust his nose under her hand, whining anxiously high in his throat. Ruth swallowed visibly, then gave Pilot's shaggy head a mechanical pat and shook her head. "No, it's all right. There now, hush Pilot, you big, silly oaf." She swallowed again. "It's all right, Georgiana, I'm not going to faint. I'm just—" She took the letter from me. Gingerly, as though she were afraid to touch it. "I'm just . . . surprised to see this again."

She glanced down at the scrawl of words across the page, then quickly back up at me again, as though she didn't want to recall what the letter said—or maybe remembered it all too well. She closed her eyes a moment, leaning against the back of the chair. And then she said, a small, fractured twist of a smile touching the corners of her mouth, "You're probably wondering who wrote this to me. Or do you already know?"

I'd been wondering, of course, all along the walk to Ruth's cottage, who G. T. could have been. The 'young charge' the letter spoke of must have been me. But the letter wasn't dated; it could have been sent to her at any time while she was with us at Pemberley. And childhood memory is so strange. I can remember certain things so clearly: the pictures in my nursery story books. The day my favourite doll was broken, and Fitzwilliam mended her for me. Feeding lumps of sugar or carrots I'd begged from our cook to the horses in the stables. Trips to London, or to visit my aunt. And of course my father's death when I was ten.

But so much of the rest is all blurred at the edges. And besides that, I suppose like most children, I wasn't terribly interested in 'grown-up' things. I don't think it ever occurred to me to wonder what Miss Granger did with herself after I'd gone to bed, or when I had a lesson with the dancing master in the afternoon.

I shook my head. "No, I haven't the least idea, I promise." A little of the colour had come back into Ruth's face, but she still looked terribly pale. "And you needn't tell me. Truly, I only came because once I'd seen the letter, it seemed only right that it should be returned to you. But perhaps I shouldn't have after all. I didn't mean to upset you."

Ruth was staring into the small fire burning in the grate, one hand still moving mechanically back and forth over Pilot's head. She shook her head slightly, though it didn't seem a gesture of denial—more as though she were trying to shake off a memory before it could take hold. And then she looked up at me, her grey eyes bright and very clear, and said, "It was Giles Tomalin. He visited Pemberley when you were eleven. Do you remember?"

Giles Tomalin. Slowly, I shook my head again. "No. I'm sorry," I added.

It seemed as though I *ought* to remember anyone who'd been so important to her.

Ruth smiled slightly. "It's all right. There's no reason that you should. He was part of a shooting party your father invited for the autumn sport. I think you only spoke to him once or maybe twice the whole time he was at Pemberley. He came . . . he accompanied us on a walk through the Pemberley woods, once. You hardly ever talked to strangers, you were so shy—grown-up men, especially. But you liked him, because he told you that if you caught a falling leaf before it touched the ground, you could make a wish."

"Oh!" I did remember, then, just a little. Not the man's face, not exactly. The best I could conjure up was a vague memory of someone tall, with broad shoulders and—I thought—very dark hair. But I could recall the day she spoke of, a little—because she and I were usually all alone on our daily walks, and it was an occasion to have someone else along. "I walked between you, holding your hands, and the two of you made a game of lifting me up on the count of three. Is that the time you mean?"

Ruth smiled just a little again, and nodded. "Yes, that's right. That was him. He was—" She stopped, her eyes fixing unblinkingly on the fire as though she were staring back across the years. She was silent so long I wasn't sure whether she meant to continue or not. But then at last she said, "I met him the day he arrived at Pemberley—before he'd arrived. It was on the road to Lambton. I'd had to do an errand in town, and I was walking back to the house. And then I heard something—a dog barking, yelping, obviously frightened and in pain. And a man shouting. Cursing, rather. And when I rounded the curve, I saw him—it was Rakes, the farm manager the Herrons used to have on their estate back then. He had a dog—some poor, starved-looking stray—down on the ground, and he was beating it, savagely, with some kind of club."

Ruth paused again. "I was just going to shout at him, tell him to stop, when another man rode up on a big black horse, swung himself down from the saddle, caught Rakes' club in one hand and jerked it away from him. Rakes was sullen—he said the dog was suspected of stealing chickens. But the other man just clenched his jaw and said that unless Rakes wanted to get a feel for his club on the receiving end, he'd better get the hell away from there. I think Rakes would have argued more. But he could probably see the man was one of the gentry, and he'd only get into trouble. And besides, the stranger raised the club and looked as though he were fully capable of making good on his threat. So Rakes ran."

Ruth came to a full stop this time. And then she said, "The stranger was Giles, of course. That was the first time I saw him. He went to kneel by the dog Rakes had been beating, and I went up and offered to help. The poor thing was so badly hurt, it was half frantic with pain, ready to snap at anything that came near. But between the two of us, we managed to get it wrapped up in my cloak and Giles' coat, tightly enough that it couldn't bite us or thrash and do itself another injury. Giles was swearing by the time we'd done, calling Rakes names under his breath. But then he recollected himself and looked up at me and said he must beg my pardon for bad language." Ruth's lips curved in another small smile. "And I laughed, I remember, and said that I should thank him for saving me the trouble of saying the words myself. Then Giles said he thought he could carry the dog on horseback, if I could take the horse's reins—because he was a stranger in this part of the world, and his mount didn't know the roads any better than he did. So I asked where he was going, and he said

Pemberley. And I told him I was governess there."

Ruth fell silent again, her grey eyes distant. And then she shook her head and looked back at me. "And that was how Giles and I met. I told him our gamekeeper at Pemberley could help with treating the dog's hurts, so we brought the poor thing there together. And then after that . . . after that Giles would make some excuse to get away from the rest of the house party at night, after dinner—that he had letters to write, or wanted to get an early start in the morning. And I would slip out and meet him, and we'd go for walks by moonlight."

"Why didn't you—" I stopped myself before I could finish the sentence. Though it didn't matter, because Ruth finished it for me.

"Why didn't we marry?" Her lips twisted again. "Because Giles wasn't just Giles Tomalin. He was *Lord* Giles Tomalin—the younger son of the Duke of Clarion."

I didn't say anything, but something of what I felt must have showed on my face, because Ruth shook her head. "I know what you're thinking—orphan, penniless governess seduced and abandoned by a scion of the upper classes. But it wasn't like that. Giles wasn't like that. He did ask me to marry him. I turned him down."

"You turned him down? But why?" I couldn't keep the astonishment from my voice. Ruth had been in love with Lord Giles—it had shown in every word she'd spoken. And I couldn't believe that the man who had written the letter in her hand had not been in love with her, too.

As though she'd picked up my thought, Ruth looked down at the folded paper and then let one hand rise and fall. "Because he *was* Lord Giles Tomalin. The younger son of a duke, whose family surely wished him to make a better match than a penniless, orphaned governess whose father had been an equally penniless clergyman. You know as well as I do what a scandal it would have made if he had married me. He would have lost all standing in society."

"Maybe he wouldn't have cared," I ventured.

"Maybe." Ruth pressed her eyes shut a moment, then opened them again. "That was what he said—that he didn't care. But how did he know that, really? His whole life, his family, friends, everything he'd been brought up to—all gone, for me. Maybe he'd not have minded at first, but in five years' time? In ten?" She shook her head. "And I wasn't going to let him tie himself for the rest of his life to a wife that everyone would despise him for." She looked up at me again with a small smile. "I know what you're thinking now, too—that I didn't want to *be* the wife that everyone of his acquaintance despised. But it wasn't that. Truly. I wouldn't have minded what other people said. It was the thought that in five or ten or even fifteen years' time, Giles *would* wake up one morning and discover that he resented me. That I was a burden to him. I couldn't"—for the first time, Ruth's voice wavered just slightly—"I couldn't have borne that."

She swallowed and shook her head again. "Besides, we only knew each other for two weeks—that was all the time he was visiting here. What did we each really know of the other's character? A marriage between us was . . . impractical. Completely against all reason and common sense."

She spoke with sudden vigour, and I could just imagine her trying to scrub and snip out her feelings for Giles as neatly and efficiently as she did all the housework of her cottage. Except that there was a note in her voice that said she hadn't even yet been entirely successful.

I hesitated, then ventured, "Haven't you ever . . . haven't you ever wondered what happened to him? Where he might be now?"

"Of course I have." Abruptly, Ruth got to her feet, crossed to the fireplace, and threw the folded up letter down onto the flames. "I've thought that he's probably bald, fat, and married with seven children by now—and that in all likelihood he doesn't even remember my name."

The dry paper caught fire at once. In an instant Giles Tomalin's letter was smouldering at the edges, the next it was blazing and crumbling into ash. Ruth blinked hard, staring down at it. Or at least I thought she did. Her voice was at any rate softer when she turned back around to me. "Thank you for bringing the letter back to me, Georgiana. I'm . . . I'm glad you were the one to find it, if it had to come to light again after all these years."

Wednesday 21 December 1814

I went out for a walk this afternoon, thinking that I might catch up to Kitty and the boys, who had gone out earlier.

Well, if I am completely honest, I was also hoping to find Edward and my brother, who rode out early this morning on a tour of the estate farms.

I didn't find Edward. But I did catch up with Kitty and the boys, just beyond Pemberley's gates. The boys were pretending to fish in the stream using sticks. And Kitty herself was sitting on a wooden stile at the edge of a field with a young man. They were too far away for me to recognise him, or to see more than that he was dressed in a red hunting coat and wore a tall beaver hat. Even at a distance, though, I could see how close together his head and Kitty's were, and that he was holding her hand while she laughed.

But then they caught sight of me, and the man, whoever he was, let go of Kitty's hand abruptly and swung himself up into the saddle of the horse he had waiting. He was off, riding down the road by the time I reached Kitty's side—though her cheeks were still flushed.

I hesitated. And then I said, "Who was your friend? He must have been in a great hurry, if he couldn't stop and wait to be introduced."

He'd been incredibly rude to depart the instant he saw me—though I didn't care about that. I was thinking of the other morning's conversation with Elizabeth.

Kitty's gaze fixed on the small square of scarlet riding coat we could still see, growing smaller in the distance as the man galloped away. She smiled—a small, secret smile. "That was Lord Carmichael."

"Lord Carmichael!" I truly was worried, then.

Lord Henry Carmichael does not live in our part of the world, but he comes once or twice a year to visit an elderly aunt on her estate near Kympton. And that fact— that he visits his elderly aunt, I mean—is probably the best thing known of him. I've only met Lord Carmichael two or three times myself—but I know his reputation; everyone in this area does. And even the handful of times I met him was enough to convince me that the reputation is richly deserved.

He is fair-haired and blue-eyed, and handsome in a rather obvious way—his is the sort of face that will grow dissolute and puffy with age. He's . . . a rake-hell is the best word for it, I suppose. He came into his title very young, and has since spent all his energies on running through the family fortune as fast as he can. He gambles, races horses, drinks to excess, and spends a fortune on clothes. The first time we met, I remember him telling me in a drawling voice that a true gentleman cannot really be considered to 'dress' unless he spends at least eight thousand pounds a year on his apparel.

And he has an even worse reputation when it comes to his dealings with women. Or, rather, with respectable, unmarried women. In London, he's whispered to have conducted affairs with the wives of half the House of Lords.

I don't for a moment think that Kitty is rich enough or beautiful enough or of a distinguished enough family to tempt him into actual marriage. But he would be perfectly willing to amuse himself by toying with her, while he's stuck on an otherwise dull family visit.

"Are you sure—," I began.

But Kitty interrupted before I could say anything more, wriggling her shoulders impatiently and rolling her eyes. "If you're going to start preaching a sermon the way my sister does, you can save your breath. Lord Carmichael"—she nodded in the direction Lord Carmichael had ridden—"is everything charming. He has five carriages—five!—and his own stable of horses. And a house in London in Mayfair. And a *vast* estate in Kent. And we've a *connection*, he and I—we share so many of the same opinions about so many things. It's perfectly remarkable. And besides, it was all quite respectable. He is thinking of buying a new barouche, and wanted my opinion as to the colour of the seat upholstery. Any project of that sort wants a woman's touch, he said. Even Elizabeth couldn't object to anything in the conversation between us." And then she smiled that small, secret smile again, and added, "Well, almost anything."

Kitty is the same age I am. But sometimes I feel far older. Or rather, she seems much younger—not much older than her nephews, really—in her single-minded determination to do exactly as she likes and take whatever pleasure she can grasp, no matter who suffers the cost.

But I also felt as though I were being the most insufferable prig—because, really, I'm not Kitty's mother nor even her older sister, and it's no business of mine to criticise how she behaves. But I couldn't stop myself from saying, "And what about Captain Ayres? Would he have found anything to object to?"

I thought—just for an instant—Kitty might have looked at least faintly guilty. But then she waved a dismissive hand. "Oh, John. What he doesn't know can't hurt him. And besides, he deserves to be punished for writing me such incredibly dull letters. Nothing in them at all except pages of how glad he is the war is over, and now he and I can settle down in peace to a quiet life." She made a face. "A quiet life! I ask you, who wants—"

Before she could finish, Thomas and Jack ran up, red-cheeked, sweaty, and panting, and demanding us to judge who had been the winner of the last race. "You both were!" Kitty proclaimed grandly. She made a ceremony of kissing each of the boys on both cheeks. And I told them they had each won the prize of picking out any sweet or pastry they liked at Mr. Todd's shop.

The boys raced off ahead of us down the lane. And Kitty narrowed her eyes at me. "Speaking of love affairs, what is the trouble between you and Colonel Fitzwilliam? Have the two of you quarrelled?"

I felt slightly sick, because if even Kitty has noticed something amiss between me and Edward, it must be obvious indeed. But I said, only, "Why should you think that?"

"Oh, well." Kitty shrugged and tossed the strings of her bonnet over her shoulders. "I just thought you might have. And if the two of you really *had* quarrelled, that would make him fair game." She looked off into the distance with a dreamy smile. "He's not the handsomest man in the neighbourhood, I suppose—but there's something quite thrilling about him all the same."

I felt my jaw drop open slightly. But there's no point in even being angry with Kitty. She really is like one of her nephews. Coming over and demanding that I loan her a particular toy that she thought I might have outgrown.

Thursday 22 December 1814

Caroline Bingley arrived at Pemberley today. I haven't seen her—nor yet even exchanged letters with her—since last May, so I wasn't at all sure what to expect. For as long as I've known her, Caroline has been the same—very proud, sharp-tongued, and excessively conscious of her own importance. Which sounds uncharitable, but it honestly is the strict truth. Caroline tried her level hardest to make my brother fall in love with her, so I had ample opportunities to observe her.

But last spring while she was staying here at Pemberley, she did fall in love—really in love, I think—with Jacques de La Courcelle, a French expatriate. Who turned out in the end to be a sham and a fortune hunter, and who married my Aunt Catherine de Bourgh—despite the twenty year difference in their ages—for her money.

I was incredibly sorry for Caroline when she left here, just after their engagement was announced. And now—

Now I suppose maybe I am sorry for her still, in a way. But I certainly have to work a great deal harder to feel so.

She looks as handsome and as expensively dressed as ever; when she arrived this afternoon she wore a dark-red velvet pelisse trimmed with gold frogging over her travelling costume that set off her dark-gold hair and blue eyes. And this evening at dinner she wore a very low-cut gold silk gown with six inches of elaborately beaded trim around the hem, and pearls both at her throat and in her hair.

My brother had some business with his estate agent in Lambton and so was dining there for the evening and planning to return to the house late. And Edward accompanied him.

But the whole point of writing in this diary tonight was to distract myself from thinking about Edward. So, Caroline:

With Fitzwilliam and Edward gone, it was just Elizabeth, Kitty, Caroline and myself at the dinner table. Elizabeth looked tired, I thought. And she ate hardly anything. Though that's not so unusual. With the baby so close to being born, she says she sometimes feels as unwell as she did at the very start.

Kitty for once hardly chattered at all. I think she was slightly awed—or at least intimidated—by Caroline, who was dressed so much more richly than Kitty was herself, and who scarcely glanced at her all through the meal.

When Caroline first arrived, what she said to Elizabeth was, "Why, look at you, Eliza. Aren't you just the picture of a sweet little mother? Never mind, I'm sure you'll get your looks and your figure back once the child is born."

Elizabeth and Caroline have never been such intimate friends that Caroline should feel free to use Elizabeth's Christian name. But apparently that fact hasn't registered with Caroline. Or—to give in to my most uncharitable speculations—it may be that Caroline simply refuses to address Elizabeth as "Mrs. Darcy."

Tonight at dinner Caroline addressed most of her remarks to Elizabeth, punctuating her speech with a good many little tinkling, silvery laughs:

"I do think it was so very, very wise of you to allow Darcy to have his time away in London. Gentlemen do need their disports, their time away from the shackles of matrimony. Such a mistake to try to keep one's husband buried in the country, constantly at one's beck and call. And we did have such a delightful time while in Town. Do you know the Rushworths? Oh, you don't? Really? How strange, they are *such* friends of Darcy's. They gave a dinner party in his honour, and everyone there was remarking on how agreeable it was to have him back in London for at least part of the Season. All his old friends have seen so little of him, these past two years since you and he married."

To do Caroline justice, I don't think she could have been any ruder or more hateful if my Aunt de Bourgh herself had scripted the entire body of her dinnertime conversation for her.

Elizabeth at least refused to be drawn; she simply smiled and said *yes*, and *certainly*, to everything Caroline said. Which annoyed Caroline far more than any direct counter-attack could have done. By the end of the meal, Caroline's laughter was sharp-edged and there were bright spots of temper burning in her cheeks.

As Elizabeth and I were going upstairs to bed, though— I don't think any of us, Caroline included, wanted to prolong the evening, so we all retired early—Elizabeth asked me, "Do *you* know the Rushworths?"

Caroline and Kitty's rooms are in the east wing with the rest of the guest rooms, which meant they had parted from us on the stairs and Elizabeth and I were alone. I looked at Elizabeth in astonishment. "You can't tell me you honestly believed everything—or for that matter *anything*—that Caroline said tonight?"

Elizabeth smiled, though I thought it seemed a little forced, and rested her hand on the curve of the baby under her evening gown. "It must be the child. Aren't expectant mothers supposed to lose all command of their good sense?"

"Well, don't even think of letting Caroline worry you." I hugged her. "I do know the Rushworths. They're passing acquaintances, nothing more. Acquaintances of Fitzwilliam's and my parents, really. And incredibly stuffy and boring. Mr. Rushworth never talks of anything but horse racing and guns. My first Season in London—before you and my brother met—I actually saw my brother consent to dance at a public assembly, just to avoid having to sit and talk with him."

Elizabeth laughed at that, and we said goodnight.

Friday 23 December 1814

I had to break off writing just now. There was a knock at my door, and my heart started pounding—even though I knew it might be only Fitzwilliam, coming to tell me that the baby was on its way sooner than expected.

It was Edward, though.

He'd been wearing evening dress: white waistcoat, black knee-breeches and probably a black long-tailed coat, as well. But somewhere between dinner with my brother's agent and here, he'd shrugged out of the coat and pulled his cravat off, too, leaving his plain white shirt open at the throat.

For a heartbeat of time after I'd opened my door, we both simply stood silent, staring at each other. And then, at the same instant, we both said, "I'm sorry."

That made both of us laugh. Edward's tight posture relaxed and he took a step forward, pulling me into his arms. I felt his breath go out in a rush, and he rested his cheek against my hair.

Finally Edward drew back a little. "Will you come downstairs with me? I don't want to wake anyone."

We ended up in the drawing room, where there were still the lingering traces of warmth from the fire in the hearth. Edward lighted the pair of taper candles that stood on the mantle, and I closed the door behind us.

I started to speak, but Edward stopped me, shaking his head. "No, please. Let me go first."

I nodded—but for all that, he didn't begin at once, but crossed to me, and pulled me towards him again, looping his arms lightly about my waist. And then he bent his head, resting his forehead against mine. "I truly am sorry," he said at last. "But before you say anything, I need to tell you that I do trust you. That I never did think you a liar. Or really believe there was anything between you and Cantrell. I was surprised to find the two of you together, true, but after that—" Edward exhaled hard again. "After that it was myself I was angry with, not either of you. I—" Edward traced the curve of my cheek with one thumb, making me shiver.

He cleared his throat and said, "I wanted—I did want—to tell you the same night I came. But it seemed" —he frowned, as though searching for the right word—

"selfish, to inflict my own concerns on you, practically the instant I walked through the door."

I looked up at him. And then I stood on tiptoe to touch my mouth to his. "Your concerns are mine already, Edward. How could you think I would not want to hear them? Anything important to you is important to me."

Edward resisted for a brief instant. And then he kissed me back, his lips lingering on mine. He pushed me away after a moment, though, setting his hands against my shoulders. He was laughing. "Stop a moment. I want—" He pushed one hand through his hair. "While I still have wits enough to string words together into speech, I want to tell you now."

He pulled me down onto the hearth-side settle with him, sitting me at one end of the bench while he took the other. "Sit there, so I'm not in danger of stopping to kiss you again, and I'll tell you."

His smile faded, though, as he sat a moment, staring into the ashes of the hearth. At last he said, "I went to London because I meant to sell my commission."

"Sell your commission!" I couldn't help from interrupting. "But Edward, why?"

Edward's father purchased an army commission for him when Edward was fifteen. Which of course is the usual way with second sons. The first son is the heir, the second becomes a soldier. If Edward's parents had had a third son, he would likely have been destined for a career in the Church. And when a commissioned officer like Edward wishes to retire from the army, he sells his commission—usually to the family of another second son.

Edward pushed a hand through his dishevelled hair, and then looked sideways at me, his face all at once earnest and intent. "If we'd not defeated Bonaparte's armies last year—if he'd not been exiled to Elba where he can start no more wars—I wouldn't have thought of it. But he *was* defeated. There's still the war in the Americas. But that can't last much longer by all accounts. And—" Edward stopped, closing his eyes briefly, then looked up at me again. "Would you think me an unutterable shirker if I said that I feel as though I want that war—and any future wars besides—to be someone else's worry, not mine?" He let out a slow breath. "I've done my duty. I hope I've done it well. But now . . . I want it behind me, the army. I want . . . I want to be free of it, once and for all. That was why I went to London."

A part of me wished—still wishes—that he might have spoken to me of the decision before it was made. But he was telling me now; that was really all that mattered. And besides, I could see the tension in his shoulders, the furrow that had appeared between his brows.

So I said, "But?"

Edward let out his breath. "Is it so obvious, then, that there's a *but*?" He shifted, gazing once more into the cooling hearth. "While I was in London, I saw a man selling matches on a street corner. A miserable-looking fellow, with one leg missing below the knee, and one eye gone, and his clothes more rags than anything else. And he'd a consumptive-sounding cough, besides. I would have tossed him a few coins and passed him by—except that I saw he wore the remains of a black Rifleman's belt. So I stopped and spoke with him—asked him whether he'd been in army service."

Edward was silent another moment. "He'd fought in Spain in '09. That was where he lost the leg and the eye. He was sent home—and was supposed to be granted a veteran's pension. Sixpence a day. Which God knows is little enough to live on, even if he had it. But the colonel of his regiment was killed, as well. Some new man took his place—one who spared little thought for making sure that the former colonel's recruits received the pensions they were owed. This man was put off with excuse after excuse when he tried to claim his pension. And then he was told he wasn't owed his pension at all. Apparently this new colonel claimed the man had been called to duty and failed to report, and used that claim to deny him all further army support."

Edward's voice was even, nearly expressionless—but still, I could see how angry he was. "This man—Mayberry is his name—what can he do to argue his case? He can't read or write to know what documents might be put before him or to make a formal complaint. He has no money to hire legal aid. For God's sake, he's selling matches on a street corner just to keep himself from starving to death."

Edward stopped again, and I asked, "What did you do?"

Edward blew out another explosive breath. "Told him I'd take up his case with his battalion's quarter-master—which I will. But I can't help . . . I can't help wondering . . . "

"You can't help feeling responsible for your men, or wondering what would happen to your regiment if you were to sell your commission and another colonel were to take your place," I finished for him.

Edward nodded. "I was a lieutenant colonel before I was one-and-twenty, in command of seven hundred and fifty men. Barely more than half of them came back from Portugal alive. And we lost half of those men last year in France." He braced his thumb against the bridge of his nose. "Not that I believe I could have saved any of those men we lost if I'd acted any differently, given different orders or employed a different strategy. Other regiments had far fewer men return alive. Still, the ones who did survive—the men who fought and starved and in winter watched their fellows in arms freeze solid to the ground while they slept. Men who left parts of themselves buried over there on foreign soil—don't they deserve at the very least to receive what they were justly promised?"

If I am to be honest, my heart had leapt at the thought of Edward's selling his commission. Of his retiring from the army and being safe—safe from the threat of ever being once again sent off to war. But the reasons Edward had just given for remaining in his post as colonel— those are the very reasons I've been in love with him since I was six years old.

So I said, "Of course they do." I slipped my hand into Edward's and moved along the bench to sit close beside him, close enough that our bodies touched. "You don't have to make any decisions tonight—you don't even have to reach any decision soon. But whatever you do decide, it will be the right choice. I know it."

Edward looked down at me, the candles' yellow glow still deepening the shadows at the corners of his mouth. "Are you so sure of that?"

"Of course I am." I touched my lips just lightly to the edge of his jaw, where I could see the steady beat of his pulse. "I know you, Edward."

Edward's arms came round me, warm and solid and strong, and he said against my hair, "What did I ever do to deserve you?"

Saturday 24 December 1814

We had a pleasant surprise arrival today at Pemberley: Edward's brother, Frank.

Or rather, it was a pleasant surprise to most of us. For Caroline, I don't think Frank's coming to Pemberley was so much a surprise as an out-and-out shock—and not at all a pleasant one.

My cousin Frank—his proper title is Lord Silverbridge—is five years older than Edward. He's not very much at all like Edward to look at. Edward takes his dark looks from his father's side of the family, while Frank has his mother's colouring: dark-gold hair and hazel eyes.

Two years ago, Frank was engaged to be married to a Miss Celia Lambeth—but she died, tragically, of typhoid before they could marry. And ever since . . . it's a bit hard to describe. Grief takes everyone differently, I suppose. Some descend into depression and despair, some people seem to grow angry at the whole world. But Frank—he was always high-spirited, but ever since Celia's death it's as though he's determined to take nothing seriously, to find all life one endless joke.

As his father's heir, of course, he needs no profession like the army—so he lives as a man of leisure in London, when he's not spending an obligatory few months on the family estate in Devon. He's always laughing and teasing and playing elaborate pranks on his London friends that get reported in the society pages of the papers. Such as the time he coated a litter of dachshund puppies in flour and unleashed them on a crowded ballroom.

That makes Frank sound frivolous, or as though I don't like him—but I do; it's almost impossible not to. He may be high-spirited, but he's never unkind or malicious. And so far as I know, he's never grown attached or even interested in any other woman since Celia died.

At any rate, today's surprise visit was very much in character.

The weather this morning was cold and very clear, with a piercingly blue winter sky and the ground glittering with frost. First thing, before breakfast, I asked Edward to come for a walk with me down to the lake, because I wanted to make a crayon sketch of the woods as they look in wintertime, all shades of grey and brown, with just the occasional bright splash of colour in an evergreen or a broken cedar bough. Edward agreed to come—and as a testament to his devotion, he said, even carried my drawing box. Though he laughed and gave me unmerciful *I-told-you-so*'s when my ungloved fingers were too stiff with cold to draw after twenty minutes or so.

We were just walking back to the house when a rider came pounding down the drive, drew up sharply and then swung himself down from the saddle at the sight of us.

"Edward! Hasn't anyone ever told you that it's a gentleman's first duty to keep his betrothed from freezing to death before the wedding?"

Edward stared at the man, who was swathed in a fur-lined greatcoat and beaver hat. And then he started to laugh. "Frank. What on earth brings you here?"

"Well, I like that." Frank's cheeks were reddened with the cold, his hazel eyes bright as he turned to me. "Two hundred miles to spend Christmas with my only brother, and he greets me by asking what brings me here?" He let go his horse's reins and stepped forward to hug me and kiss my cheek. "Come to think of it, I've a mind to quarrel with him in any case for proposing to you, young Georgiana, before I could get a word in."

He extended a hand to Edward, then, and Edward took it, still grinning. "Not worth trying, Frank. If she's mad enough to want to marry me, I'm afraid she's still wits enough to know to steer clear of you."

Frank gave me a theatrical look. "Sad, but too true. Georgiana always was the sensible one."

The two men embraced, then, laughing and pounding each other on the back. They live such different lives that they don't see each other very often—I've not seen Frank since Edward and I have been engaged, and I don't think Edward has, either. But the two of them get on well together and always have.

We all walked back to the house, Frank and Edward still talking. Frank had been planning to spend the holidays at the family estate. But a snowstorm to the south had made travel to Devon impossible. And so Frank decided on impulse to ride for Pemberley, instead.

At least, that's what he told Edward and me.

The rest of the company was at breakfast when we arrived back at the house: Fitzwilliam and Elizabeth, Kitty and the boys, and Caroline. Thomas and Jack were playing at highway bandits when we walked in, and Jack had just upset a pot of hot chocolate all over the carpet, so that in the general uproar I don't think anyone else noticed Caroline's face when she saw Frank walk into the room. I saw her, though. All the colour drained from her cheeks and her eyes looked first stricken—and then, after a moment, angry. She turned pointedly away and concentrated on looking out the window all the time the cocoa was being mopped up and Frank simultaneously was making his greetings to the rest of the group.

Finally when the spill had been cleaned up and Kitty had taken the boys out of the room, Elizabeth said, "Caroline, I don't think you've ever met Edward's brother?" She turned to Frank. "Frank, may I present to you Miss Caroline Bingley—"

Caroline interrupted before Frank could say anything—before he could even finish his polite bow of acknowledgement in her direction. "We've met," she said. Her voice was angry, too, hard and clipped.

Sunday 25 December 1814

It seems wrong to be so happy myself, when everyone else is so very distressed just now. Of course, come to that, I *am* distressed as well, and worried, too. And I'm sorry for Kitty, which I wouldn't have expected. I suppose I ought to be angry with her for spoiling an otherwise perfect night, but I find I can't be.

I ought to tell this in the proper order, though.

Between Edward and finding Ruth's letter and everything else that's happened, I completely forgot to mention before that despite our Christmas celebrations being so quiet, we were to hold a ball here at Pemberley, just as we have done every year—ever since my grandfather started the tradition more than fifty years ago.

I know my brother would have been happy to cancel the celebration this year, for Elizabeth's sake. But she wouldn't hear of it, only said that this baby was after all a Darcy, and as such, it couldn't dream of disrupting a fine old Pemberley custom by choosing the night of the ball to be born. Which made my brother laugh—and so the preparations for the ball went on.

At any rate, the ball took place tonight. Or rather last night, I suppose I should say, since I've just looked at the little clock on my mantle and found that it is in fact two in the morning.

Elizabeth came to my room, just as I was finished with dressing and about to go downstairs to greet the guests. She looked a little pale, I thought—but she smiled when she saw me and said, "Good heavens, Edward had better put his name down on your dance card quickly—every gentleman in attendance will be clamouring for a dance with you tonight."

I laughed. "Well, you know what they say about fine feathers making fine birds."

I was wearing a new gown—and it *is* very pretty. White silk embroidered with touches of silver, tiers of vandyked lace around the hem and pearl rosettes around the neckline. And I had tiny white rosebuds for my hair.

Elizabeth shook her head. "No, it's not just the dress. You look—" And then she smiled and squeezed my hand. "You look *happy*, and I'm so glad for you. You and Edward both."

"Thank you. But you're looking lovely, too. Are you feeling all right?"

Elizabeth truly was lovely, in an ivory satin gown with a pale-green spider-gauze overdress, embroidered in gold and trimmed with silk roses in a deep pink colour. She put a hand over the swelling of the baby, and said, "Apart from feeling as though I ought to be black and blue with all the kicking going on inside me." And then her smile faded. She was still holding my hand, and even through her evening gloves and mine I could feel her fingers grow tense. "Georgiana, have you noticed your brother—" She stopped abruptly.

I waited, but she didn't say anything more. "Have I noticed my brother . . . ," I finally prompted.

But Elizabeth shook her head. "No, never mind, it can wait. We'd better go down. The guests will be arriving soon."

This time, I might have pushed her further. For it's not usual at all for Elizabeth to question me about Fitzwilliam; anything she wants to know of him, she would ask him herself. But at that moment, Kitty came bursting out of her room, demanding whether Elizabeth had any spare pins, because Kitty had accidentally torn a few inches of lace off the hem of her gown by stepping on it, and could Elizabeth come and help her? Because she'd already sent the maid away.

She'd banged back into her room—to get her slippers on, she said—before Elizabeth could answer.

"I'll go," I told Elizabeth quickly. "You go ahead downstairs. Because the one thing I do know of my brother is that he'd never forgive me if I let you bend down to help Kitty with the hem of her dress tonight, when I'm perfectly capable of doing it myself."

I did help Kitty with re-pinning the lace. And listened to her talk the whole time about who was to be at the ball, and how many dances she was going to grant each of the men she expected would ask her. Thomas and Jack came knocking at her door just as she was standing before the looking-glass on her dressing table and pinching her cheeks to make them red—and Kitty and I both promised to smuggle a sampling of all the cakes and pastries on the supper table to them up in the nursery. I can remember my brother doing that for me when I was too young to attend the Christmas ball.

And then we went downstairs.

Every time the seasons change at Pemberley, I think that whatever month it is must be my favourite time of year here. When the trees are all covered with the first green-gold new leaves of spring, and the daffodils are opening like tiny drops of sunshine. When summer comes, and all the roses in my mother's garden bloom. When autumn turns the sunlight into golden amber, and the woods are a riot of oranges and yellows and reds.

I love them all. But I think I love Pemberley House— just the house itself I mean—best of all at Christmas time. It looks so beautiful, with swags of greenery on all the mantles, holly sprays in vases, and the smell of paper-white narcissus in the air, and fires in every hearth.

Tonight the downstairs hallway had been decorated with wreaths and garlands of holly and ivy and evergreen, all twined with ribbons of red and gold silk. All the candles in the chandeliers had been lighted, and the musicians in the ballroom had already started to play when Kitty and I came down. The room was filling quickly with the guests who had already begun to arrive, handing their cloaks and hats and wraps to the servants, greeting Elizabeth and my brother, who were standing just inside the door.

And I scarcely saw or heard any of it, because Edward was waiting for me at the foot of the stairs.

I did see Kitty dart away at once—and I felt another prick of worry, because I could see that she made straight for Lord Carmichael. He was looking very dashing in a gold brocade waistcoat, with an emerald-headed tie pin in his cravat—the complicated folds of which must have taken him an hour or more to arrange.

But then Edward took my hand, and I forgot all about Kitty—and about everything else.

He was wearing his army uniform for the formal occasion: red coat trimmed with gold braid. And just for a moment as our eyes met I felt overwhelmed by the realisation: that he truly is mine, and I'm his.

He was smiling as he took my hand. "Hello."

"Hello."

Edward's smile deepened as he drew me with him through to the back of the hall and into the parlour , which was empty of guests, since everyone was moving from the hall directly into the ballroom or the billiard room for some of the men. He didn't say anything, though, just stood smiling at me, his dark gaze moving over my face slowly, as though he were trying to memorise every feature. "What are you thinking of?" I finally asked. It was quiet, here, the sounds of music and the crowd outside muffled, and somehow it seemed right to keep my voice to barely above a whisper.

Edward laughed at that. "I was thinking that none

of the practised lines seem to fit with you."

"Practised lines?" I repeated, puzzled.

"The ones you're supposed to say to girls at a ball. *I must be in heaven, for you're surely an angel.* Or, *Who stole the stars for you and put them in your eyes?*"

We were both laughing by that time. "Men actually practise saying things like that?"

Edward's shoulders moved, and he grinned. "It saves you from sweating over whether you'll trip over your own feet or tread on the hem of some girl's dress during a dance, at least." And then he sobered, interlinking his fingers again with mine. "You are beautiful, though."

He drew back, though, before his lips touched mine, and shook his head. "Wait. I didn't drag you back here for this—I brought you in here because I have something I want to give to you."

"What is it?"

"Your Christmas present." Edward grinned again as he reached into the pocket of his uniform coat. "Close your eyes first."

I did close my eyes—and as I did, I felt myself thinking, *Please let me like whatever it is he's giving me.*

Because I had no idea what Edward would have chosen for me. Gifts are so hard—even my brother hardly ever gets me *exactly* what I would have chosen for myself. And this was such a lovely night—it would spoil it a little if I had to pretend to be delighted. Or if Edward realised my delight was just pretence.

But then I felt him place something into my gloved hand. I opened my eyes—and instantly drew in my breath. "Oh, how lovely!"

It was a ring, but the design was unlike any I'd seen before. Two tiny golden hands clasped a heart fashioned from a sea-green emerald, which itself was topped by a golden crown.

"Do you really like it?" Edward asked. He was watching my face. "They're fairly common in Ireland. *Claddaugh* rings, they're called. They're often given as betrothal or wedding gifts. The hands are for friendship, the heart is for love, and the crown for loyalty, so the story goes. I saw this one in the window of a jeweller's shop in Galway, and it made me think of you, somehow. But if you'd rather have something else—" he added quickly. Probably because my eyes were starting to brim over with sudden tears.

"It's perfect." I wiped my eyes with the tips of my gloved fingers and gave him a shaky smile. "I'm sorry—I've always thought crying from happiness completely idiotic. But I can't seem to help it. I love the ring." I took off my glove and slid it onto my finger. The gold already felt warm against my skin. "It's absolutely, completely perfect."

So was the rest of the ball, really.

A group of mummers from the village dressed in spangled paper caps and coloured ribbons came in and performed a play of Saint George and the Dragon. And then the Christmas cake was brought in and cut and served. And Edward and I talked and danced.

I did look around for Kitty a few times. But I couldn't see her anywhere. Though I did see Caroline, looking very grand in a bright-yellow gown, the skirt and sleeves slashed with pale-green silk and the neckline embroidered with green rosettes. Frank was speaking to her. And they were too far away for me to overhear what he was saying, but it looked as though he were asking her to dance. And Caroline was refusing, a peevish-looking frown on her face.

I also saw Caroline inveigle my brother into dancing

with her. Fitzwilliam and Elizabeth were sitting on the settee at the side of the ballroom—because of course Elizabeth finds it tiresome to be on her feet for any great length of time. Edward was a short distance away, talking to Mr. Waterstone, who has an estate some ten miles away. Moments before, we had both been speaking to him—but I excused myself to Mr. Waterstone and went to check on Elizabeth, to make sure she was feeling all right and to ask whether there was anything I could get for her.

That was when Caroline came flouncing up in a swirl of yellow skirts and dropped to perch beside Fitzwilliam on the settee. "Come, Darcy." She put a hand on his arm. "You must dance at least once tonight. You are our host, after all." I give her credit that she didn't go so far as to bat her eyelashes at him. But she spoke in a low, throaty tone, teeth flashing in a smile. She gave Elizabeth a brief, dismissive flick of a glance. "I'm sure you won't mind my borrowing your husband for a short while, will you? It does seem so very unfair that he should be unable to enjoy the festivities at his own ball as much as the rest of us."

My brother's face stiffened and went blank of all expression—the way it does when he's either offended or angry. He opened his mouth, and I'm sure he was going to refuse. But Elizabeth stopped him before he could, smiling brightly and saying in a very level tone, "Yes, Darcy. You must dance. Caroline is quite right."

There was very little my brother could do. I could see he had no wish to dance with Caroline. But after what Elizabeth had said, there was also no way he could in courtesy refuse. He did look at Elizabeth a moment more, seeming to hesitate. But then he bowed to Caroline and held out his hand, and they moved off together onto the dance floor.

Someone else came up to speak with Elizabeth. And Edward came to find me again for the dance. And then after that, supper was announced.

I leaned against Edward as the guests began to stream into the supper room, and he put his arm around me. "Tired?"

"A little." We'd been dancing and circulating among all the rest of the party for hours. But I turned in Edward's arms to smile up at him. "I think what I'd really like, though, is to find some quiet spot. Then you can thoroughly compromise my reputation by being alone with me there. And I'll have no choice but to marry you."

Edward's arms tightened about me. "Done."

The drawing room and even the morning room were filling with the guests who had spilled out of the crowded supper and card rooms. So we ended up in the gallery upstairs, which was dim and cool after the heat and noise of the ballroom, though the scents of the wax candles and pine boughs still drifted on the air.

Edward gave me his arm, and we had started to walk along—just slowly and idly—under the rows of family paintings that line the gallery walls. And it was only then that I thought to ask, "Edward, are you all right?" I stumbled a little over the words, because I didn't wish to spoil our night. But I could still remember the taut, strained look his face had worn during the last ball we'd held at Pemberley in the spring. The fine tremors that had run through his whole frame, however hard he fought against it. And I felt guilty that this was the first time all evening that I'd thought to ask. "With all the noise and crowd and everything else, I mean? I'm sorry—perhaps I should have suggested we get away sooner. I just completely forgot—"

I stopped. Because Edward's brows had risen, as though with surprise. And then, slowly, he shook his head. "Do you know, I completely forgot, too." He frowned a little and his gaze seemed to turn inward, as though he were taking his own measure or examining his own internal response. "I forgot even to think about the noise. But"—a slow smile started at the edges of his mouth—"I'm . . . fine. Just fine."

And that was when we heard it: a soft, scuffling sound, a rustle of clothing and a muffled laugh or indrawn breath, coming from the shadowy far end of the gallery. Edward turned to me, his brows rising again—in both surprise and silent inquiry, this time. I shrugged and shook my head. I suppose really I ought to have guessed who it was. It wasn't as though I'd had no warning. But still, when Edward took the candle from one of the wall sconces and crossed to the shadowed corner in several swift strides, I still felt my jaw drop open with shock. The candlelight was dim, but perfectly bright enough for me to make out the identities of the man and woman on one of the stiff brocade sofas. It was Kitty and Lord Carmichael.

Monday 26 December 1814

I did not break off at that point in the story last night just for dramatic effect. Kitty knocked on my door, and I had to quickly close this journal and slide it out of sight into the drawer of my dressing table. Because whatever she's done, it would be needlessly cruel to let her know that I was recounting the whole ugly little story in my diary.

To tell the story in order from the point where I left

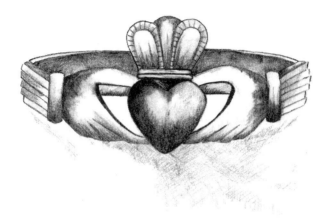

off, though:

Edward stopped short at the sight of Lord Carmichael and Kitty, and the hand that was holding the candle jerked with surprise, sending a spatter of hot wax onto the floor. But then he turned to me and said, very calmly, "Georgiana, I think you'd better escort Miss Bennet to her room."

Kitty opened her mouth and looked sulky, as though she were about to argue. Her hair was coming down, her lips were slightly swollen, and her cheeks were flushed. But then she glanced at Edward's face, and whatever she saw there must have made her change her mind, for she ducked her head and went swiftly past him towards the passage to her room.

I looked at Edward. He looked angry, but in a measured, composed way, and not the frighteningly controlled fury I've sometimes seen in him before. So I followed Kitty down the hall.

Though really I should not have bothered. She was

alternately sullen and defiant and said only that she
hadn't done anything so very dreadful, and no one here
could punish her in any case, and that she would run
away if anyone tried to stop her seeing Lord Carmichael
again.

Finally my fingers were twitching with the urge to
take her by the shoulders and shake her until her teeth
rattled. So I walked out and shut the door on her and
went downstairs to my brother's study. Since the ball
was still going on, I assumed that was where he and
Elizabeth and Edward would be found.

And in fact they were there, Edward and Fitzwilliam
standing together at the hearth and looking grave, Elizabeth sitting on the sofa, her dark lashes sparkling with
tears.

I slipped into the room and came to stand by Edward,
putting my hand into his. "What's happened?" I asked
him. "Where is Lord Carmichael?"

Edward turned, and the lines of worry and temper
on his face lightened a little as his fingers tightened
around mine. "Gone."

"Edward, you didn't—"

"Hit him?" Edward finished for me. He gave me a
quick, wry flash of a smile. "No. However much I may
have wanted to. He left here wholly unharmed. The
trouble is, he refuses point-blank to marry Kitty. He
says he has no reputation to lose, and he has no concern
whatsoever for hers."

I wasn't surprised, really—although I did wish that
my opinion of Lord Carmichael's character hadn't been
so accurate.

Because of course marriage to Lord Carmichael would
be the only solution, as far as saving Kitty's public character is concerned. Only Edward and I saw her and

Lord Carmichael in the gallery—but that's only so far as we knew. Others might have seen them if anyone besides Edward and me went upstairs. Or some of the servants might. And others could well have seen them slip away from the ball together, which in itself would be enough to ruin Kitty's reputation, when a man of Lord Carmichael's character is concerned.

It may be cruel, it may be unfair to think that Kitty could be ruined forever, where nothing worse happens to Lord Carmichael than that he is confirmed as a rake. But it is the truth.

My brother cleared his throat. "He might be persuaded, though." His mouth twisted with distaste, but he said, "The fellow plainly likes money. He might—"

Elizabeth stopped him, though. "No!"

I've rarely seen Elizabeth truly upset; she's so good at seeing the humour in almost anything. But she was upset last night. Her eyes were swimming and twin spots of angry colour burned on her pale cheeks. "No, Darcy, I won't let you!" Her hands clenched. "It's unthinkable that you should be forced into buying a husband for yet another of my empty-headed sisters!"

She meant, of course, that just over two years ago when her youngest sister Lydia eloped with George Wickham, he would never have married her if my brother hadn't intervened to settle Wickham's copious debts and buy him a place in the army.

Fitzwilliam sat down at once on the sofa beside her and pulled her towards him, cradling her head against his shoulder and stroking her hair. "You can't think that there's any price I wouldn't pay to spare you worry, love."

Elizabeth shut her eyes and rested her head against him, tears slipping from under her closed lids. My brother hugged her harder. "Please, Lizzy, don't cry." He searched through his pockets for a handkerchief and finally found one, using it to wipe her cheeks. "Listen to me, love. We'll find some solution. I promise you." He kissed her temple.

Finally Elizabeth took the handkerchief from him, pressed it against her eyes, and then gave him a watery smile. "I'm sorry. I seem to be living up to everything everyone always says about women close to confinement."

Edward's eyes met those of my brother over the top of Elizabeth's head, and Edward cleared his throat. "Why don't Georgiana and I go back to the ball and see if any rumours are circulating about Kitty and Lord Carmichael? If anyone else did see them together, we'll surely soon pick up word of it. And that will help determine what's to be done."

My brother nodded to that. "Thank you."

Kitty must either lead a charmed life—or else Fate was simply sparing Elizabeth worry—because Edward and I didn't hear so much as a whisper about Kitty or Lord Carmichael all the rest of the night.

I even sought out Caroline. Because if anyone knew of any scandalous rumours, I was sure it would be her. And that she wouldn't in the slightest mind repeating them. But she didn't say anything—even when I ventured to remark that Lord Carmichael had left the ball very early.

Finally the ball ended. Edward had found Frank at some point during the night and told him what had happened. And Frank offered to see Elizabeth up to bed while my brother and I bid good-bye to the departing guests. Fitzwilliam asked Edward if he'd come and talk things over with him now that the guests were gone. So Edward kissed me goodnight and went off with him—

and I came back to my room. Which was when Kitty interrupted me just as I was writing down what had occurred.

And that was when I did begin to feel genuinely sorry for her. Her face was all splotched and her eyes red and swollen. And she must have tried darkening her lashes for the ball last night, because her tears had made the kohl or whatever it was run in black stripes down her cheeks.

She asked in a tear-clogged voice whether she could come in and talk to me, and then flung herself down onto the cushions of my window seat when I said she might.

"What's going to be done with me?"

She still sounded sullen, but somehow I didn't feel the same impatience I'd felt before.

"I'm not entirely sure," I told her honestly.

"Elizabeth will never let me stay. Not now." Kitty picked disconsolately at a loose thread on one of the cushions. "She's so—" But her voice broke before she could finish. Her face crumpled and she started to cry: great, ugly, tearing sobs. "All I wa-wanted," she finally choked out, "was to change my life like my sis-sisters did. Like Lizzy and Jane. They both made brilliant matches. Jane is married to Mr. Bingley—who is very wealthy indeed. And look at Lizzy. Mistress of a place like this!" She gestured all about her. "And I thought—I thought, why shouldn't I do just as well as they? They're not so very much pr-prettier than me. Why can't I be wealthy and have carriages and jewels and beautiful gowns, too?"

She was still crying, but the words tumbled out faster and faster. "Ever since I can remember, all my mother has talked about is how we girls must all find husbands and marry as soon as we can. Because of my father's estate being entailed away. Do you know what it's like to grow up that way? It's hor-horrid! And it only got worse, not better, when Lizzy and Jane married so well and went away. And Lydia, who was the only one of my sisters who was ever any fun, is married and gone now, too. It's just me and Mary left at home for my mother to parade around and push on any eligible man who sets foot within five miles of the house—never mind if the man is old or ugly or has false teeth and stinking bad breath. John asked me to marry him, and I said yes, just so that my mother would stop and I could finally get away. But do you know what my life will be like if I marry John? Just like my mother's! He has no estate of his own—he's a younger son. What if I have daughters? I'll be left spending all my time scheming to get *them* married off, pushing *them* at any rich men who happen to come their way."

Kitty scrubbed furiously at her eyes, then lifted her head. "Maybe Henry—Lord Carmichael—will still offer for me, though. I know he likes me. And he did ask me for my opinion on the upholstery of his new barouche. Don't you think that shows he *must* have serious intentions? I think it was his way of hinting that I would be riding in the barouche myself a great deal in future."

I looked at her, with the eyelash tint smearing her face, the pretty pink gown she'd worn for the ball looking crumpled and her hair bedraggled as the curls she'd laboured over began to unwind. Maybe I ought to have told her what Lord Carmichael had said of her. Maybe it is crueler to let her have false hope than none at all. But I could not do it, even so.

All I finally said was that it was very late, and she ought to try to get some sleep if she could. And Kitty yawned, scrubbed at her eyes again, nodded and went quite quietly back to her room.

That was last night; I have not seen her yet this morning.

I did see Edward, though. He was alone in the breakfast room when I came down, since Elizabeth was still upstairs in bed and my brother with her. Edward wasn't eating, just standing in front of the window and looking out towards the winter-bare trees.

We didn't speak for a moment, just stood together. And then: "Edward, what are you going to do?" I asked.

Edward slowly shook his head. "I don't know." There was a furrow between his brows. "On the one hand, it's not really any of my business to interfere." He rubbed the space between his eyes. "God, I feel like some gossiping elderly spinster just thinking about it. And yet on the other . . . on the other, John Ayres is one of my officers. A friend. What kind of a friend would I be if I let him marry Miss Bennet in ignorance of all this?"

"What kind of man is Captain Ayres if he can't see Kitty's character for what it truly is?"

Edward turned from the window and looked down at me. "You think I ought to say nothing? Communicate nothing to John?" He didn't sound angry or as though he were arguing, only tired and as though he honestly wanted my opinion.

"I don't know." In a way, it doesn't seem fair that Kitty should suffer no consequences for what she's done. She has treated Captain Ayres appallingly badly these last weeks, even if he knows nothing of it. Besides which, if she *had* been seen last night by anyone but Edward and me, the scandal would have rebounded not only on her, but on Elizabeth, as well, since Elizabeth is her sister—which I'm sure Kitty didn't even for a moment consider.

But I was sorry for Kitty last night—and I am still, now. I can remember what it was like last year, when my Aunt de Bourgh was determined to see me wedded to the suitor of her choice. And I had my brother and Elizabeth both to support me and argue against my being pushed into a match.

I was remembering, too, the last thing Kitty had said to me the night before, just as she left my room— which was to beg me to ask Cook to save some of the pastries from last night's supper for Thomas and Jack. "I completely forgot to bring them up any sweets from supper last night," she said. "And I promised them so faithfully."

"I don't think you should say anything," I finally said to Edward. "Let me speak with Kitty before she leaves. She clearly can't stay here, not with Lord Carmichael still in the neighbourhood, and I'm sure Elizabeth will want her to go. But let her break the engagement to Captain Ayres herself. She can do that without any lasting damage to her reputation in the eyes of the world. And I'm sure I can get her to promise that she'll do it. She doesn't really want to marry him."

Edward looked surprised—and then he let out his breath and relaxed. "You're absolutely right. That's much the best way." He slid one arm around me and pressed a kiss into my temple. "I think I'd better turn into one of those thoroughly cowed husbands who always do everything their wives tell them. You're obviously much better at all this sort of thing than I am."

He was smiling, but the furrow between his brows hadn't entirely smoothed out. "Edward, are you . . . all right?" I asked after a moment's hesitation.

"Yes . . . no." Edward rubbed his forehead again. "Just

a headache, that's all." And then he saw my hand and reached down to lift it in his. He smiled again—a quick, flashing smile. "You're wearing the ring."

I was, of course. The heart-shaped emerald of the *claddaugh* ring flashed deep green fire in the morning light. I tugged Edward's head down and kissed him. That's really why I'm so sorry for Kitty. Because she hasn't found her own Edward—and probably never will, if she keeps on the way she's begun.

"I never took it off last night," I whispered against Edward's lips. "I'm not *going* to take it off—not ever."

Later . . .

Kitty is gone.

I did speak to her about Captain Ayres, as I promised Edward. I told her that Edward had agreed not to mention anything of Lord Carmichael to John Ayres. But that she really ought to end the engagement.

I felt more than awkward, saying such a thing to her. Because we are the same age, and it isn't in any way my business to dictate to her. But she didn't argue, just nodded and said, "You're right. I know you're right." Her eyes filled with tears, but she blinked them away and swallowed. "I'll write to him as soon as I get back to London. Poor John. He'll be so upset. But he doesn't deserve to be married to me. And I ought to let him know as soon as possible, so that he's spared the trouble of coming to Longbourn to see me when next he gets leave."

By now she'll be well on her way back to her parents' home at Longbourn. Though she departed a little later than was planned. First thing this morning she came to Elizabeth and asked whether she could take

Thomas and Jack with her. The boys would be perfectly welcome at Longbourn. And, Kitty said, it had been her responsibility to look after the boys, and it wasn't fair that Elizabeth should have to take them on instead because Kitty herself had misbehaved.

She looked . . . not exactly defeated. But at least more subdued and sad than I've ever seen her. Her eyes looked red and swollen, still, and beneath the brim of her travelling bonnet, she'd pulled her hair back into a plain, simple knot without any of the usual curls.

Elizabeth's eyes were red-rimmed as well. And she looked as though she couldn't decide whether to comfort Kitty or shake her. But in the end Elizabeth kissed her cheek and said that of course she could take Thomas and Jack—that they were welcome at Pemberley, but they'd break their hearts missing Kitty after she was gone and would do better with her back at Longbourn.

Friday 30 December 1814

Today was our annual open house for my brother's tenants, and we were busy all day with the families coming to pay the rents and bring apples and hams and other gifts of the season.

I offered to take Elizabeth's place as hostess—she was looking tired, especially after all that had happened with Kitty. But she wouldn't hear of it, and took her place among the proceedings as usual, greeting the tenants and their wives and children and helping Mrs. Reynolds with seeing that the supplies of cakes and spiced wine didn't run out.

Towards the late afternoon, though, I noticed Elizabeth was sitting down on one of the sofas. Her face looked pale and her breathing was a little quicker than usual. I sat down next to her and asked, "Are you—"

Elizabeth stopped me, resting her head against the cushions, her eyes sliding briefly closed. "If you succeed in being the fiftieth person to ask me today whether I think the baby will be coming soon, I will be obliged to murder you." She opened her eyes and smiled. "And that would be a shame, because you happen to be my favourite sister-in-law."

I laughed. "I'm sorry. I suppose it must get very tedious—especially in a group of other mothers like this one, where it seems the natural topic of conversation to everyone who speaks with you. I won't ask. I just thought you looked a little—"

I stopped again, this time because Elizabeth had drawn in a sharp breath, her hands resting on top of the curve of her belly. "Are you all right? Should I call for someone to help?"

Elizabeth shook her head, though. "No, it's nothing. Just a stray pain—and they've been coming for a week now. My sister Jane told me she was just the same, all through the entire last *month* before baby Amelia was born." Her eyes rested on Fitzwilliam. He was shaking hands with old Mr. Gibbons, who works as a horse trainer on the home farm. "I do hope it means this child is coming sooner rather than later, though."

Saturday, 31 December 1814

If this entry is nearly illegible, it's because my hands are shaking almost too badly to write.

Elizabeth's baby really is on its way. Which is good news, of course. It's just I never imagined it happening quite this way. In the middle of a snowstorm, with my brother gone—and with the roads too impassable even to send to Lambton for the midwife.

I must go. I only stopped in my room to change my clothes and to scrawl this down. But I have to get back to Elizabeth.

Sunday 1 January 1815

It's morning, now—and the snow has finally stopped. A pale winter sun is making the icicles outside my window sparkle like crystal. I've just read my entry from yesterday. Which really is as incoherent as I thought. Elizabeth would laugh if she saw it.

A new year today—I had to stop myself from writing '1814' at the top of this page. And a new member of our family.

I'll try to tell—more comprehensibly—just what happened.

Yesterday morning, first thing, my brother's agent came in to ask whether my brother could come out to settle a disagreement between two of the tenant farmers over grazing rights. This particular quarrel stretches back generations. But the sons of the two families who've taken up the feud now are hot-tempered—and I think given to drink, though Herbert, my brother's agent, didn't say that exactly—and the quarrel was threatening to turn ugly.

So my brother said he would come. Though he hesitated to leave Elizabeth. We were all sitting at breakfast, and Fitzwilliam asked how Elizabeth was feeling.

Elizabeth said—as shortly as she's capable of saying anything—that she was perfectly fine and wasn't an invalid. But then she smiled and apologised for being in such a bad temper. And said that my brother should go and take full advantage of this opportunity to get away from her, if only for the morning.

But then, just as my brother was about to take his leave, Elizabeth followed him to the doorway.

My chair was closest to them, so that l heard Elizabeth say, as she caught my brother's hand, "Darcy? Is there anything wrong?"

I hadn't noticed it until Elizabeth spoke—but my brother did look . . . not troubled, exactly. But preoccupied. Or at least tired, as though he'd not been sleeping well.

Fitzwilliam shook his head though. "No, nothing. I'm just wishing I didn't have to ride out in this filthy cold weather to play nursery governess to a couple of overgrown schoolboys, that's all." He glanced at the window, and the skies that looked still more leaden and heavy than the day before. "It looks as though we'll have snow before nightfall, and this particular property is close on five miles' ride from here."

And then, before Elizabeth could answer, Caroline came sweeping into the room.

Frank had been unusually silent up until then. But at Caroline's entrance he sprang up and gave Caroline an engaging grin. "Miss Bingley. May I offer to get you some toast—or some cold ham from the sideboard? Your wish is my command."

I thought Caroline turned a shade paler and she pressed her fingers to her mouth. But then she drew herself up and said, in a frosty tone, "Thank you, but no," turned her back on Frank, and asked where my brother was going.

Fitzwilliam told her about his errand. And Caroline said, "How excessively fortunate! I was just wishing to go into Lambton to the apothecary's to buy some hartshorn. I've not been sleeping well at all, and I was wondering how I was to procure anything for my relief." She gave Darcy a smile. "And now you can take me with you, and leave me off in Lambton on your way."

My brother agreed—there was really very little else he could do. Though before he followed Caroline out the door he stopped and kissed Elizabeth on the mouth. "I should be back by dinner time."

Caroline hadn't so much as glanced in Frank's direction again. But Frank had been watching her all the while; I'd seen him. I think Edward had, too—for I saw him looking at his brother closely and he said, "Miss Bingley doesn't seem entirely enamoured with you, Frank."

I thought something crossed Frank's gaze, swift as a shadow. But then he smiled and said, "Hard to credit, isn't it? Still, it's only a matter of time before she succumbs to my sterling character and sparkling charm." Frank pushed back his chair and stood up. "I'll see you all this afternoon," he said. He bowed to Elizabeth and me and said, "I've a mind to ride into Lambton for a while."

Edward went to his room after that, since he said he wanted to write letters as promised on behalf of Mr. Mayberry, the destitute former soldier he met in London. Elizabeth took up some sewing and I sat on the window seat and sketched.

But when Elizabeth had run the needle into her thumb for the third time—I could tell by her exclamations of annoyance—she set the baby's gown she was embroidering aside and said, "Who on earth ever decided that fancy work was an agreeable way to pass the time?"

I looked up from the drawing I was making of Edward as he looked when he arrived at Pemberley, in his red-coated army uniform. "Don't look at me. I loathe sewing."

"At least *you* do it well, however."

I laughed. "Well, and so do you." Elizabeth does sew beautifully—when she cares to.

Elizabeth sucked a drop of blood from the pad of her thumb. "Not today, apparently." She folded the infant's gown away. "And unless this poor child wants a dress with equal parts bloodstains and embroidery for decoration, I think I'd better give up for now." She rubbed the base of her spine. "My back's been hurting all morning, and I'm just—"

Elizabeth shook her head and then stood up with sudden decision. "Will you go and find Edward and ask him if he'll take us for a ride in the phaeton? Darcy and Caroline"—I thought her voice altered slightly on the words—"will have taken the carriage. But I'd love some fresh air—and it may be our last chance if Darcy is right about the snow."

I found Edward sitting at the writing desk in his room. He wasn't wearing a jacket or tie, and his sleeves were rolled up. And he was rubbing his forehead as though it ached. But he smiled when I passed on Elizabeth's request and said that of course he would oblige, he'd nearly finished the letter in any case.

It was bitterly cold outside—and of course the phaeton is an open carriage, that we usually only use in summer. Elizabeth and I were wearing pelisses and bonnets and both had fur-lined muffs for our hands, and thick rugs over our laps. But my toes were still tingling with cold and my cheeks felt numb before Edward had even driven us past our gatekeeper's lodge.

Elizabeth bit her lip and shifted on her seat every time the phaeton hit a bump or a rut in the road. And before we'd gone more than two miles, she touched Edward's shoulder and asked him to stop. "I'm sorry. I know this was my idea—but maybe it wasn't such a good one after all. Do you think—could I get out and walk, just for a little while?"

Edward told her gravely that she was officially exempt from having to apologise for anything, drew up on the horse's reins, and swung himself out of the driver's seat to help Elizabeth down. I got down with her and we walked for a few hundred yards, with Edward driving the carriage slowly behind us.

A few flurries of snowflakes were just starting to swirl through the air. And cold as it was, it was good to be out-of-doors. Or at least it was until I heard Edward give a sudden shout, and I looked round—and then we were hit by a sudden, moving wall of snow.

That really was what it felt like. I've never known a snowstorm to come up so fast—but this one did. One moment the snow was so light as to be barely noticeable. And the next Elizabeth and I could scarcely see more than a few feet ahead of us.

Edward vaulted down from the seat again and said, "We'd better get back to the house—quickly."

But Elizabeth didn't move, only gave a sudden sharp gasp and caught hold of my hand. At first I thought she was frightened because of the storm. But then I looked down and saw that her skirts were wet, and that her free hand was clutching the swollen curve of her belly. "Oh, dear heaven." Her eyes were wide with panic under the brim of her bonnet. "The baby—it seems to be coming *now*."

Edward was wonderful. Without missing a beat, he

simply picked Elizabeth up in his arms and carried her swiftly back to the phaeton. He turned to help me in, too, but I shook my head and scrambled in without any help. "I'm all right. Let's just get back to the house."

The snow was coming down hard and fast, though— so fast that in what seemed like no time at all, we couldn't even see the road ahead of us. Road, fields, pasture—it all blurred under the thick covering of endless white. And the horse was starting to panic, half-blinded by the snow; it tossed and turned its head and tried to kick at the traces until Edward finally got down from the driver's seat again and took hold of the reins.

He settled the horse, talking quietly to it and rubbing its neck and ears. And then he came back to Elizabeth and me.

Looking at Elizabeth on the seat opposite mine, I realised I'd never seen her truly frightened before—any more than I'd seen her upset before the other night at the ball. But her eyes were still wide and panicked-looking, and beneath the colour the wind and cold had whipped into her cheeks, her face looked white.

Edward gave her a quick glance, then came over and spoke in an undertone to me. "There's nowhere nearby we could take shelter, is there? Nowhere closer than the house?"

I shook my head. "No. There's old Mrs. Bates' cottage —but that's nearly a mile from the main road, and I don't promise I could find it in all this snow."

Edward nodded. Elizabeth seemed not to have heard us. She was breathing quickly and clutching her middle again, her eyes squeezed tightly closed. Edward leaned over the side of the phaeton and took hold of her hand. "Listen to me. It's going to be all right. We're not more than a mile from Pemberley House. I can lead the horse that far."

A little of the terror seemed to ebb from Elizabeth's face. She gave him a shaky nod, and Edward let go of her hand. "All right. You just sit tight back there and I'll get you home. I promise you."

I would have moved across to sit next to Elizabeth, but I didn't want to throw off the phaeton's balance; the wheels were having a difficult enough time finding purchase in the snow. So I stayed where I was on the seat opposite and held Elizabeth's hands. The labour pains must have started, because every so often her fingers would clench hard around mine. But once she smiled a little at me and said, "That's quite a man you've chosen to marry, you know."

And I smiled back and said, "I know." We hit another bump in the road then and Elizabeth gasped—and I told her, "If Edward promises he'll get you home, he will."

I didn't doubt he would—not really. But I don't know how he kept his sense of direction. I would never have been able to find my way back to the house—and I've lived here my whole life and travelled that stretch of road more times than I can even begin to count.

Finally, though, I felt the carriage wheels begin to crunch over what felt like gravel instead of earth underneath all the snow. And the next moment I could see the lights of the house up ahead.

Edward drew the phaeton up to the front steps, helped Elizabeth down, and then picked her up again and carried her inside. Probably giving our footmen the shock of their lives when he burst through the front door. I ran up the stairs behind them and followed Edward into the drawing room, where he was setting Elizabeth down beside the fire.

He turned to me when he'd settled her into the hearth-side chair and took my freezing hands in both of his. "Are you all right?"

I nodded. "Of course. I'm fine. Edward, I'm so glad you were with us. If you hadn't been—" And then I stopped, looking at Elizabeth. Because really there wasn't time to think about what could have happened if Elizabeth and I had gone out on our own.

"I should go and fetch Mrs. Reynolds," I said. I kept my voice low—though Elizabeth was leaning her head back against the chair cushions, her eyes closed. "Clearly there's no question of going for the midwife, not in this snow. I don't suppose you also happen to know how to deliver a baby, as well as navigate in the middle of a snowstorm?"

Edward gave me a lopsided answering grin and pushed the snow-wet hair out of his eyes. "I have done it in the past." And then he grinned again at my look of disbelief and said, "But I'd much prefer to leave it to Mrs. Reynolds, I promise you. You go ahead and fetch her. I'll stay with Elizabeth."

Mrs. Reynolds was in the stillroom, supervising the making of soap; the air was steamy with the scent of boiling lye and the rose oil Mrs. Reynolds always puts in.

It is completely impossible to alarm or rattle Mrs. Reynolds. So she didn't gasp or wring her hands when I told her Elizabeth was going to have the baby today. But she did look grave. "Well, now. I've had the four babes of my own—but that were thirty-odd years ago. And as for delivering one, well, that's something I've never done."

"But if there's no one else?" I asked her. Because Mrs. Reynolds is the only one of the household servants who *has* had children of her own. All our housemaids and kitchen maids are of course young and unmarried; all girls in service are. "Do you think you can?"

"Oh, aye, I suppose so." Mrs. Reynolds still looked grave, though, and she pursed her lips as she added, "So long as nothing goes wrong."

Edward was sitting beside Elizabeth, talking to her quietly when we got back to the drawing room. Whatever he was saying seemed to have helped, because some of the colour had come back into Elizabeth's face and she was even smiling a little.

Another pain struck just as Mrs. Reynolds and I came in, and Elizabeth shut her eyes and bit her lip. But she looked up when it had passed, smiled a little at Mrs. Reynolds, and said, "I'm sorry to be making such a fuss. I know women have babies every day."

If Mrs. Reynolds still had doubts, at least she didn't let Elizabeth see it. Her broad face was completely unperturbed. "There, now, lamb, no need to be sorry." Mrs. Reynolds clucked her tongue in sympathy and patted Elizabeth's shoulder. "Every mother's afraid with her first-born. Let's get you upstairs, shall we?"

Elizabeth's face paled again as she caught sight of the snow outside the window and she turned back to Edward. "Darcy? And Caroline and Frank—what if they're—"

"Darcy will have had sense enough to take shelter in one of the tenant cottages." Edward stopped her. "And as for Miss Bingley and my brother, there's no need to worry for them. They're surely in Lambton and can stay at the Inn there until the storm has passed."

Mrs. Reynolds helped Elizabeth towards the door and I turned to Edward. "I should go with them and see if there's anything I can do to help."

"Of course." Edward kissed me lightly. "You go ahead." He glanced at the window, where thick white flakes were still swirling outside the glass. "I'd ride out again if I thought there was any chance of fetching Darcy home for her. But I don't think there is, not with him five miles away."

A shadow of a frown crossed Edward's brow, but then he shook his head and said, "You go ahead up to Elizabeth. I'll be here if there's anything you need me to do."

Upstairs in Elizabeth's room, Mrs. Reynolds efficiently stripped the bed and then bustled away with the armload of linen, saying she'd be back with some old sheets and quilts to use.

I'd sat down with Elizabeth on the little chaise in front of the dressing table. "How are you feeling?" I asked her.

"I'm all right." Elizabeth's hands were clasped hard together, so tightly I could see the knuckles turning white. "It's just . . . I wish Darcy were here. Or Jane. Or—" And then she laughed a little, and bit her lip again. "I never in five hundred years thought I'd say it, but right now I even wish my *mother* were here."

She broke off, shutting her eyes as another pain struck. When the pain had passed, she looked up at me and put her hand into mine. "I'm so glad you're with me, though." And then a shadow of fear crossed her face—the same fear I'd seen in Edward's gaze downstairs, the same fear I could feel pressing up like a physical force under my ribcage. "You don't think Darcy could have been caught—"

"Of course not." I spoke firmly—and with much more certainty than I truly felt. "Fitzwilliam will have taken shelter in one of the cottages he was visiting just as Edward said, I'm sure of it. It's barely noon now; he wouldn't have yet started back to Pemberley when the snow hit. Believe me. I know Rory Barnes and Tom Hutchins—there's no possible way even my brother could have settled the quarrel between them this quickly."

Elizabeth smiled just a little. And a moment later Mrs. Reynolds came back with an armload of old quilts and sheets. Betty and Joan—two of the housemaids— helped her make the bed and build the fire up in the grate so that the room would stay warm. We'd drawn the curtains and lighted the lamps, but I could still hear the wind outside and the hissing patter of snow against the windows.

I helped Elizabeth to change out of her gown and into a nightdress. And when Mrs. Reynolds had finished arranging the room, she told Elizabeth, "All right, lamb, all's ready now. You should stay on your feet—walk a bit, if you feel you're able."

Elizabeth still looked pale, and she didn't speak—but she did nod, and with my help got to her feet.

I'm not sure how long we walked, or how many circuits of the room we made. It all felt like a blur: slowly walking from the bed to the hearth to the dressing table and round again. Holding Elizabeth's hand and feeling her fingers tighten on mine every time a pain struck.

I know once Elizabeth turned to me, still breathing quickly from one of the pains, and said, "I'm sorry, this must be horribly boring for you."

"Well, you did ask me to come for a walk." I squeezed her hand. "And don't be a ninny, do you think there's anywhere else I'd be when my very first niece or nephew is about to be born?"

I did notice after a time that the pains seemed to

be coming closer and closer together—and that they were getting stronger. Elizabeth started to bend over, clutching her middle and gasping every time one hit. Her dark hair was soaked with sweat, and the nightdress clung damply to her body. And then finally she made a little sound, half whimper, half groan, through her clenched teeth and said, "I can't walk anymore. I have to—"

Mrs. Reynolds had been sitting, quietly knitting something grey and wooly in a chair by the hearth. But she was there at once, helping Elizabeth onto the bed. She rubbed Elizabeth's shoulders a little and said, "There, now, my dear, you're doing splendid. I'm afraid you'll only be comfortable again when you can hold the babe in your arms. But that won't be so long, now."

I looked at the clock on the mantle—and was shocked to see that it was nearly eight o'clock in the evening. Elizabeth seemed scarcely to have heard Mrs. Reynolds. Her eyes were tightly closed, and she groaned again as another pain struck. She rolled to one side, as though instinctively trying to escape the pain. And I saw there was a bright stain of blood on the quilts where she'd been lying.

Mrs. Reynolds had moved to the hearth to stir up the fire, and I crossed to her and asked, in an undertone, "Is anything—does that mean something's wrong?"

Mrs. Reynolds glanced at the blood and shook her head. "That? Nay, there's nothing wrong there. It's a good sign, if anything—means the babe will be coming sooner, not later. Most first babies are much slower to come. I mind when your lady mother were brought to bed with Master Fitzwilliam, she laboured all through the night and the next day." Mrs. Reynolds' kind grey eyes focused on Elizabeth, lying limp and spent, her eyes still closed, in the aftermath of the pain. "This one'll come before midnight, I shouldn't wonder."

There was a line between her brows, and I said, "That's good, surely?"

Mrs. Reynolds nodded—though the deep furrow between her brows remained. "Oh, aye." And then she added, more to herself than to me, and in a voice so low I could barely hear, and Elizabeth certainly could not, "Aye, so long as the babe's not backward. Or it doesn't strangle on the cord." And then her eyes refocused on me, as though she were only just realising fully that I was still there. She shook her head and said, in an entirely different tone, "You oughtn't to be here, Miss Georgiana. An unmarried girl in a birthing room? It's not proper."

I nearly laughed. Except that that would have hurt Mrs. Reynolds' feelings, and she'd been so wonderful through everything so far. Instead I kissed her cheek. "I think it's a little late to try and persuade me that new babies are found under cabbage leaves in the garden. And besides—" I broke off, watching as Elizabeth writhed through another pain on the bed. "Besides, you and I seem to be all that Elizabeth has right now."

Mrs. Reynolds pursed her lips together. But then she seemed to give up, for she shook her head and said, "You'd best go and change your gown, Miss Georgiana. Put on the oldest one you have, if you mean to stay all the way until the babe's born."

I did as she said and ran back to my room—that was when I scribbled down yesterday's diary entry. And when I got back to the room, Elizabeth was groaning and there was a dark, wet stain spreading out from under her on the bed.

"She's started to push," Mrs. Reynolds said. "Won't

be long now." She pushed me towards the head of the bed. "You help Mrs. Darcy—talk to her, hold her hand." She settled herself near Elizabeth's feet. "I'll see to the babe."

The rest . . . I'm not even sure I can put it down here into words. I did know technically speaking where babies come from, of course—and yet before today, I really had no idea at all just what the birth of a child is like.

Elizabeth grasped my hand so hard I could feel the bones grinding together, and her face reddened with the effort of pushing the child into the world. She kept biting her lip and trying not to scream, too. Until Mrs. Reynolds patted her knee and told her, during a break between pains, "You go ahead and make all the noise you like, my lamb. Be a good lesson to those flighty housemaids of mine not to let the stable lads take any liberties."

Which made Elizabeth hiccup a laugh before the next pain struck.

It seemed to go on for hours, though. I could see how exhausted Elizabeth was growing; she kept her eyes completely shut, now, and every time a pain left her, she would collapse back onto the pillows, utterly limp and spent—until the next time. I was beginning to get frightened. And then suddenly Mrs. Reynolds said, "That's the way—that's the way, now. I can see the babe's hair!"

Elizabeth's eyes flew open as the next pain struck and she said, "I can't—"

"Yes you can!" The room was over-warm with the heat from the fire; Mrs. Reynolds had said it would need to be, for when the child was born. Sweat was dripping down my ribs under the old gown I'd put on. I held onto both Elizabeth's hands. "You can do it, I know you can! Did you hear that? Your baby's hair!"

"Aye, a fine head of black hair, just like its father's, I reckon," Mrs. Reynolds said from the foot of the bed. But Elizabeth really didn't hear her this time. Another pain had struck and she was groaning and curling forward, straining and pushing and shouting—and I could hear myself shouting with her, telling her she could do it, and how amazingly well she was doing, and then—

And then there was a sudden wail, and Mrs. Reynolds was lifting something red and wet and coated with slime and laying it on Elizabeth's chest. And I realised that it was all over—the baby had been born.

Elizabeth was laughing and crying at once—all three of us were. Mrs. Reynolds found a linen towel and rubbed the baby dry and then put a blanket over it and Elizabeth both. And I wiped my eyes and asked, "Is it a boy or a girl?"

Mrs. Reynolds looked at me blankly, and wiped tears from her own cheeks with the corner of her apron. And then she laughed, the closest to completely nonplussed I'd ever seen her, and said, "Do you know, I were that flustered I never even thought to check?"

Which made all three of us laugh again. Elizabeth lifted the blanket. The baby had stopped wailing and was just lying on her breast, blinking swollen little eyes. "It's a boy," she said. Elizabeth's hand came up to cup the tiny head, fuzzy with damp curls of black hair. With one finger, she traced the line of the baby's shoulder and arm, ending at the tiny fingers, clenched fist-tight. She swallowed and then whispered, "Hello there, little man."

When I left Elizabeth's room, she was propped up against some pillows, with the baby at her breast. I touched her shoulder lightly before I went. "Do you need anything else?" I asked. "Or do you want me to stay?"

Elizabeth's eyes were drowsy, but she yawned and then shook her head. "No. You go on and get some rest yourself." She yawned again and then took hold of my hand. "Thank you, Georgiana. And tell Edward *thank you* from me, too."

I found Edward still sitting in front of the drawing-room fire when I went downstairs. He looked up quickly when I came in, face taut and alert. "Is she—"

"Elizabeth is fine," I said. "The baby's a boy."

And then I realised abruptly how tired I was, and sat down next to Edward on the sofa, curling against him and resting my head against his shoulder. He put an arm around me and drew me closer. "Do you want anything to eat? We could send for—"

I shook my head, though. "No, that's all right. I'm too exhausted to eat—and I'm not even the one who did all the hard work."

Edward's laugh was a breath of warmth on my temple. I turned around so that I could look up at him and said, "Did you really once deliver a baby?"

"I really did." The ghost of a smile lifted the corners of Edward's mouth. "And in weather not unlike today's, in fact."

"Will you tell me?"

Edward doesn't usually talk about his experiences on campaign. He seemed to hesitate. But then he settled back against the arm of the couch, one arm still around me. "It was in Spain—on a retreat over a mountain range. We'd been marching day and night almost without rest for days. And the weather had turned cold, with driving snow. It was . . . bad. Men were dropping in their tracks from exhaustion. But then I suppose I told you of that part before. And then—in the middle of the second night—I saw one of my men fall out of the column of marchers with his wife. She was in the family way—and close to her time—so I went back to see if I could be of any help. Privately not giving much for their chances of surviving the night. If I'd still had my horse, I'd have given it to them in an instant. But the poor beast had already died and been slaughtered for its meat." Edward's eyes had gone distant. "I had no idea what I was doing, of course. But the woman's husband was half-dead himself with hunger and cold. So I stayed with the both of them, and . . . an hour later, just as the final supply waggons were rolling past us on the road, the child was born."

"And what happened to them?" I was so tired I asked the question before I realised. But then regretted it the instant I heard the words leave my mouth. Because it seemed as though the answer couldn't possibly be a happy one.

But Edward smiled again. "Do you know, they all three survived? Husband, wife, and child? We were in a skirmish with some of the enemy the next day and I lost track of them. But the next time I saw them they were all three alive and doing better than I could have hoped. The husband lost a leg a few months later, so they were sent back to England. But I saw them just a few months ago. The baby—it was a boy—is four years old now, and has two younger sisters, as well."

We were quiet a time. The heat of the fire was making me feel even sleepier, and I leaned against Edward again and stifled a yawn—and then said, "Oh, I nearly forgot. Elizabeth said to tell you *thank you*."

"She's very welcome," Edward said.

I must have fallen asleep after that, because the next thing I knew, I was vaguely aware of Edward lifting me up in his arms and carrying me up the stairs. I don't remember him bringing me to my room or setting me down. But I woke up in my own bed, under the blankets Edward must have drawn over me.

It's still early morning now, and the house feels hushed, as though all the snow outside is insulating it from the rest of the world. Outside, the branches of all the trees on the lawn are bowed nearly to the ground by the weight of the snow on them.

And now that I've written all this down, I'd better finish dressing and see how Elizabeth and the baby are today.

Later . . .

I'm back in my own room again. Though I did go to see Elizabeth.

The door was open just a crack, so I pushed it open and peeped in. The curtains were drawn, and it was early enough that the room was still dim, but after a moment I could just see Elizabeth and the baby, sound asleep in the bed, the baby just a little red-faced swaddled bundle—a little like a caterpillar—against Elizabeth's side.

The fire had gone out and the room was chilly—but I didn't want to wake either of them by ringing for anyone to come and bring more coals. So I just slipped into Elizabeth's dressing room, intending to get an extra blanket to spread over them. I did find the blanket and was standing just in the dressing room doorway, about to go back into the bedroom when I heard running footsteps racing up the stairs, taking the steps two at a time, or so it sounded like.

And the next moment my brother was in the room. I let out a breath of relief—because although I hadn't *really* thought he might have been caught somewhere on the road in the storm, a part of me had still feared he might, and I was so thankful to see him returned safely home.

Fitzwilliam passed within ten feet of the doorway where I stood, but he didn't see me, nor even glance in my direction. If he'd knocked me over and had to step over my prostrate body to get to Elizabeth's bedside, I'm not sure he would have noticed I was there.

He had a look on his face I'd never, ever seen in him before, and I saw his hand shake as he steadied himself on the bedpost, looking down at Elizabeth and the sleeping baby.

Elizabeth's eyes fluttered open, and she blinked—and then she sat up and said, "Darcy!"

My brother, his voice turned husky and uneven, said, "Elizabeth—oh, God, you're . . . are you—"

"I'm fine. Splendid, in fact." I could hear the smile in Elizabeth's tone. "And if you come over here, you can meet your son."

I drew back a little into the shadows of the dressing room. But not too much, because I didn't want to risk making too much noise. I didn't mean to eavesdrop—but I didn't want to come bursting out and spoil their first few moments of being together, either. So I stayed where I was.

Fitzwilliam had sat down on the edge of the bed, his arms around Elizabeth and his face buried in her hair. His shoulders were shaking. And that made me freeze, completely forgetting all question of eavesdropping. Because I've never seen my brother cry. Not even when our mother and then our father died.

When he raised his head, his eyes were wet, though, and his hand still trembled as he smoothed the dark curls away from Elizabeth's brow. "Oh, God, I've been half out of my mind these last weeks. I was certain I was going to lose you."

"Lose me?"

Fitzwilliam exhaled and wiped his eyes with the back of his hand. "That's how my mother died. When I was seventeen. She was nearly forty. And the birth was too much for her. She died. And the child died, too. And I was afraid—" he broke off to exhale hard again, then closed his eyes and rested his forehead against Elizabeth's. "There's nothing I wouldn't do for you. Nothing I wouldn't protect you from. But whatever I did, however much I wanted to, I couldn't protect you from this. You could have died, and I'd have been powerless to do anything at all."

Elizabeth pulled back and was staring at him. "*That's* why you've been so distant and strange these last weeks? *That's* what's been troubling you?"

Fitzwilliam ran a hand down his face. "I'm sorry. I should have known you'd notice. I did try not to let you see anything was wrong. I didn't want to burden you—or make you afraid."

Elizabeth was laughing. Laughing and biting her lip, trying to make herself stop—which made her snort a little. "I'm not supposed to laugh too much. Mrs. Reynolds said it might do damage. But—" she gave up the struggle and started to laugh all over again.

"I'm not entirely certain I see the joke." My brother was smiling, though.

Elizabeth shook her head and finally managed to stop. "I'm sorry. But I thought . . . I thought you were upset—angry—about Kitty's behaviour." Her smile faded and she said, soberly, "I thought perhaps . . . that perhaps you'd begun to regret connecting yourself to my family. I even wondered whether you were wishing you'd married Caroline instead of me."

"Caroline? Caroline *Bingley*?" It was my brother's turn to stare. "Are you joking, Lizzy? And as for connecting myself to your family—" Fitzwilliam stopped and exhaled hard again. "Elizabeth, love, I know . . . I know I've been called too reserved at times. It's . . . it's my weakness, I suppose. I've never found it easy to share my feelings. But if you can honestly think—if you doubt how much I love you—"

"I don't doubt it." Elizabeth ran her fingertips lightly through the springing black curls on my brother's brow. "I never did. Not really. But I did think . . . you've a certain rank and station in the world, Darcy. You've grown up your whole life destined to be the master of Pemberley. The most respected and looked-up-to member of the most prominent family in this part of the world. And with Kitty—your wife's sister—apparently bent on creating all manner of gossip and scandal, I thought—"

"Listen to me." Fitzwilliam had taken hold of Elizabeth's shoulders. "I wouldn't care if every single member of your family decided to run naked through the streets of London and throw rotten oranges at the Prince Regent. At least, I wouldn't care, except in so far as it caused you worry or pain."

Elizabeth laughed, a little unsteadily this time, and Fitzwilliam went on. "If I've learned one thing these past three years since I first met you, it's that pride of place means nothing—nothing—compared to who you want at your side. And that's you. No matter what. For always." And then he stopped, looking down at the little bundle lying cocooned at Elizabeth's side. "And now—" He stopped and cleared his throat as he reached out and wonderingly touched the baby's swaddled form. "And now this little lad, too."

"Do you want to hold him?" Elizabeth asked.

My brother's face looked . . . almost afraid, awed and wondering, as Elizabeth put the sleeping baby into his arms. "He's—" Fitzwilliam stopped and cleared his throat and then wiped his eyes again. "Have you chosen a name yet?"

Elizabeth shook her head. She was smiling. "I wanted to wait for you. But I was thinking maybe James? After your father. And Edward for the second name."

Thursday 5 January 1815

Tonight is the annual Twelfth Night ball at Pemberley—which is as much a tradition as the Christmas one, though we weren't sure whether we would have it this year. With baby James safely born, however, Fitzwilliam and Elizabeth decided to go ahead with the festivities. So all day we've been busy finding costumes and making preparations.

The Twelfth Night ball is always a masque ball, and in addition to wearing domino-masks, all the guests always play at Twelfth Night characters, besides. So Caroline, Elizabeth, and I sat in the drawing room, writing the names of characters on cards for the guests to draw from boxes at the doors. Each character is part of a pair, and it's the guests' task to find their partner for the evening—as well as to play the part of whatever character they've been assigned.

Last year, Elizabeth was Madame Topnote—which

meant she spent the evening singing very high scales. And my brother happened to be her match—Signor Croakthroat, who was supposed to be constantly clearing his throat in an effort to sing.

This year we were determined to think up new characters. Or rather, Elizabeth and I were. Caroline consented to help with bad-tempered grace and spent most of the time disagreeing with every suggestion. Finally baby James, who had been asleep in his cradle beside Elizabeth, let out a loud wail and Elizabeth smiled and picked him up. "I'm afraid he'd much rather have his dinner than invent new characters. I'd better take him upstairs and feed him."

Which meant that Caroline and I were alone when Frank came into the room. I felt Caroline stiffen beside me, but she didn't look up from the card she was inscribing with the name Mrs. Candour. Frank sat down opposite us at the table we were working on and looked through the cards we'd already written on.

"Here's one for you, Miss Bingley," he said. He looked up at Caroline and passed one of the character names across. Caroline's cheeks flushed and she let the card drop to the table as though it had burned her fingers. That was when I saw the name inscribed on it—one of Elizabeth's inventions—*Miss Princess.*

"And here is one for you." Caroline thrust another card across the table at Frank, so viciously that I only caught a glimpse of the character name. But I think it was, *Signor Coxcomb.*

Frank left us soon after that. I thought a quick spasm of pain crossed Caroline's face as the door closed behind him. I hesitated, then asked, "You said you had met Frank before—was it in London that the two of you formed an acquaintance?"

Caroline's face hardened again and she tossed her head. "We met a few times at Almack's; that's all. He's amusing, I suppose, in his way. But the type of young man whose attentions grow quite tiresome, after a while."

Friday 6 January 1815

I don't think I've ever in my life wanted to murder anyone as much as I wanted to murder Caroline Bingley tonight. I haven't much time for writing. I promised Elizabeth and Fitzwilliam that I would go to Caroline's room and speak with her. But if I'm to manage *not* to slap her face or call her rude names, I first have to talk myself into being at least slightly sorry for her again.

The ball began well enough—very well, really. The ballroom was decorated again with white lilies and ropes of greenery and gold foil stars. All the guests arrived in their cloaks and masks, and had great fun in drawing the names of their characters for the evening from the box at the door to the ballroom. I drew Miss Playful and Edward was Farmer Stump. Elizabeth came downstairs for a little while—though of course she's still supposed to rest a great deal, and had to leave soon in any case to feed James. And Mrs. Reynolds had organised the traditional Twelfth Night cakes, decorated with painted sugar.

Ruth Granger found the pea that had been baked into the cake—which made her queen of the ball. And elderly Mr. Herron found the bean, which made him king. They looked a little like the spirits of the Old Year and the New dancing together, maybe—what with Ruth's shining coppery hair and bright face and Mr. Herron's old-fashioned powdered wig and white side-whiskers.

And Ruth had managed to make even her ball gown—
a dusky, deep-purple satin—look sensible and plain.
But it didn't matter, somehow. Ruth was laughing and
Mr. Herron was beaming at being the centre of the festivities.

But none of this is what I set out to write about,
which was Caroline's behaviour.

She drew the character card she'd written herself—
that of Miss Candour. I frankly wouldn't be at all surprised to find she marked it in some way so that she
would recognise it. Or never added it to the box at all,
but just kept it with her and pretended to pick it at the
appropriate time.

She spent the entire ball circulating among the guests
and telling them—with extreme candour—exactly what
she thought of their costumes, their dancing skills, and
their manners.

She told poor Mrs. Herron that her maroon velvet
dress made her look, "Exactly like an overstuffed blood
sausage." And she said to Miss Felicity Tillsdale, "I de-
clare, Miss Tillsdale, you really would be almost pretty
if it weren't for the unfortunate configuration of your
teeth."

There was a great deal more besides, I'm sure—those
remarks just happened to be the ones I overheard. Which
were unpleasant and spiteful, certainly. But it wasn't
until we were all seated at the supper table that Caroline said anything with the potential for *really* serious
effect.

She was seated next to Lord Carmichael. Whom
Elizabeth and Fitzwilliam debated inviting after what
happened with Kitty. But it was finally determined that
it would only create more talk if he were excluded from
the guest list, and that people might begin to speculate

about Kitty's sudden departure from Pemberley. So Lord Carmichael was sent an invitation—though I don't think we really imagined he would be so bold as to come.

But he was there. Wearing a mask that was decorated with brown and gold feathers and a beaked nose to give him the look of a hawk.

He flirted a good deal with Caroline, who was, to pay her her due, one of the handsomest of the unattached ladies here tonight. I saw them dancing together at least three times, and sitting down in an alcove of the ballroom. And then at supper, Lord Carmichael must have paid her some compliment or other—because Caroline turned to him in the character of Mrs. Candour and said, "La, Lord Carmichael, how you do go on! But I warn you, I am quite determined not to believe a word you say. Everyone knows how dangerous you are to a lady's reputation. Why, just the other night I saw you and poor Miss—"

Caroline happened to have spoken—or maybe it wasn't happenstance at all, and was really planned—during a lull in the general conversation. Everyone in the room could hear her. I saw Fitzwilliam stiffen at the head of the table, and Elizabeth, across from him, went pale.

I was sitting nearest to Caroline, on her other side from Lord Carmichael. And I couldn't think what to do. Let her go on, and she'd drag Kitty's name out and do her best to create the scandal we'd managed to avoid. But interrupt, and everyone would know there was something we wished to hide.

The white soup had just been served; a steaming bowl had just been placed before me. So I pretended to reach for my wine glass and in the process knocked the entire bowl into Caroline's lap.

I must say the result was very satisfactory. Which is probably a terrible testament to my character, morals, and capacity for Christian charity, but there you are.

Hot, oily soup splashed all over the front of Caroline's very expensive gown and she jumped up, shrieking.

I stood up, as well. "Oh, no, Caroline, I am so sorry! How terribly clumsy of me. Please, let me help you," I said. I dabbed—not very effectually—at the dripping stains with my napkin.

Caroline gave me a look that—if looks truly could kill—would have sent me into an early grave. She brushed aside my offer to help and stalked out of the room, saying that her gown was permanently ruined and that she would have to retire upstairs to change.

I sat back down. The supper-time conversation resumed. Though Edward, who was sitting on my other side, was shaking with silent laughter, and he said in an undertone, "Remind me not to do anything to vex you while we're at table."

I smiled. "You ought already to be terrified of vexing me at any time."

And now the ball is over, and I must—as promised—go and speak with Caroline.

Sunday 8 January 1815

I did speak to Caroline last night. Though I'm not at all sure I accomplished anything.

Out of the whole of the party, I was chosen to be the one to speak with her about her behaviour because I'm the closest thing she has here at Pemberley to a friend.

By which I mean that before Elizabeth and Fitzwilliam married, back when Caroline was still hoping that my brother would marry her, she did her best to fawn on me and cultivate my acquaintance as a means of growing closer to my brother.

At any rate, I went along to her room last night after the close of the ball and knocked on her door. I hadn't been entirely successful in talking myself into pitying her. Well, to be strictly honest, I hadn't been at all successful; I could still cheerfully have seen her, if not strangled, at least bundled into a carriage and sent away from Pemberley at once.

Caroline made some reply to my knock, too muffled by the wooden panel for me to understand. But I thought I caught the words, "Come in," so I turned the knob and entered.

Caroline was by the wardrobe, undressed and wrestling with the laces on the back of her long corset. She let out a little scream at the sight of me, snatched up a purple silk dressing gown from the bed and clutched it to her chest. "For goodness' sake, Georgiana, I said *don't* come in," she said snappishly. "Have you been afflicted with deafness?"

"I'm sorry," I said. And then I frowned. "Why on earth are you trying to unlace your own corset? You brought Mason with you."

Mason is Caroline's lady's maid, who accompanies Caroline wherever she goes. And Caroline doesn't seem at all the sort to do anything for herself when someone else might do it for her.

"I didn't want Mason." Caroline's voice was still short, and she avoided meeting my gaze. "She was being stupid and clumsy tonight, and I sent her away."

She finally succeeded in untying the knot at the base of the corset, loosened the strings and stepped out of it, all the while holding the dressing gown one-handed in front of her, like a shield. She stepped behind the dressing screen in the corner of the room, and when she came out she had put on the dressing gown. And her eyes were narrowed with accusation. "You did that deliberately," she said. "Spilled soup all over my gown at the supper table."

I was relieved, in a way, by the directness of the attack, since it meant I didn't have to bother with pretence or with dancing politely around the subject. "Can you wonder that I did?" I said. "It's one thing to flirt outrageously with my brother and try to make Elizabeth jealous." Caroline made a small sound of angry protest at that, but I spoke over her. "That is more pathetically futile than anything else, since you'll never manage to make real trouble between them. But it's another thing entirely to deliberately cause a scandal that would drag Kitty's name into the gutter and cause Elizabeth a great deal of pain, as well."

"Well?" Caroline tilted her chin up and met my gaze defiantly. "And why shouldn't I?"

I took firm hold of my temper with both hands. "Why should you? What have my brother and Elizabeth ever done to you, that you should repay them in such a way?"

For a moment, Caroline continued to look defiant. And then quite suddenly her face seemed to crumple, and she broke into noisy sobs. "They're ha-ha-happy together," she choked out. "Isn't that enough?"

"Oh for goodness' sake, Caroline, do be quiet!" I snapped. I still wasn't of a mind to be terribly sorry for her.

At least she was surprised enough to leave off crying and look up at me with a sound midway between a gulp and a snuffle. I looked at Caroline. Her face was tear-blotched, her nose reddened. But her fingers were also so tightly clasped together in her lap that the skin stretched over her knuckle bones. I took a breath and tried to speak more quietly. "Caroline, what is all this about? Is it—" I ventured a guess: "Is it something to do with Edward's brother Frank?"

Caroline made a harsh, ugly sound that was like a laugh. "Frank? Yes, you could say that it has everything to do with Frank. Since I'm going to have his child."

I was so startled I must have stared at her for a full half-minute before I could gather my wits enough to speak. "You're—"

"Going to bear Lord Silverbridge's by-blow?" Caroline's mouth twisted as she cut me off, her voice hard. "Yes. I am. Unless I'm lucky enough to miscarry."

"You don't mean that!"

To my surprise, Caroline's chin quivered and she started to cry all over again. "No. I don't. Of course I don't. I'm just so miserable, and—" She broke off, wiping her eyes with the back of her hand and swallowing the rest of her sobs. "You can't tell anyone." She gripped my hand, so hard I could feel her nails leaving dents in my skin. "I mean it, Georgiana. You can't tell one single person what I've told you tonight, or I'll . . . I'll say the child is your brother's."

I would have thought myself past being shocked by anything Caroline could say, but that momentarily took my breath away. "You'll do what?"

Caroline's eyes slid away from mine, but she said, "I'll say the child is Darcy's. That it was conceived while we were in London these past weeks."

I drew in my breath. "And if you do, I'll make it publicly known that you stole my Aunt de Bourgh's pearl necklace last spring at the instigation of Jacques de La Courcelle."

Caroline's eyes widened and she gasped. "You would-n't!"

"Oh yes, I would. I will."

Caroline stared at me, shocked. Though her expression quickly changed to one of aggrieved resentment. "What's happened to you, Georgiana? You used to be such a meek, quiet little thing."

"I'm sure you would very much prefer it if I were, still," I said. And then I asked, "Does Frank know?"

"It doesn't matter." Caroline's voice wavered as though she were fighting tears, but she gritted her teeth and said, "It doesn't matter. And you can't tell anyone, either, Georgiana. It doesn't matter what you threaten me with." She folded her arms protectively over her middle with another sobbing breath. Her whole body was tensed, shivering. "I'm ruined in any case."

Tuesday 10 January 1815

Edward asked me to come for a walk today after breakfast. We couldn't go far. It's been so cold that the snow hasn't yet melted, though our gardeners have cleared off enough paths that we could walk down to the lake.

It's been two days since the Twelfth Night ball. Two days since Caroline told me of her expectations. Which of course explains why she's been dressing herself and sending her maid away; I suppose she wishes to keep Mason from finding out for as long as may be.

What I cannot understand is what is really the state of affairs between her and Frank. Frank obviously followed her here to Pemberley. And he's been nothing but attentive to her ever since. While Caroline has been nothing but scornful of him, and done her best to push him away at every turn.

Maybe Frank does know about the child, and offered her an irregular arrangement rather than marriage? And Caroline is angry? That doesn't seem entirely like Frank. But it would explain Caroline's behaviour, I suppose.

At any rate, I had made up my mind to tell Edward the truth today. Whatever Caroline threatened two nights ago, I cannot imagine her actually risking arrest for thievery—which means she won't really try to claim the child is my brother's. And I don't think any of us wishes to have her stay much longer at Pemberley unless *something* about her situation is sorted out or changed.

Last night at dinner, Frank seemed entirely unlike himself. Morose, and lost. He drank more than he ought, as well. He wasn't angry or ill-tempered with it, because Frank could never be that. But his speech did grow slurred and his eyes were glazed. And Caroline sniffed a great deal and made pointed, haughty comments about men who couldn't hold their drink.

So I was going to tell Edward today—he of course can speak with Frank much more easily than I could. But I never got the chance.

Edward was very quiet as we started out for our walk. His brows were furrowed and he seemed lost in thought. About halfway to the lake, he turned to me and said, "There's something—something I wanted to talk to you about. About whether or not I should stay in the army." He stopped walking and turned to look down at me. "What do you think I should do?"

I felt my heart contract. Because part of me—a large part—wishes that he'd sell his commission now, at once. And some days, maybe I can persuade myself that that would be best for Edward, too. But would it really—or am I only being selfish in wishing that? It's so hard—I never realised quite how hard—to see matters objectively when someone you love is involved.

Besides, didn't I read some hideously sentimental poem once—something about *true love speaks not of chains, but of freedom's wings*? The verse may have been uninspired, but maybe the sentiment is true.

So I swallowed and said, "What do you *want* to do, Edward?"

Edward let out a long breath and thrust his hands deep into the pockets of his coat, frowning down at the ground. "I want—I believe I want to stay in the army. Or at least, not exactly want. But I feel I ought to, somehow. At least for now."

A strange feeling swept over me, then. A kind of biting cold that had nothing to do with the icy wind whipping at our faces and tearing at my hair. I could imagine it gnawing its way through to my bones.

But I pressed tight against Edward, twining my arm through his, and said, "Then that's what you should do."

Edward smiled and bent down to kiss me. But he still seemed . . . abstracted, I suppose is the word. And I couldn't bring myself to add to his worries by telling him about Frank and Caroline.

Thursday 12 January 1815

Baby James took ill tonight. It was so sudden—that was the most terrifying thing. He's so tiny, still. And he doesn't smile yet—babies don't until they're a few weeks older than he, according to Mrs. Reynolds. But the last few days, he's just begun to open his eyes and truly seem to take in his surroundings. Yesterday when I held him he stared and stared at my face, very solemnly. He has Elizabeth's eyes, but for the rest he looks so much like my brother that I kept halfway expecting him to open his small mouth and speak in Fitzwilliam's voice.

He was perfectly well when we all retired to bed. Elizabeth refused to have a nursery maid, so James sleeps in a small cradle next to her and Fitzwilliam's bed— or bundled into the bed between them, Elizabeth says. Because they both like to have him close.

But tonight—or I suppose I should say last night, since it's nearly dawn now—James woke up crying and coughing at once. Short, harsh, barking coughs that made my own chest ache to hear them. Elizabeth came to my room, holding him, and asked me to go and fetch Mrs. Reynolds. And my brother went to wake one of the footmen and send him for Mr. Broyles, the physician. Fitzwilliam was doing his best to reassure Elizabeth, but I could see how worried he was.

Babies *do* die. Especially in winter. And looking at James's small face, all scrunched up with the effort he was making to breathe, his life seemed so fragile— barely three weeks old. Even a slight sickness could be enough to snatch him away. And this was not slight at all. Besides the cough, I could hear a whoop of air with every one of his laboured breaths.

The whole house wound up being roused, Edward and Frank and Caroline, as well. And it was decided that Edward and Frank would ride out for Mr. Broyles. They could take their own horses and cover the distance to Lambton more quickly than one of the footmen. And it was safer for two of them to go than one, in case one horse foundered or lost its footing in the snow.

They left just as Mrs. Reynolds came bustling into

Elizabeth and Fitzwilliam's room. I know she was worried, too. But she was splendidly calm. She took one look at baby James, clasped tight in Elizabeth's arms, and said, "Ah, it's the croup, that's what ails the poor lamb. I'll go and tell the kitchen maids to start boiling water. We'll need clean towels and a great deal of steam."

When the copper kettles of boiling water arrived, she fixed a kind of tent using the towels and two chairs, and directed Fitzwilliam and Elizabeth to sit inside with James, letting him breathe the moist air.

While my brother took a turn with James under the tent, Elizabeth came over to Caroline and me. She was terribly pale, but she tried to smile. "There's no need for the two of you to go without sleep for tonight," she said. "I'm sure he'll be all right. My youngest sister Lydia had croup when she was one or two, and my mother treated it just this way. Which I would have remembered if I'd not been so panicked before."

Her eyes still looked dark with fear, though. Because of course there is a great deal of difference between a baby of just three weeks and a child of one year or two. I took her hand. "Of course I'm not going back to bed. Unless you'd rather I didn't, I'll stay right here in case there's anything I can do to help."

Elizabeth squeezed my hand and said, "Thank you."

I would have expected Caroline to leave. I was a little surprised that she had come out of her room in the first place. But she said, her voice only a little awkward rather than snappish or short, "I have some camphor in my room. I always travel with it in the winter time. I'll fetch it if you like, and you could add it to the boiling water. I've heard friends of mine—the friends who have children—say that it's very effective in cases of croup."

Elizabeth's eyes widened slightly with surprise, as I'm sure did mine. But she was too distracted by worry for James to say anything but, "Thank you. Yes, please fetch it." She turned to look back at the steam tent, where Fitzwilliam was holding James cradled against his chest. "Thank you, that's very kind."

Caroline must have run all the way to fetch the camphor from her room, because she was back in what seemed no time at all. "Here you are." Elizabeth had gone back under the towels to sit with my brother and James, so Caroline gave the packet of camphor powder to Mrs. Reynolds. But then instead of leaving, she crouched down to kneel beside the steam tent on the floor and touched Elizabeth's arm. "He really will be all right, I'm sure of it," she said. She spoke quietly and more gently than I'd ever heard Caroline speak before. "My school friend Maria Gibbon's little daughter had croup when she was not much older than your little boy. And she recovered perfectly well. She's three years old now."

And the camphor or the steam or both did help at last. Fitzwilliam looked down at James, still curled small as a kitten against his chest, and said, "I think—" He stopped and cleared his throat. "I think he's breathing more easily, now."

He was. The laboured rasp of his breathing was nearly gone, and his tiny face was relaxed, peaceful in sleep.

Edward and Frank returned a few minutes later with Mr. Broyles. Who had nothing to do but examine his small patient and say that James was well on his way to being cured, and that his treatment had been exactly what was required.

Everyone broke into gasps and exclamations of relief.

Mrs. Reynolds started to cry, and Elizabeth laughed, her eyes bright with tears, too. My brother drew her to him with one arm, resting his forehead against hers, with James cradled close in between them.

And then all the commotion woke baby James, who blinked indignantly at us from Fitzwilliam's arms, as though wondering why we were disturbing him, just as he'd finally got to sleep—which made everyone laugh. Even Caroline. Though it was just after that that she ducked out of the room and into the hall.

I was standing next to Edward, leaning against him. Edward was saying something to my brother. But I saw Frank turn and go after Caroline a moment later.

I murmured, "Excuse me a moment," and went out into the hall, too.

Caroline and Frank were standing together at the head of the stairs at the far end of the hall. Frank's back was to me, and his voice was too low for me to make out the words. But I could see Caroline's face, pale and icy-hard as she shook her head. "No. I'm not listening to any more."

She whirled and ran away down the hall, back towards her own room. And Frank stood still a moment at the top of the stairs, watching her. He hadn't noticed me. But I could see the mixture of anger and pain on his handsome face, the bleak unhappiness in his eyes. And then he passed a tired hand across his face and started down the stairs, his shoulders bowed.

I hesitated. And then I went after Caroline.

I caught up with her just around the corner of the passage to the east wing. It was as though once she was out of sight of Frank, all her energy had abruptly deserted her. She had not even reached her room, but was sitting slumped on one of the velvet benches that lined the hall. Tears were running in silent tracks down her face.

She looked up at my approach. But she didn't bother to hide or even try to check her crying.

"Caroline—" In that moment, I did begin to feel sorry for her. She looked the picture of exhausted misery. I sat down beside her on the bench and said, "Can you tell me what's wrong? What did Frank say to you just now?"

A flicker of resentment crossed Caroline's gaze as she drew the edges of her dressing gown more tightly together. "Why should you care? It's not as though you even like me. Why should you? I've been horrible to you—to all of you. You and your brother and Elizabeth." More tears slid down Caroline's cheeks, and she dashed them impatiently away with the back of her hand. "I don't mean to behave so. But I'm so unhappy, all the time. It makes me feel as though there's something terrible inside me, goading me to be rude and spiteful. As though I want to . . . to lash out at the whole world." Caroline's breath went out in a hiccuping sob. "But what does it matter? You've every reason to despise me"

I suppose that's one of the saddest truths of life. That so often people who are the most in need of friendship and kindness are the very ones who behave in a way calculated to drive everyone around them away.

I said, "I don't despise you. And Frank is my cousin. He'll be my brother-in-law in a few months' time. And I saw his face just now when he you left him. He looked . . . he looked more unhappy than I've seen him since the girl he was betrothed to died. Is he unwilling to marry you, despite the child?"

Caroline looked at me, and then her breath went out in a long sigh and the small spark of defiance in her gaze seemed to fizzle and blink out. She dragged the sleeve of her dressing gown across her tear-streaked face and said, "No. Just the opposite. He keeps asking me to marry him. And I keep telling him no."

"You keep telling him *no*?" I stared at Caroline. "But why on earth? Frank is . . . I mean, I should have expected you to—"

Caroline's mouth twisted up. "To jump at him?"

I'd been too much surprised to speak tactfully. But it was true. Frank is his father's eldest son, wealthy and heir to the title of earl, besides. He is exactly the kind of man I should have expected Caroline to jump at. To be honest, I should have thought Caroline would leap at the chance of marrying a great deal less handsome and good an earl's heir than Frank, if only for the prospect of being a countess one day.

Caroline stared straight ahead, the words tumbling out in a flat, exhausted rush. "Last spring, when I fell in love with Jacques—and then he married your aunt, solely for the sake of her fortune—I decided that I was through with love. Or with trusting men or anything they say. When I went to London—I was staying with my sister Mrs. Hurst and her husband—I made up my mind that I was going to do anything to get myself a husband. Who it was didn't matter, so long as he was rich and had a position in society. I told myself I was willing to do anything—anything at all—to force some man into marriage."

Caroline scrubbed at her eyes again. "It seemed a means of getting revenge on Jacques, in a way. Punishing the entire male race by forcing one of them into marrying me. And then"—Caroline's voice wavered and she swallowed—"then I met Frank. He was . . . different from the other young men of the *Ton*. He made me laugh, for one thing. And he was . . . was *real*, when all the other men were just pride and manners and false compliments—" She stopped, looking down at her clenched hands. "But that doesn't matter. I told myself that he was the perfect candidate—an earl's son, and wealthy besides. And connected to your brother—but outranking him at the same time. It felt as though marrying him would be the perfect way of . . . of punishing your brother for choosing Miss Elizabeth Bennet for his wife instead of me. So I—" Caroline stopped and swallowed again. "I deliberately got myself with child. I set out to seduce him—I planned the whole thing. And then . . . three weeks ago, as soon as I was sure, I went to Frank and told him. And he offered to marry me, straight away."

I shook my head. "Then why—"

Caroline interrupted before I could finish. "Because in that moment when he said that he would marry me, I realised what I had not been willing to let myself admit to before." She turned to look at me with dull, reddened eyes, and took another hiccuping breath. "I love him. I do. And I've done my best to entrap him into marriage— by the most dishonourable means imaginable. Frank said he would marry me, because . . . because he's a good, honourable man. But how can I say yes? How can I? He doesn't love me. He's only offered me marriage out of duty, of obligation. And if I married him—" Caroline's hands balled themselves into fists. "If I married him, I'd be a burden to him. An unpleasant duty—and one he'd come to resent. How could he not?" She let out her breath again. "I won't do that to him. I love him too much to let him tie himself to me for the rest of his life, just because of my bad behaviour."

"Is that why you got my brother to invite you to

Pemberley?" I asked.

Caroline nodded. "I wanted to get out of London, and—" She broke off. "I never in a hundred years dreamed that Frank would follow me here. But he did. Because he feels sorry for me—because he thinks it his fault about the baby, his fault that I'll be ruined in the eyes of the world." Caroline's voice shook. "A few days ago, I even told him the truth—that I had planned the whole thing, hoping to entrap him into marriage. I hoped it would make him despise me enough that he'd leave here, stop asking. But he only said it didn't matter. That the child was still his, and he still wanted to give it his name—"

Caroline pressed her eyes shut and her chin jerked up and down as she struggled not to cry. Finally, she looked up at me again. "Did you see the way your brother looked at the two of them just now—at Elizabeth and little James?" she asked. "They're his whole world. You can see it in his eyes, every time he looks at them. Hear it in his voice when he so much as mentions one of their names. And that's—" Tears leaked from Caroline's eyes again, but this time she didn't even bother to brush them away. "Seeing them together tonight, the three of them, I realised—more clearly than I've ever realised anything in my life—that that's what I want. A husband who looks at me and my baby that way. I'll never have that, now—never. But if I can't have that, I'd still rather bear the scandal and have this child alone than watch Frank grow to hate me, to hate how I manipulated him into marriage."

Caroline stopped speaking and was silent. And I sat beside her, wondering what I should say. What *could* I say? I didn't—I don't—blame Caroline for feeling as she does. In her place, I wouldn't go through with marrying

Frank, either. And yet I couldn't see any other solution.

"I'm sorry," I finally said. "I wish there was some way I could help."

"That's all right." Caroline passed a hand across her eyes. Her voice was dreary. "You have helped, in a way, just by listening. Thank you. I think—" She stopped. "I think I'll leave Pemberley tomorrow. First thing. I don't think I can face your brother and Elizabeth. Not after the way I've behaved. Will you . . . do you think you could convey my good-byes to them? And tell them how sorry I am?"

I said that of course I would. And Caroline thanked me again and went back along the hall to her room.

Friday 13 January 1815

I've so much to write that I'm not sure I know where to begin. Caroline did leave Pemberley at first light this morning. The whole household was still asleep and quiet after last night's scare with James. But I woke to the sound of gravel crunching on the drive, and looked out the window to see Caroline's carriage—or rather her brother-in-law's carriage, emblazoned with the Hurst family crest—rolling away.

I had only been asleep for a few hours. But I couldn't fall back to sleep after that. I lay awake, thinking about Caroline and about Frank. And when I heard the sounds downstairs of the servants setting out breakfast, I got up.

I did tap lightly on Elizabeth and Fitzwilliam's door as I went down. My brother answered. Elizabeth and James were asleep, still; I could see them over Fitzwilliam's shoulder, both of them curled up in the big four-poster bed.

"Is James—" I whispered.

"Much improved." My brother came out into the hall with me, shutting the door behind him so as not to wake Elizabeth and the baby. "Mr. Broyles said to repeat the steam treatment if he had any other episodes. But so far he seems not to need it at all. He and Elizabeth have been asleep for a few hours, now."

"And you?" I asked. Because my brother's eyes looked tired, the marks of last night's worry still plain. "Did you so much as close your eyes?"

Fitzwilliam smiled briefly as he shook his head. "No. I sat up, counting James's breaths—torn between being terrified he'd suffer a relapse, and thanking God that he was well. But he *is* well." My brother passed a hand across his face and smiled again. "I'd better steel myself, I think, or I'll suffer a nervous collapse when he gets to be of an age to ride horses and climb trees."

I laughed. "You certainly will, if James turns out anything like you. Do you remember the time you broke your wrist because you were determined to ride Father's new Arabian stallion?"

"I certainly do. I'm not sure which hurt more—the broken wrist or the thrashing Father gave me for disobedience."

I asked whether Fitzwilliam would come down to breakfast with me, but he shook his head. "No. Can you ask Mrs. Reynolds to send up a tray? I don't want to wake Elizabeth and James, but—" My brother's eyes strayed to the closed door behind him. "But I would rather stay with them, for now."

Caroline was right. You really can hear in Fitzwilliam's voice just how much baby James and Elizabeth are the centre of his whole world.

I said that of course I would ask Mrs. Reynolds to

see that some food was sent up—which I did. And then I went to find Edward. Because that was what I had decided in all the time I had lain awake after watching Caroline drive away—that I had to tell Edward about his brother and Caroline.

Edward had already finished breakfast by the time I got downstairs. I found him in the library, reading a letter—something official-looking, written on thick paper with a heavy wax seal. I thought Edward looked tired this morning, too. But he smiled when he saw me, setting the letter aside. "Good morning." He pulled me towards him and onto his lap almost absently, as though the movement were so instinctive as to be a reflex, and kissed the crook of my neck.

I kissed him back. But then I said, "Edward, can I speak with you? It's about Frank."

Edward listened while I told him everything that Caroline had told me. He looked troubled when I had finished. He rubbed a hand along his jaw, and he said, "So that's it. I knew there was something between my brother and Miss Bingley. But this—" He shook his head. "God, what a mess. Frank ought to have his head kicked for being such a fool."

"Caroline said it was all her—," I began.

But Edward stopped me with a raised eyebrow. "It can't have been *all* her doing. Frank can't have been entirely unwilling, or there wouldn't be a child coming into the world, with Miss Bingley as the mother and Frank the father." He stopped, shaking his head. "Frank has been . . . I'm sure you have noticed it, too, but Frank has been different ever since Celia died. Unwilling to care about any other woman, not seriously. I can understand it, in a way. Losing someone—anyone that you care about—it makes you wary of ever caring for anyone again. You think if you could just close yourself off from all friendships, from feeling—"

Edward broke off. His eyes had darkened, and I knew he was thinking of all the friends he himself has lost in battle over the years.

I touched his cheek lightly, and he seemed to come back from wherever his mind had been wandering. The hard bleakness faded a little from his gaze and he said, "But whatever he does—or doesn't—feel for Caroline Bingley, he still has a duty to her. And to the child."

I rested my head against Edward's shoulder. "But she doesn't want to be a duty. That is why I came to speak with you about it, Edward. What is to be done?"

Edward shifted me gently from his lap and pushed up from the chair. "I don't know. But I'll speak to Frank. He ought to know Miss Bingley has left Pemberley, if he doesn't already. And I'll try to find out what his feelings are—whether he wants to go after her and try to force her to see sense."

"Force her to see sense?" I repeated. "But she refuses to speak with him—refuses to even consider the possibility of marriage to him. I can't blame her for that, either."

Edward smiled slightly at the indignation in my tone. "I wasn't suggesting Frank kidnap her and drive her kicking and screaming to Gretna Green. But whatever Miss Bingley may have planned, the child *is* still Frank's— Frank's as much as hers. She hasn't the right to refuse to let him be a part of the child's life, if he wishes it."

Put like that, I couldn't help but agree. I slipped my arms around Edward's neck and tugged his head down to kiss him. "You're right—I know you're right."

Edward pulled me to him. I could feel the hard muscles of his back and shoulders through the fabric of his coat as he kissed me again. "Caroline Bingley," he said after a long while. He shook his head. "Poor Frank."

"She's not that bad!" I protested. "You should have seen her last night. She was . . . different than I've ever seen her. I wasn't just sorry for her, I was even starting to like her after we had talked awhile."

"Maybe." Edward's smile was easier this time, and the lingering tension in his face was all but gone as he reached to cup my cheek with one hand. "But he can't possibly ever be as happy with her as I am with you."

We went to find Frank after that. I offered to let Edward speak with him alone—Frank is his brother after all. But Edward shook his head. "No. You can tell him more accurately than I just what Miss Bingley said last night. Frank ought to hear that. And you can step between us if I'm tempted to thrash Frank for being such a cork-brain as to get himself into this predicament in the first place."

Frank was in the game room, aimlessly driving the balls about the billiard table. He looked up when Edward and I entered, and I said, without preamble, "Frank, Caroline has told me all about the two of you. And I think you should know that she's gone from Pemberley, now. She left at dawn."

Frank nodded. It was so strange to see Frank's face as it looked this morning: weary and without even a flicker of the usual humour.

He seemed entirely unsurprised by my words. Or maybe it was simply that he could not bring himself to care whether I knew of his relations with Caroline or not. He pushed an exhausted hand through his hair and said, "Well, that's that, then."

"That's that?" Edward repeated. "That's all? You're just going to let her go? Don't you care at all—"

"Don't I care? Don't I *care*?" The words were an explosion, the weariness in Frank's face changing to sudden anger. "Why do you think I followed her to Pemberley in the first place?"

"Wait a moment," I said. I took a step closer to Frank, looking up into his face. "Are you saying—are you in love with Caroline?"

"No, I'm in the habit of seducing young women that I don't care a fig about." Frank spoke with nearly as much violence as before. His hand clenched around the billiard cue. "Of course I'm in love with her. I—" He stopped and ran his hands down his face. "One of the first times I spent any time with her—just a few weeks after we first met—we went riding with a large party, out into the countryside. One of the party—Christopher Glass—had an estate that we all planned to take luncheon at. But Caroline and I got separated from the rest of the party. And then a rainstorm blew up. We were completely lost—with no idea of which direction the house was in, and nowhere else to take shelter. We were both of us drenched to the skin in minutes. And Caroline—I didn't know her at all well then, but you know how she first appears. A typical, haughty society girl of the *Ton*—all those expensive clothes and fine jewels and proud manners. Looking at her next to me, completely soaked by the rain, I thought I was in for the most unpleasant afternoon of my life. I was expecting her to demand I take off my jacket and lay it on the ground in front of her, just so her horse wouldn't have to step through mud and risk her riding habit being splashed."

Frank stopped and drew in his breath. "And then—I don't know how it happened, maybe her horse balked or lost its footing. But all at once Caroline simply pitched straight off her mount's back and into a deep mud hole. I scrambled down to help her. But somehow I slipped and managed to fall in myself, as well. We were both of us soaked, covered in mud, staring at each other. And then Caroline . . . Caroline started to laugh. We both did. We laughed and laughed—like a couple of lunatics, I suppose. But that's when I realised that Caroline was— that she's different, when she lets herself be. When she forgets to worry about how she looks and what all of society is thinking about her. After that, we used to meet in secret—we'd go for long rides. One time it had been snowing, and we stopped and had a snowball fight, just the two of us. That was the day I realised I had fallen in love with her. And I thought—" Frank broke off again, then shook his head. "But I was wrong. If she'd rather face public disgrace than marriage to me—"

I stopped Frank, putting a hand on his arm. "You're wrong. Caroline does love you. She told me so last night. It's for your sake that she has been refusing to marry you. She didn't want to burden you, or force you into a marriage based solely on duty."

Frank stared at me, looking as stunned as though I had just started to sprout wings. I squeezed his hand. "She's in love with you, Frank. Really."

Frank stared at me a moment more. And then without a word he turned and almost ran from the room.

"Where is he going?" I asked.

Edward grinned. "After Miss Bingley, I assume. Do you think we should follow?"

"Us follow? Why?"

"For one thing, I don't imagine Frank has the least

idea where he's going, or what direction Miss Bingley has taken. And for another—" Edward stopped and grinned again. "Call it sheer nosiness. But I won't believe Caroline Bingley has really changed until I see it with my own eyes."

We did ride after Frank, both Edward and I on horseback. And as it happened, we caught up with them barely a mile away from Pemberley's gates. A wheel had come off of Caroline's carriage, and it stood half in a ditch, listing crazily to one side. Caroline's coachman was at work on trying to make repairs—without making much progress, so it appeared. And Caroline was sitting on a rock by the side of the road, her face both furious and tear-stained beneath the brim of her ostrich-plumed bonnet.

Frank must have arrived on the scene only a few minutes before Edward and me. He was saying something to Caroline while she shook her head. The first words I was able to distinguish were Caroline's:

"Oh, go away, can't you?" Caroline scrubbed ineffectually at her eyes with a scrap of lace handkerchief. "Go away and let me be! That was the whole point of my going away today—that I would never have to see you again. And I wouldn't have, if not for this cursed carriage wheel!"

"All right." Frank had one hand on his horse's reins, but held up the other in a gesture of defeat. "All right. I will promise to go away and never bother you again. But on one condition. That you listen to what I have to say to you now."

Caroline lowered the sodden handkerchief and looked at Frank. Then she nodded, the gesture a mixture of sulkiness and resignation. "Very well. I'll listen. What was so important that you had to come riding after me to say it?"

"I love you."

Caroline's head snapped up. "*What* did you say?"

Frank drew in his breath. "I said I love you."

Caroline's eyes widened. And then she started to shake her head. "No you don't—you can't. Or you would have said it before now."

A brief flicker of a smile touched the edges of Frank's mouth. "I don't recall your giving me much of a chance to say anything before now." And then he sobered. "I should have said it, though. God knows I wanted to. But I . . . I suppose it was fear. Or pride. I thought you didn't care for me; I'd no wish to burden you with declarations of love you couldn't return. After all, if you hated me so much that even for the sake of the child you couldn't bear the thought of marriage to me—"

"*Hate* you?" Caroline broke in, looking up at Frank. She was still crying, but she had started to smile, just a little bit through the tears. "How could you believe I could ever, ever hate you? I think I've been in love with you since the first day we met, even if I didn't let myself admit to it at the—"

Her last words were lost as Frank caught her in his arms and kissed her. And then he drew back, just enough that he could say, "Caroline Marissa Bingley, will you do me the honour of becoming my wife?"

Caroline said yes, of course. She and Frank are on their way to Gretna Green now. Because of her condition, there was no time to be lost in arranging the wedding. But I don't think she and Frank would have wanted to wait in any case.

I helped Caroline pack her things for the trip to Scotland. And while we were in her room together she said, "Do you know, I've been unhappy for so long that it seems quite strange to be so happy now. I think . . . I think I may have to practise thinking happy thoughts, instead of being angry at the whole world. But I *am* going to try."

I truly think she will. She bid Elizabeth such a warm good-bye, and apologised so sincerely for her past behaviour that Elizabeth blinked. Elizabeth is incapable of holding a grudge, though, even if she tried. So she kissed Caroline's cheek and wished her all the happiness and joy in the world.

All of us—Elizabeth and my brother, Edward and I—watched the two of them drive away early this afternoon. "Will your parents mind?" I asked Edward as the carriage vanished around the curve of the drive.

At the last moment, Frank had tasked Edward with the job of writing to their parents and giving them the news that Frank had eloped with Caroline and would be bringing his new bride to meet them as soon as Frank and she were returned from Scotland.

Edward shook his head. "Not likely. They've been desperate to see Frank married and settled for years now."

I thought Edward seemed unusually quiet, though—worried, or at least abstracted, as we made our way back into the house. Elizabeth went off to feed James, who was waking up from his morning sleep. My brother went into his study to take care of estate business. And I followed Edward into the library and asked, "Edward, is something—is there anything wrong?"

"Do you mean besides the fact that I'll have to get

used to having gained Caroline Bingley for a sister-in-law?" Edward's brief smile faded, though. "Nothing's wrong. Not exactly. It's just that letter." He nodded to the official-looking document he'd been reading this morning, still lying where he'd set it down on the library table. "It's from Wellington himself."

"The Duke of Wellington?" I looked up, startled. "What has he to write to you about?"

Edward took up the letter, fingering in the heavy wax seal. "He's asked me to join his staff. As one of his aides-de-camp. If I agree—" Edward glanced down at the words written in a bold, black hand across the page. "If I agree, I am to travel to Vienna, to attend him at the Congress. That is where our delegates are meeting with representatives of all the other powers—Russia, Prussia, Austria—all trying to impose some kind of order on the bloody hash Bonaparte made of Europe." Edward drew me to him, then, resting his cheek against my hair. "If I go, I'll have to leave in just two weeks' time."

Tuesday 14 February 1815

It's been weeks since I wrote in this diary. But that was by choice—I wanted to spend every moment I could with Edward, not alone writing in this book.

Edward is gone now. He left yesterday.

He accepted the place on the Duke of Wellington's staff. I suppose I never did write down his final decision —but he wrote to accept the duke's offer the day after Frank and Caroline eloped. It's a chance for Edward to help with forging the new order of the world—whatever that is to be—at the Vienna Congress. Besides which, as one of Wellington's aides-de-camp, Edward will be in a position to prevent abuses of power and corruption—

like those suffered by the old veteran Mr. Mayberry.

So long as Edward is to remain in the army, it's a wonderful opportunity for him, and a great honour, besides.

I'm being completely selfish in wishing that he hadn't had to go, that he were still here at Pemberley, now.

Saturday 18 February 1815

No word from Edward yet. But of course, there wouldn't be. I suppose it will be weeks before I can expect that any letter he sends will arrive here.

This morning Elizabeth and I did have a surprise visitor—Ruth Granger, come up from her cottage to pay a call. She doesn't usually come so far in the wintertime —for of course she doesn't keep a horse or carriage—but she said she'd accepted a ride for part of the way from Mr. Smith, who was coming this way in his farm cart. And she'd walked the rest.

Ruth doesn't usually walk so far, either, on account of her health. But today she did not look any worse for the exercise. She was wearing a dark-purple coloured Spencer over her gown, and the wind had whipped colour into her cheeks. And even apart from that, there was something—something different about her. A feeling—a kind of restless energy or hidden drive. I couldn't entirely describe it, even to myself. But I noticed it right away, from the moment she sat down with us in the drawing room.

She wanted to see baby James, of course. Who has grown so much since he was born I can scarcely believe it. I suppose that's what everyone always says about babies—but it really is true. James has started to smile now, too—anyone who comes to pick him up from his cradle gets rewarded with a huge, toothless grin.

Ruth held him and bounced him up and down on her knees—which earned her another gummy smile. She'd brought Pilot with her—which rather scandalised Mrs. Reynolds—but James waved his fists and made excited baby sounds at the sight of the big dog. Elizabeth and I laughed and Elizabeth kissed the top of James's head and said, "I keep forgetting how much of the world he still has to discover. He's never even seen a dog before today."

And then James started to fuss a little—which usually means he's hungry or tired or both—so Elizabeth took him upstairs to feed him and put him down to sleep.

Ruth and I were alone, then, after Elizabeth had gone. And almost the first thing she said to me was, "I'm going away."

"Away?" Even though I had noticed something altered in her, I was still more than surprised by the words. "Ruth, what do you mean? Away where?"

"To Brussels." Ruth was sitting up very straight in her chair, her hands clasping and unclasping in her lap. "I'm— A former employer of mine has offered me a job there. Lady Denby. I was only with her about a year—this was before I came to Pemberley—and then her little girl was sent off to school. But she—Lady Denby—has kept in correspondence with me ever since. She and her daughter are now living in Brussels—a number of English families have gone there to settle, since the end of the war. Lady Denby says that society there is very fashionable and gay. But her own health has suffered in the last months, and she wishes that I would come out to her and serve as companion to her daughter Jane."

"Of course you should go, if that's what you wish," I

said slowly. "But very fashionable, very gay society—are you sure that's truly what you want?"

"I want—I want a change, at least." Ruth's fingers moved restlessly against the arms of her chair. "I've been quiet so long—because of my health. But I'm stronger now. I haven't had any attacks or shortness of breath for months. And I've decided—I've decided that I don't want to be an invalid for the rest of my life. There's a whole world out there—and I've seen barely anything of it at all."

"I can understand that," I said. And then I hesitated. Ruth is such a very private person—and I didn't want to pry. But something still made me ask, "Ruth, are you leaving because . . . does this have anything to do with the letter from—the letter I found?"

"Giles' letter." Ruth's voice was expressionless. "It's all right, you can say his name. And—" She let out her breath and her hand moved mechanically from Pilot's collar to stroke his ears. "No. Yes." Her shoulders moved. "Maybe a little. It's just—" Ruth broke off, her eyes focusing on a point in the middle distance. "It's just that ever since you showed me that letter I've been . . . reminded, I suppose. Of what I used to want for my life. The plans I used to have. Not Giles, I don't mean. He was never . . . was never anything I planned on." The words came out in a rush. "But I used to want to travel. Accomplish things. I—" Ruth stopped again, her eyes refocusing on me. "It's not that I haven't been happy here. And I'm so grateful to your brother for giving me the chance to stay when I needed it, four years ago. But I think it's . . . it's time for me to move on, now."

I told her that I understood, and that of course she should go if she felt that way about it. But that I would miss her. And I will, very much. And Ruth asked whether my brother might help her with finding a tenant to rent her cottage—for she wishes to keep possession of it, even though she'll be living in London. And I told her that of course I was sure he would.

Just as she left, though, she hugged me—and I felt I had to ask, "Are you . . . should I be sorry that I ever brought that letter to you? Would you rather I had just put it back in the trunk and never told you it had been found?"

Something flickered briefly across Ruth's face—something sad, lost-looking, that made her look for a moment younger and far less certain than she usually does. But then she shook her head. "No. Don't be sorry, Georgiana. I'm glad the letter was found—and that you were the one to bring it to me. It's just—" She stopped and rested her hand on Pilot's neck, and then shook her head again as though trying to push something away. "I don't feel I can stay here any longer, that's all."

Monday 27 February 1815

I had a letter from Edward today at last! He is arrived in Vienna—and writes that the Congress progresses slowly, due to the acrimony the various powers' delegates bear for one another. And the fact that the ambassadors and princes—Prince Metternich of Austria, Prince Karl August von Hardenberg of Prussia—spend a great deal of time trying to outdo each other in the lavish balls and entertainments they host. Edward says that he has spent more time dancing than practically anything else.

And then at the close of the letter he wrote, *Will it sound like something from a bad romance novel if I write that I am counting the days until I can see you again? Romance novel or no, I am.*

Tuesday 7 March 1815

I have had two more letters from Edward since my last entry—dated one day apart from each other, though they arrived at the same time.

Edward sounds well. A little tired, perhaps. But otherwise fine.

So why have I been sitting here, staring at the emerald stone in my ring, turning it round and round my finger? Maybe it's just that Vienna seems so incredibly far away right now.

I am lucky this journal cannot talk, or it would ask why I neglect it for weeks and then take it up again only to complain.

I did have another letter, too—this one from Caroline, writing from Frank and Edward's family seat at Drayford Hall. She sounds so happy as to seem completely unlike herself. She and Frank were married in Scotland, just as planned. And Frank's parents have been everything kind and charming to her in welcoming her to their home.

And to end on another happy note, here is a drawing of Elizabeth and baby James, who are sitting together in a chair nearby mine. Elizabeth makes faces at him, and James pats her cheek and coos. And then they stare at each other and smile.

Wednesday 15 March 1815

I am sitting curled up on the window seat in my bedroom, watching a March gale beat against the windowpane outside. And writing this because there is nothing else I can do. I can't scream. I can't cry. Or rather, I could, but it would not do any good.

Napoleon Bonaparte has escaped from his exile on the Isle of Elba. Word of it is spreading like wildfire all over the district—all over England, I am sure. Mrs. Reynolds had been into Lambton to do some shopping and brought the news home. At first Elizabeth and I thought it must be false, or only some exaggerated rumour. But old Mr. Herron came to call on us this afternoon—very worried that we should have heard the news and been upset by it. He heard it himself from his son, who lives in London and is a member of the Prime Minister's cabinet. So it really is true.

The former Emperor Napoleon has escaped from Elba, regained control of the French army, and is even now marching on Paris, intent on evicting His Royal Highness the King of France from the throne. He may even have conquered Paris by now; news from the Continent can take weeks to reach our part of the country.

I have not heard from Edward yet—though of course he must know of Napoleon's escape. Everyone is saying that Wellington is sure to be recalled from Vienna to face the threat.

Because Napoleon tried to conquer Europe once, and no one doubts that he will again. Which will mean another war.

Thursday 6 April 1815

Finally, a letter from Edward. It was brief, stiff. Just a scrawled note, really.

The Duke of Wellington has been recalled from Vienna and is to travel to Brussels; I suppose he may even have arrived in Brussels by now, since Edward wrote the letter before they departed.

Edward is to accompany the duke, of course. As one of Wellington's staff.

Edward did not say anything beyond that. Nothing of what will happen when they reach Brussels, or what the end result of all this will be. But the newspapers are all filled with news of Napoleon's advance into Paris and beyond. The latest reports put him on the border between the United Netherlands and France, backed by an army tens of thousands of men strong. Our troops are to be strung out along the border. No one knows where or when the French army's invasion may occur— only that Napoleon will invade, and our troops will be called on to fight.

I wish I could write more. I wish I had something

else to write, if only because it would distract me.

I never finished my drawing of Edward in his army uniform. I'll complete it and paste it in here.

Monday 17 April 1815

I have not yet heard from Edward. I cannot even write to him, since I do not know where in Brussels he and the rest of the general's staff are to be billeted, and anything I sent would only go astray.

But I did hear from Ruth. She of course is also in Brussels now—and likely to remain, since her employer Lady Denby does not think that Napoleon's armies pose enough of a threat to drive them back to England.

According to Ruth's letter, Brussels society is almost entirely unaffected by the threat of war.

It's unreal, she writes. *Across the border, Bonaparte is massing what reports hold to be a vast army. And yet here in Brussels there are balls and dinners and entertainments every night. The Duke of Wellington himself holds balls or routs every week, attends every party, and walks in the park with dozens of his admirers every afternoon.*

She says that morale among the troops is very high. And the Duke of Wellington himself appears to all eyes completely unconcerned.

Monday 1 May 1815

Here is the letter I received from Edward today:

Dear Georgiana,

I have been thinking about you constantly, all day long. And now that I finally have a few moments to write to you, I am too tired to do more than scrawl a few lines. We are arrived in Brussels. Which in many ways is Vienna all over again—balls and parties and routs. Except that every day brings another report of Napoleon's massing his troops just beyond the border.

War seems inevitable. And part of me dreads it. And in part—in part as much as I abhor the thought of another battle, a part of me feels relieved. I know how to be a soldier. Sometimes I am not sure I know how to be anything else— and I wonder whether that is not the true reason I elected not to sell my commission and resign.

God, I'm sorry. I should probably tear up this letter and start again and try to write something less complaint-ridden.

I do wish you were here.

All my love,
Edward

Monday 15 May 1815

I am to travel to Brussels.

I was hoping that writing it would make it seem more real. And I suppose it does in a way, seeing it there on the page. Though I am still afraid that something will happen—that the fighting will break out sooner than anyone thinks, or some other unforeseen circumstance may occur to stop my going after all.

Come to that, I have been nearly prevented from even thinking of the journey already.

My brother stared at me a long moment when I told him of the plan, then rubbed a hand across the back of his neck and said that he would have to be out of his mind to allow his sister to travel straight into the heart of a war-torn land.

We were sitting at the breakfast table. With baby James sitting propped up on Elizabeth's lap and gnawing with fierce concentration on a spoon she'd given him. Elizabeth shifted the baby into her arms and took my brother's hand and said, her voice quiet, "Darcy, if you were the one who had gone to war—and I had the chance of seeing you at least once more before the fighting began—do you think anything could stop me seizing that chance?"

It was only then that my brother agreed.

But I should start from the beginning and tell properly everything that occurred.

This morning, a letter arrived for me from Kitty. I had not heard from her at all since she left Pemberley. And even Elizabeth has had only one short letter from her, which said that Kitty had indeed written to Captain Ayres to break off the engagement between them.

But this morning's letter was addressed to me. And in it Kitty said that her friend Mrs. Harriet Forster's husband—who had been a colonel in the militia—had been called to duty in the regular army. So many of our troops were sent to the former American colonies last year that the Duke of Wellington—despite the confidence Ruth described—is reported to be in dire need of men. Colonel Forster is in Brussels already, serving with the 1st Guards. And now Mrs. Forster is to join him there and has asked Kitty to come as a companion for her. And Kitty's letter asks whether I would not like to join the party.

Colonel Forster has rented a house in Brussels already, so we will have somewhere to stay when we arrive. And it has all been arranged. Elizabeth and I will leave Pemberley in a week's time and travel to Longbourn. Elizabeth says that baby James is overdue for a visit with his grandmother and grandfather in any case. And then from Longbourn, Kitty and I will travel to Ramsgate, where we will embark for Ostend. We are to set sail on the 10th of June.

I've written to Edward of course, to tell him that I'm coming. But given the state of the mails, I may arrive before the letter does.

Which if I am completely honest, I am glad for. There is a part of me that is afraid that if Edward had time to personally approve the plan, he would tell me that it is too dangerous, that I ought not to come.

Saturday 10 June 1815

I'm writing this in the parlour of our inn at Ramsgate—the Traveller's Arms, the inn is called. It's very early in the morning; Kitty and Mrs. Forster are still asleep, but I can hear the innkeeper and his wife arguing in the kitchen and the maidservants beginning to clatter pots and pans.

We're to set sail this afternoon and, depending on the winds, should reach Ostend sometime tomorrow night.

I had never met Mrs. Forster before, though I have heard of her from Elizabeth. Elizabeth's sister Lydia was staying with Mrs. Forster and her husband in Brighton when she—Lydia, I mean—eloped with George Wickham two years ago. Given that history, I was more than a little surprised that Mr. and Mrs. Bennet consented to let Kitty go with Mrs. Forster to Brussels. But after meeting Mrs. Forster—or Harriet, as she insists I should call her—I think I do understand.

Harriet has been married to Colonel Forster for these three years already, but she is very young—only a few months older than I am. She has a round, pink-cheeked face and round brown eyes and bouncing brown curls. Now that I have written that, it sounds rather patronising. But I don't mean it that way. I do like her—it is impossible *not* to like her. I can see why Elizabeth hasn't managed to cherish any resentment over her small part in Lydia's elopement.

Harriet is chubby and bouncing and friendly—and anxious to please—as a new puppy. And very sweet and kind. She offered to change rooms with me last night at least three times, just because the room I'd been assigned to was at the back of the inn, overlooking the stable yard, and Harriet was afraid that I might be woken by the noise. And she is sincerely attached to her husband. It's not only that she can talk of little else but the prospect of being with him again. There is a kind of glow that comes into her face whenever she speaks his name.

And besides all that—and which Kitty didn't mention in her letter to me—we are to be accompanied to Brussels by Harriet's grandmother, Mrs. Metcalfe, who will serve as chaperone for us all.

Mrs. Metcalfe is as unlike her granddaughter as it's possible to imagine: fine-boned, bird-thin and ramrod-straight instead of plump and round, with snowy-white hair scraped back into a plain knot under her cap. Her movements are all sharp and very decided, as is her voice. And she has a small, withered-apple face and the keenest pair of black eyes I've ever seen.

She caught me watching her last night while we sat down to the dinner of steak and kidney pie that the inn had provided. "I suppose you'll be wondering what an old woman such as myself is doing, gallivanting off to the Continent in this way when I should be sitting by the fireside at home?"

Her eyes seemed to bore into mine—which I had always thought an exaggerated figure of speech until now. But her gaze seemed as though it ought to penetrate clear to the back of my skull. So I gave up the half-framed polite response I'd been composing and answered frankly, "Actually, I was trying to guess at what your age might be."

That seemed to please her, for she laughed. Her voice is old and cracked-sounding, but her laugh is surprisingly young. "Well, you're honest, at any rate. I cannot abide dishonesty in young females—or all this wrapping a truth up in a lot of flowery-sounding rubbish when it would take three words to say what you really mean." And then she stopped, fixing me with the same penetrating stare as before. "Your room is next to mine upstairs. You don't snore, do you? Or talk in your sleep?"

I was startled, but told her I didn't—at least, not so far as I knew.

Mrs. Metcalfe nodded her head, making the ruffles on her cap bounce. "Well, see that you don't tonight. I'm an old woman and need my sleep." And then she closed one eye in a wink that surprised me nearly as much as the question had. "Sixty-nine years old, to answer your question from before."

A maidservant has just been in to offer me tea and hot rolls for breakfast. Maybe I will go outside and look around Ramsgate for a little while after I have eaten. It is very strange to be here again—and in these circumstances, preparing to set sail for the borderlands of a war. I have not been in Ramsgate since I was fifteen.

Sunday 11 June 1815

I am sitting on the deck of our packet boat. It is nearly eight o'clock at night—which means we have been aboard more than a day, now—and the sea is millpond smooth and stained rosy-gold by the fire of the sunset. It would be beautiful—well, it *is* beautiful, but would be more so if it weren't for the fact that the utterly calm sea means we are stranded some miles still from Ostend without a breath of wind to push us towards the shore.

Kitty and Harriet have been horribly seasick almost from the moment we set sail; they are down in the ship's cabin, lying on the hard wooden bunks and groaning feebly. I have never been aboard a ship before, so I had no idea whether I would be sick or not. I haven't been for a moment, though, not even last night when the sea was quite rough. I feel slightly guilty saying so, when Kitty and Harriet are so miserable, but I really do love the sensation of the boat rocking and swaying under my feet.

Mrs. Metcalfe is the only one of our party besides me not affected by sickness. At the moment, she is also on deck, lecturing one of the ship's crew about the hygienic arrangements on board. Which honestly do leave something to be desired, but between the voyage and the prospect of finally reaching Brussels within the next few days, I haven't noticed very much.

I was just reading through what I wrote yesterday morning at the inn. Mostly to keep myself from growing impatient over the delay in reaching shore. But it has reminded me that I never wrote about the conversation I had with Elizabeth just before Kitty and I left for Ramsgate.

Our visit at Longbourn was lovely—though we were busy from morning until night with Elizabeth's family and all the neighbourhood callers who came to see her during our stay. And then, too, Elizabeth's sister Jane came to visit with her husband Charles Bingley. They brought their daughter Amelia, who is nearly a year old now. Amelia looks exactly like Jane, the same golden-blonde hair—though Amelia's of course is as yet just wispy curls—the same blue eyes. She was so funny with baby James; every time she saw him she would give a kind of high-pitched baby shriek and crawl towards him at full speed. And then she would grin and chuckle and try to gum his cheek or poke her small fingers into his ears.

James started to be able to roll himself over while we were there.

But none of this is what I started out to recount, which was that on the night before we were to depart Longbourn, Elizabeth came to my room. She had a parting gift for me—a little bottle of lavender water to use on my handkerchiefs. But then once she'd given it to me she sat down on the bed and seemed to hesitate, looking uncertain or as though she were trying to make up her mind whether or not to speak.

Which is so unlike her that I asked whether anything was wrong.

Elizabeth shook her head. "No, there is nothing the matter. Or at least, I hope that there will not be anything the matter. It's just . . . " she gave me a small, rueful twist of a smile. "I have been debating whether or not to tell you this all day. I don't want to upset you. But then, that's rather condescending, isn't it? Trying to decide what you should and should not know. And besides, you ought to be prepared if—" Elizabeth stopped again and drew in her breath. "To speak plainly, my mother had a letter from my sister Lydia three days ago. Lydia is the worst correspondent in the world, of course, and hardly ever writes. Not unless it is to ask for money. But in this letter to my mother, she wrote that her husband George Wickham's regiment has been called to foreign service and is already embarked to join the Duke of Wellington's force in Brussels."

I think I said, *Oh*. Or something like that. And Elizabeth leaned forward and asked whether I was all right.

I nodded. "Yes. I'm . . . surprised. Though I suppose I shouldn't be. I didn't know he was now in the regular army, but the chances were always going to be great that he should be called to fight with the rest of Wellington's troops."

I know last year I forced myself to write out the full story of how George Wickham nearly persuaded me into eloping with him four years ago, when I was fifteen. It is embarrassing now, to remember how naive I was, how easily taken in by his unctuous declarations of love. And I still despise myself a little—even if I was only fifteen—for being so spineless that I was too afraid to tell him *no* when he asked me to run away.

But at least I have the comfort of knowing that it was after all four years ago, and I am not that girl anymore.

I sat back a little against the pillows on the bed. And then looked up at Elizabeth. "I am surprised. But I don't think I am worried or distressed. The army is thousands and thousands of men strong—it's surely not very likely I should meet him. And besides, even if I did, I don't think I would care."

And it is true. I don't think I would care, not now.

Last spring, George Wickham went so far as to come to Pemberley in an attempt to blackmail my brother. Wickham *could* damage my reputation by spreading the story of our near elopement. Even though nothing more untoward than a single kiss ever occurred. And my brother would have paid to stop Wickham's doing it—but I told him he mustn't. I refuse to live my whole life in fear of what Wickham may choose to say. And Edward already knows the whole truth of the affair in any case.

Even being in Ramsgate yesterday—which was where Wickham instigated his courtship of me—didn't so much bring it all back as make me feel more than ever as though all that were part of entirely another life from the one I have now.

I have to stop writing. Mrs. Metcalfe has been talking to the captain, and apparently there is a chance of some of the crew rowing us to shore; she has just come over to tell me she'll need my help in dragging Kitty and Harriet from their berths.

Monday 12 June 1815

We are in Ostend at last. I was too exhausted to write anything when we finally found our beds last night. So it is morning now. Late morning, to judge by the angle of the sun streaming in through my window, though there is no clock in my room and I have not yet been downstairs.

We are staying in the home of Mrs. Pamela Elliott, the wife of General Elliott, who commands the garrison here.

Mrs. Elliott is an older woman, grey-haired and pink-cheeked and sensible-looking. Though I think she must have been quite pretty when she was young. She and the general never had children of their own, so she makes it a habit to befriend and take an interest in the younger people who come into her acquaintance. Mrs. Elliott also happens to be a second cousin of Harriet's on her mother's side. And it was arranged between Mrs. Elliott and Harriet before we set sail from England that we should come to the Elliotts' home when we arrived.

We were rowed to shore from the packet boat last night. Which is why the cover of this book is now slightly damp; the splash of the oars and the occasional swell of a wave would come over the side of the boat and soak our luggage. We wound up on a stretch of sandy beach just before midnight, surrounded by all our bags. And Mrs. Metcalfe asked—well, I suppose commanded would be strictly speaking more accurate—the sailors who had rowed us in to take us on to the town.

And so here we are, at General and Mrs. Elliott's. I had better go downstairs now, since Kitty has just come in to inform me that Mrs. Elliott is holding a ball tonight, and we ought to help her prepare.

Tuesday 13 June 1815

Poor Kitty. I would never have believed it was possible to be so completely sorry for someone and so completely exasperated with them at the same time. But I am with her right now.

It is two o'clock in the morning, and I am sitting up in bed in the room Mrs. Elliott assigned to me for our stay. It is a very pretty room, though the furniture is all very much in the French style and so heavily gilded it's dazzling even by the light of the single candle by my bed.

This morning, when Kitty told me, was the first I had heard about the ball that General and Mrs. Elliott were to hold tonight. But Mrs. Elliott had apparently been planning it for weeks, and had written Mrs. Forster that if we should arrive on or before the twelfth of June, we should be able to attend. In all honesty, a ball was the absolute last thing I wanted to even think of after our journey. And—though I realise that I sound like the drooping heroine of a melodrama all over again—all I have wanted from the moment I left Pemberley has been to reach Brussels and Edward as quickly as possible.

It is not just gothic heroine fancies. There's a kind of strung-up tension about the whole city of Ostend—the whole countryside around here. We went out in the late morning to walk around the city a little while. And it's beautiful. Cobbled streets and houses of coloured bricks. And breathtaking cathedrals, built of grey stone, with impossibly high spires and windows of coloured glass. But all the while we were walking, children—little street urchins—were crowding around us and simultaneously begging for pennies and cursing Napoleon and the French. *Success to the English, and destruction to the French*, was what they called out over and over again. And in the few shops we went into—a sweet shop, a lace-maker's, and a book stall—the owners said almost exactly the same. Everyone was full of war-talk. Fiercely eager to tell us of how Napoleon was hated here for his taxes and for having conscripted all the fine young men to die in his cursed army.

But the ball:

Unlike me, Kitty had heard about it from Mrs. Forster

before we set sail and had been looking forward to it ever since.

Greatly looking forward to it; back aboard the packet ship when I went in to help Mrs. Metcalfe with getting Harriet and Kitty up onto deck and into the rowboat, Kitty had groaned and pulled the blankets over her head at first. And then she sat bolt upright and asked me what day it was. And when I told her it was the eleventh of June, she dragged herself up and shook Harriet and said that they had to go or they'd not be at Mrs. Elliott's before the twelfth.

I remember at the time thinking it was strange—though everything was in such confusion what with rounding up our bags and paying the ship's captain that there was no chance to ask her to explain. And then yesterday—Kitty spent the entire day debating and changing her mind over what she should wear and worrying that the spots the sea-water had left around the hem of her gown—pale-lavender silk with an overskirt of deeper purple sarsnet—would show.

And now I know why: Lord Henry Carmichael was among those in attendance here tonight.

I was sitting off to one side of the dancing with Mrs. Metcalfe—who had donned for the ball the most incredible turban of silk and gold lace—when I saw Lord Carmichael come in. He was with a large party of other guests—three other gentleman and four ladies. And one of the ladies—an exquisitely pretty woman with four ostrich plumes in her red hair and a very low-cut gown of emerald chiffon spangled with gold and pearls—was clinging to his arm. I recognised Lord Carmichael. And felt a lurch of dismay, because Kitty saw him at the same time and started straight for him.

I'm *not* Kitty's mother. I'm not even responsible for

her behaviour on this journey. But I still felt I ought to do something to try and stop her coming to any worse harm than she already had.

Except I needn't have worried. Not about Lord Carmichael trifling with Kitty's affections, at any rate.

I had excused myself to Mrs. Metcalfe and gone after Kitty, so that despite the music and the crowds of people all around I was near enough to hear the exchange between her and Lord Carmichael. She put out her hands and said, "Henry! How utterly enchanting to see you again!"

And Lord Carmichael gave her a completely blank look through his gold- and jewel-encrusted quizzing glass and said, "I beg your pardon. You seem to have the advantage of me. Have we been introduced?"

I was behind Kitty and could not see her face. But before she could reply, Lord Carmichael had been hailed by someone further into the ballroom and moved off, the red-haired lady still clinging to his arm. I took a step forward and touched Kitty on the shoulder.

She had rouged her cheeks again; when she turned around I could see that all the natural colour had drained from her face and the paint stood out on each cheek in two garish stains. She looked as though she were on the verge of tears, too—so I caught hold of her hand and pulled her with me into a little curtained-off alcove at the rear of the ballroom.

There was a courting couple there already—a plump girl dressed in curry-coloured satin and young man in a black superfine coat and very tight pantaloons. They gave us—or me, rather—indignant looks, but pushed past us and rejoined the ballroom when it was clear Kitty and I meant to stay. Once they had gone, I pushed Kitty onto the stiff brocade cushions that formed a kind of bench around the alcove's rear wall. It was like moving a wooden doll—she went wherever I directed her, her movements jerky and stiff. And when I wasn't trying to get her to move she came to a total standstill, her eyes fixed straight ahead.

When I had sat down next to her on the bench, though, Kitty turned her head to look at me, her eyes still swimming with tears. "He doesn't remember me." Her voice was choked. "He had not the smallest idea of who I was."

"I know. I heard." I didn't even think Lord Carmichael had been guilty of deliberate cruelty, or that he had merely pretended not to know Kitty's name.

He might have flirted with Kitty shamelessly at Christmas time. But now, six months later, he quite simply had no memory whatever of the girl whose reputation he had nearly ruined. "I know it is not much help to you," I added, "but I am truly sorry."

"I thought—" Kitty's breath caught on a sob, but she clenched her hands and blinked hard, staring at the tasselled curtain in front of us. When she spoke, the words tumbled out in a rush. "I didn't tell anyone—not even Harriet—but that was the whole reason I came on this journey. To see Henry again. Harriet didn't know the full story of everything that happened between us at Pemberley. I only mentioned to her once that I knew him. And so she told me, just in passing, that she had had a letter from Mrs. Elliott mentioning that Lord Henry Carmichael was staying in Ostend with some friends. Harriet only thought I might be interested to hear news of an—" Kitty's voice choked up again. "An acquaintance. But I thought if I could just get to Ostend myself—see Henry in person. I thought now that I'm not engaged to John anymore, perhaps—"

Kitty broke off with a sharp gasp as the curtain that separated us from the ballroom was lifted aside. I would have expected another couple. But it was a dark-haired young man wearing the dress of an army officer: red embroidered coat with gold frogging and epaulettes, tall black Hessian boots. Kitty's eyes went wide at the sight of him and she lost what little colour in her face she'd regained.

The man bowed. "Kit—" he checked himself. "Miss Bennet. I saw you come in here, and thought you appeared . . . distressed. May I be of service in any way?"

Kitty only stared at him, her hand at her throat, and the man turned to me and bowed again. "I apologise for the intrusion. I know we have never been introduced. But I think you must be Miss Bennet's sister-in-law, Miss Darcy?"

Kitty at last came back to life. A red flush of colour suffused her face and she stammered, "I—Georgiana, I'm sorry. This is—I mean, allow me to present John. Captain John Ayres."

I couldn't blame Kitty for being shocked. If the scene had been part of a novel I was reading, I would have said Captain Ayres' sudden appearance at the precise moment Kitty spoke of him was too great a coincidence to be believed. I gave him my hand, though, and he took it and said, "Your servant, ma'am." And then he straightened and gave me quick flash of a smile. He was not handsome, exactly—his face was too thin and his jaw a little too square. But I liked him at once. His expression was easy and friendly, and his dark eyes were both intelligent and very kind, with crinkles of humour around the corners.

I returned the greeting. And then I felt my heart lurch, and without meaning to, I tightened my fingers around his. Because I had realised that as an army officer, Captain Ayres might have news of Edward.

He shook his head when I asked him, though, and said that he has not seen Edward since he joined General Wellington's staff.

After Captain Ayres had given us the latest news—of which there is really none, save that Napoleon continues to gather troops across the border—he turned to me with another of his quick, ready smiles. "I believe—if you'll permit me—I can look after Miss Bennet from here." He turned to Kitty. "Would you do me the honour of allowing me to escort you in to supper?"

They were together all the rest of the night. Captain Ayres never said anything, and his behaviour was throughout that of a friend rather than a lover—but he was very gentle with Kitty, and careful of her in a way that made me think he might have overheard the exchange between Kitty and Lord Carmichael, too.

Thursday 15 June 1815

I have only a few moments to write this, and my hands are shaking so much that I've already upset the inkwell twice.

We arrived in Brussels this afternoon. And the fighting is expected to begin tomorrow. The war has truly begun.

Later . . .

I am so tired. My eyes ache as though they've had salt shaken into them. But sleep is impossible tonight. Literally impossible, since the streets outside are full of confusion and noise: shouts and snatches of army song, marching feet and the creak of waggon wheels. And every so often the air is split by a roll of drums and a bugle call to arms.

The army is assembling; they're to march out at dawn.

And since I cannot sleep, I might as well write out a better account of today. Since my last was scribbled down in the few minutes I had between dressing and leaving for the ball.

Our carriage arrived in Brussels at around four o'clock this afternoon. Harriet of course had given our driver the address of the house her husband the Colonel has engaged for her stay here—a very pretty townhouse on a street near the *Parc* that lies at the heart of the city. We had barely rolled up outside the door, though, when it burst open and a very stout woman in a white mob cap and apron came flying out. She is Madame Duvalle, the local woman whom Colonel Forster hired for a house-keeper, though we didn't know that at the time. She seized first Mrs. Metcalfe's hands, then Harriet's and Kitty's and mine, all the while pouring out a torrent of French. I speak French—and sufficiently well, I always thought—yet I could scarcely understand what she said.

But finally the meaning of the words became plain. The French—*the French devils*, Madame Duvalle called them—attacked an outpost held by our Prussian allies today. Reports of the outcome are still coming in—some say the French will be in Brussels by tomorrow noon if they are not checked, some hold that the Prussians drove them off. But in any case, Wellington's army would be moving out tomorrow to meet their attack. *And unless they can cut those French devils to pieces, what is to become of us? Napoleon's soldiers will trample us underfoot and kill us all*, was what Madame Duvalle said.

Even writing this, not even a day later, the next hour or two seems all jumbled and blurred together in my memory. We were all tired after the long journey, and it made the news—even all the people thronging the street, anxious to hear the latest reports that might come in—seem almost unreal. I know we came into the house, and Madame Duvalle, still alternating between expressions of fear and curses against Napoleon, served us little frosted cakes and blackberry cordial to drink.

Kitty and Harriet looked terrified. And even Mrs. Metcalfe—who had merely snorted something about hysterical females in the face of all Madame Duvalle's flood of alarms—looked grave, her lips pressed together in a thin line.

And then, somewhere about dinner time, Colonel Forster himself arrived back at the house.

Harriet jumped up with a little cry and ran to him when he came into the room, and he caught her against him. Colonel Forster is several years older than his wife—about Edward's age, I suppose. With curling, reddish-blond hair that is starting to recede a little from his high brow, and a square, strong-boned face. He held Harriet tightly a long moment, and then set her gently down.

"Thank God you are safely arrived," he said. "Though I wish to God you were anywhere but here."

He looked tired, with lines of strain bracketing the corners of his mouth. I don't think any of us really needed to ask him to know that the reports of a French attack were true. But Harriet did ask him what the latest reports were, and whether the army was really to march out tomorrow. And Colonel Forster said that the Duke of Wellington was keeping his plans very secret so as to prevent spies from bringing word back to the

French. But that all his senior officers had been given orders to be ready to move out at a moment's notice.

Colonel Forster sat down on the couch, then, with one arm holding Harriet tightly against him. She looked as though she might cry as she clung to her husband's hand. Kitty, Mrs. Metcalfe and I all stood up to go—all wishing, without any words needing to be spoken, to give them as much time alone together as we could. I couldn't stop myself from asking, though, "Do you—" I had to swallow against the tightness in my throat. "Have you any idea of the whereabouts of Colonel Edward Fitzwilliam? He is one of the duke's aides-de-camp."

We were in a front room of the house, and I could see the street outside through the window: soldiers' red coats and white belts everywhere. Flemish drivers were working to load waggons, and horses were being harnessed to commissariat trains. I had no idea of how I might ever find Edward in all the confusion and uproar.

Colonel Forster had closed his eyes as he rested his cheek against his wife's hair. He looked up at me blankly an instant, then slowly shook his head. "I'm sorry. I have no idea. Though he might be at the Duchess of Richmond's tonight. She is holding a ball." A faint smile gathered at the edges of his mouth. "Too grand an affair for a commoner like myself to have been issued an invitation, of course. But all of our more aristocratic officers have been invited to attend. Wellington himself is planning to be there, or so I heard."

"A ball?" It was my turn to look completely blank. This seemed like one more piece of unreality in this utterly unreal day. "On the eve of battle?"

Colonel Forster's lips twisted slightly. "The event is one of long standing. And I believe Wellington was heard to say by one of his staff that it would stiffen public morale if he and his officers were seen there tonight—seen to behave as though utterly unconcerned by the threat of war barely ten miles away."

We left Colonel Forster and Harriet alone then, and went upstairs to the rooms we had been assigned. Mine—the room I am writing in now—is small but comfortable, with a fireplace of tulip-painted tiles and a pink satin coverlet on the bed. I sat down on the edge of the bed, vaguely aware of a maidservant coming in with a ewer of hot water for washing, shaking the wrinkles out of my gowns and hanging them in a carved wooden wardrobe. I suppose I thanked her, because she curtsied and went out. And I got up and went down the passage to Kitty's room.

Kitty's door was still partly ajar; when I looked in, she was sitting in a chair by her own fireplace, her fingers crumpling and twisting a lace-edged handkerchief over and over again. She looked up when I came in. But before she could say anything, I said, "I want to go to the Duchess of Richmond's."

Kitty's eyes widened and her mouth dropped open slightly. "The Duchess of Richmond's ball? But how can you? You've not been invited. Are you even acquainted with her?"

"I am. Or slightly acquainted, at least. I met her in London during my first Season."

Which was true. The Duchess of Richmond is a dragon of the London society scene. She's—

I was trying to think of a more polite way of putting this. But I am too tired—and there is another call to arms sounding even now in the street outside. Besides, this is only my own diary. So I will say that the Duchess of Richmond is considered by all who know her to be arrogant, overbearing, snobbish, acid-tempered—and utterly ruthless in her determination to find rich husbands for her seven daughters. I lived in London for two years and never met a single person who truly liked her.

After I met the Duchess for the first time, I heard that she considered me very stupid and shy, and in no way to be compared to her own Georgiana—her daughter, I mean, who has the same name I do. I could just imagine what opinion she would have of Kitty and me when she saw us arriving at her grand ball, uninvited, unescorted, and unannounced.

But I did not say any of that to Kitty. I only said, "Do you want to see Captain Ayres?"

"John? I haven't—I mean, I don't—" Kitty's cheeks flushed, then drained of all colour, leaving her face icy-pale once more. "We didn't decide on anything that night in Ostend. Only that we hoped to see each other again here in Brussels. I'm not at all sure—"

"He is to march off to war tomorrow, Kitty. Do you want to see him before he goes?"

Kitty locked her hands together. She gave a small, shaky nod. "Yes. I want to see him."

"Then come with me to the ball."

Kitty hesitated, but nodded. "All right. When ought we to leave?"

I think Mrs. Metcalfe would have gone with us—she nearly insisted on it, on the grounds that her presence would make our attendance at the ball more respectable. But she looked tired by the journey and the ill-news of war—though I was very sure she would never have admitted it. And besides, Colonel Forster had left the house again after spending a bare hour with his wife, and Harriet needed the comfort of Mrs. Metcalfe's presence more than Kitty and I needed a chaperone. Which was what I told Mrs. Metcalfe—and she reluctantly agreed.

I should have expected the Duchess to have engaged the ballroom of one of the city's grand hotels for her ball. But it was held in a long, low out building—a kind of annex—to the villa the Duke and Duchess of Richmond had engaged for their stay in Brussels. The villa had once belonged to a coach-maker, and the building had been used by him to store his coaches—or so I heard one of the other guests say.

The Duke and Duchess's villa was all the way across the city—they live in the lower part of town—and it took nearly two hours for our carriage to arrive there. The streets were crowded with soldiers and supply waggons—and of course all the other carriages driving towards the Duchess's ball.

We did finally arrive at the villa sometime around ten o'clock. And our fears of being turned away were unfounded. Or at least irrelevant. Calls of reveille were already being sounded, and the streets echoed with the sounds of marching as the soldiers left their billets to assemble at the Palace Royale. Officers, too, were leaving the ball to make ready for marching out tomorrow. Which meant that all Kitty and I had to do to get in was slip past the confusion of farewells and leave-takings at the door.

We did come in time to see the last of the dancing by a group of soldiers from one of the Scottish regiments— sergeants from the Gordon Highlanders, I think. And it was—I'm not sure I can find words to do the per- formance justice. Especially not now, tonight. But if anything could have made me forget the coming battle just for a little while, it would have been the Scottish soldiers marching slowly into the ballroom while their pipers played a haunting, melancholy, lilting song. And then the way they danced, bowing and leaping in their kilts and plaids—I had never seen anything like it before.

Just as the dancing was finished and the last mournful notes of the pipes dying away, I heard Kitty's and my names being called and turned to find Captain Ayres threading his way towards us through the crowd. My heart leapt—because if Captain Ayres was there at the ball, it seemed at least possible that Edward might be, as well. But before I could even open my mouth to ask, Captain Ayres shook his head.

"Miss Darcy. Miss Bennet." He bowed to each of us, and took Kitty's hand before saying, "I'm sorry to tell you, Miss Darcy, that Colonel Fitzwilliam has been sent to Vivorde with a message from Lord Uxbridge to Colonel Taylor of the 10th Hussars."

I can—vaguely—remember Edward telling me once that Lord Uxbridge commands the cavalry, but little more than that; he never wished to speak very much about the army or even the other officers he knew. But now I wish I had *forced* him to tell me as much as he could: names, ranks, records of service, everything. Not, I suppose, that it would really be of very much use even if I did have all that knowledge at the ready now.

But as it is, all I really know of Lord Uxbridge is that he scandalously seduced the Duke of Wellington's sister-in-law into leaving her husband, and that as a result his wife—formerly Wellington's brother's wife—is not socially received.

I would have left the ball immediately, if I'd had only my own wishes to consult. But of course I couldn't leave Kitty there on her own and without the carriage to convey her back to the Forsters'. And it would have been cruel even to try to make her leave the ball while Captain Ayres was still there.

Captain Ayres would have tried to serve as escort to both of us—he was very gallant and kind. But I wanted to let him and Kitty have as much time together as they could, so after a few minutes I made an excuse about wanting to visit the ladies' retiring room and slipped away, off into the crowds.

It is strange: my memories of the ball now seem to be all in fragments, with me walking through them like a ghost, unseen and unnoticed by anyone around me. Which isn't quite true. I know a few of the younger officers were in their cups enough to ask me to dance, though without having been properly introduced. And I even did dance with one of them, because he was so young—he looked barely seventeen. He was a little drunk on the Duchess's champagne and more than nervous about what he was to face tomorrow. He kept patting my hand and saying I needn't worry, our British boys would give Old Boney what for. And looking absolutely terrified all the while.

But for the rest, I spoke to no one, just wandered around the edges of the long, candlelit room—and fought a losing battle to keep from thinking of Edward.

It's stupid—I know it's stupid. But all throughout the day, I had had a strange, superstitious feeling that if only I could *see* Edward—even just once before he left—it would somehow guarantee his safe return.

I saw the Duke of Wellington and some of his staff officers come in sometime around midnight, I think. I had never seen him in person before—it was startling to be in the presence of a man who truly has grown into something of a legend. The only man capable of beating Napoleon, or so the newspapers and rumours always say.

The duke has lean, proud, aristocratic features. Handsome, in a very austere way. I could imagine him being charming when he chose. But tonight he looked as though his mind were far away and racing behind the careful social manners with which he greeted those guests he knew.

Once I happened to be standing nearby, and overheard someone ask whether the rumours were true, and Napoleon really had commenced his attack. And the Duke of Wellington looked very grave and said that yes, it was quite true, and the army would march out tomorrow. And then a young man in a staff officer's uniform came in with a message for him—bad news, I think it must have been, because Wellington's face turned grimmer still, and he turned and asked the Duke of Richmond whether he had a good map on the premises.

I think it was soon after that that Kitty and Captain Ayres found me. Captain Ayres was leaving the ball. Nearly all the officers were, as word spread that our Prussian allies had suffered worse casualties at the hands of the French than had previously been supposed.

To our astonishment, the Duchess of Richmond tried to bar the doorway, begging them not to spoil her ball by leaving so soon, and pleading that surely they could stay 'just a little hour more.'

Which would have been almost funny had it not been so grotesque. I suppose she thought that Napoleon would surely not be so impolite as to attack before the close of her ball?

Captain Ayres escorted both Kitty and me to our carriage and took his leave of us. Kitty's lips were trembling, but she did not cry—and she gave Captain Ayres her cheek to kiss and said, "Do take care, John."

She is sitting across the Forsters' parlour from me as I am writing this, slow tears rolling down her face. I hope he comes back to her. And Colonel Forster to Harriet. And Edward—

I have been trying not to think of him. But it is impossible not to. I have rubbed my thumb a hundred times over the emerald in the *claddaugh* ring he gave me, as though it could conjure up some sort of magical spell to protect him.

My last fragment of memory of the ball is from when we were already in the carriage, waiting for the driver to clear enough of the other carriages that we could be on our way. Just by chance, the Duke of Richmond happened to be standing quite close by to where our own vehicle stood.

The Duke of Richmond is a man of fifty or there-abouts, with a paunchy frame and a melancholy, jowly face. It is said he drinks to excess—though most people excuse him that, on account of his wife. He was bidding farewell to an older man—one of his friends, I suppose—both of them standing in the glare of light cast by one of the torches that had been set at intervals along the drive. The wind blew the flame into a tattered banner of fire over their heads. And carried their words across to where I was sitting in the carriage.

The duke must have been speaking of his time alone with Wellington tonight. Recounting to his friend what Wellington had said while they were alone in the Duke of Richmond's study, consulting the duke's maps.

"He said Napoleon had humbugged him." The duke's words floated to me across the sweep of gravel drive. "And then he underlined a place on the map with his thumbnail and said, *That is where I will stop the French. At Waterloo.*"

Friday 16 June 1815

If I thought last night was terrible, today has been so, so much worse.

I have just spent the last five minutes at least sitting here, staring at that first sentence I wrote and wondering what more I can say.

I do not know how to sum up these last twelve hours—because practically nothing occurred, and practically no information reached us of what was taking place outside the city.

I never realised before that the two most exquisite tortures in the world must be uncertainty and boredom.

We did finally go to bed last night, sometime near dawn. I don't think any of us wanted to. But Mrs. Metcalfe gathered us all up and herded us upstairs, saying that she was an old woman and didn't propose to sit up on a lumpy horsehair sofa all night. And I did fall asleep for a few hours once I had lain down on my bed—I was too tired not to.

The city felt eerily empty and quiet when we got up this morning, after the uproar of last night. As soon as we had all breakfasted—or pretended to, I don't think Kitty or Harriet managed to eat any more than I did—we went outside, to see if we could gain any news.

No one could give us any—no one could tell us anything of the French or the Prussians or our own army. And then, sometime about midday, we were walking through the *Parc*, and we heard it: a thundering cannonade of gunfire, sounding near enough to us to be within the city walls.

Our army must have come under attack as soon as they marched out this morning.

People—civilians—were running everywhere, crying

out, exclaiming, wringing their hands in fear. But no one knew anything for certain. Some said the battle was six miles off, some said ten. Some claimed at every moment to believe the cannon fire sounded as though it were surely moving closer.

We stayed in the *Parc*—I'm not sure why, except that it seemed as though we might be first to hear the news, should any come in. There was no news; what we heard, at nearly every moment, were moans and wails that we had surely been defeated and the French would be marching through the streets of Brussels by morning. They were rumours only—I knew they were only rumours, because even those who had ridden down the road in the direction the army had taken had brought back no definitive word of the battle. But I still felt as though I were going to scream—or take the next person who moaned of defeat by the ears and shake him until his teeth rattled.

I was walking beside Mrs. Metcalfe, with Kitty and Harriet following behind us. Finally, one small, reedy little man wearing spectacles came hurrying past us and said he planned to flee Brussels as soon as he could— and strongly advised us to do the same—because our army had been cut to pieces and was retreating in the utmost confusion.

Mrs. Metcalfe stepped forward, seized him by the ear as though he had been a twelve year old boy, and calmly informed him that he should by all means take himself off as quickly as possible. "And," she said, "I will box your ears for you, my lad, if I catch you repeating such pernicious twaddle to a single other person here."

That made me smile, despite myself.

It is ten o'clock at night, now. I am back in my own room. We came back to the Forsters' around half-past nine, when finally the noise of the gunfire ceased. Though still—

I had to stop writing just now when Harriet knocked on my bedroom door to give me the latest report. Finally, finally, there is actual news.

An acquaintance of Harriet's, Sir Neil Campbell, had brought it to her just now—and since he had it directly from a Colonel Scovell, who was on the field of battle today, Harriet felt we might believe it to be true.

Colonel Scovell had left the battle at around half-past five—and the last he knew, 'all was well.'

Which I suppose is comforting—though of course half-past five was hours ago, and a full four hours before we heard the gunfire cease. From what Sir Neil told Harriet, the French had encountered some of our troops on the march at a place called *Quatre Bras*, about fifteen miles from Brussels.

It was only a few regiments of our troops; they had no cavalry and very little artillery—and yet even still, they managed to hold their ground against the French. The 92nd, 42nd, and 79th Highland Regiments suffered the worst of the French assault. They received the combined attack of the French cavalry and infantry. But throughout the day, they kept charging and driving the French back. Until they were finally overpowered by the sheer force of the French numbers. Colonel Scovell reported that the Highland regiments had been cut to pieces, almost to the last man.

Kitty gave a little sob of distress when Harriet repeated that part of the news. And then she swallowed and shook her head when Harriet turned to her. "I'm sorry." Kitty scrubbed impatiently at her eyes. "It's just—the Highland regiments. We saw some of them last night, Georgiana. Do you remember? They danced at the Duchess's ball. And now they must all be dead."

I do remember; I'm remembering it now: the haunting music of the pipes, the sway of the young men's kilts and their shouts of laughter after the dancing was done. Our having seen them at the Duchess of Richmond's ball *shouldn't* make their deaths any more affecting—they'd be just as young and just as dead if I'd never laid eyes on them—but somehow it does seem to bring the day's losses—

I had to stop writing again. The rest of this likely will be illegible, because my heart is still hammering so hard against my ribs it feels as though they ought to crack.

Just as I was writing that last sentence, there was a tremendous alarm in the street outside: a rumble of heavy military carriages. And then—from everywhere it seemed—people shouting, crying out that all was lost, the British defeated and in full retreat. I ran downstairs—and nearly collided with Kitty, who had come out of her room at the same time—and we stepped out onto the street to see if there really was news.

There was not—at least, I don't think there was, only more rumours: the Belgian townspeople declaring over and over again that the French had been seen advancing through the woods to take Brussels. Everywhere people were rushing about, harnessing horses and flinging bags into carriages—ready to flee to Antwerp.

Finally Kitty and I went back inside, and found Mrs. Metcalfe and Harriet in the front hall, wearing dressing gowns hastily thrown over their night-dresses. At first I blinked and thought I must have absorbed one too many terrors today or be more tired than I had realised. Because next to Mrs. Metcalfe the first thing I saw was one of the maidservants, drenched to the skin, hiccuping and sniffling and mopping up a puddle of spilled water on the floor.

But then Harriet explained in a whisper that apparently the girl had had hysterics over the alarm outside, and Mrs. Metcalfe had emptied the jug of water from her wash basin over the girl's head.

Kitty and I repeated to them what we had heard. And Harriet said in a small voice that her husband the Colonel had wished her to go to Antwerp in the event of danger.

I half expected Mrs. Metcalfe to snort and dismiss such rumours out of hand again. I was very nearly counting on it. I have only known Mrs. Metcalfe a handful of days, but I discovered I was depending on her to scoff at all fears as she had the housemaid's—which would be a small measure of reassurance in itself.

But instead Mrs. Metcalfe sighed and looked all at once weary, and older—her face suddenly seemed to show every one of her sixty-nine years. Her voice, when she spoke, sounded weary, too. "Well, girls, there's a choice to be made here. Even if this latest alarm is stuff and nonsense, that is no guarantee the next one won't be real. And for three young, pretty women like yourselves"—she looked from one of us to the other— "the middle of a city that falls to French soldiers is about the last place on earth anyone that cares about you would want you to be. Harriet's friend says the great battle—the one that decides matters once and for all—is to be tomorrow or the next day. So do we stay here, or do we go?"

I had to clench my teeth so hard my jaw ached, trying to stop myself from saying that I wished above all things to stay. It's not fair to the others. The danger is real enough, even if the outside rumours are not. No one is making up or imagining what the end could be if the French do defeat our armies. And I do not think I am especially brave or heroic—I don't feel it at the moment, at any rate. But somehow, after this day of uncertainty, everything in me is screaming against the thought of leaving Brussels and moving to Antwerp—where we would surely be in the same uncertainty for days before we heard reliable word of whether the battle had been a victory or defeat.

There was a long moment's silence. Harriet's round face had a white, strained look, and her hands were shaking. I was certain she would wish to leave for Antwerp as soon as the carriage could be brought round from the stable. But instead Harriet said in the same small voice, "I think . . . I think I would rather stay here. At least until we know for certain whether there is more immediate danger."

My breath went out in a rush as I felt relief sweep through me. I said that I would stay, too. And Kitty surprised me by saying that she would rather stay in Brussels, as well.

So it is decided. We are to stay. Mrs. Metcalfe took Harriet away to dose her with hartshorn in the hopes that she might get some rest tonight. She gave some to me and to Kitty, but I poured mine away into a potted plant without her seeing. I am tired—but I don't want anything to make me sleep tonight.

Saturday 17 June 1815

Edward is still alive.

My hands are shaking again with relief just writing that.

Yesterday I was afraid even to write down what I feared, all the time we were listening to the noise of the guns—as though writing that I was sick with the fear that Edward had been killed might somehow make it true.

But he is alive. Alive and unharmed. Or he was, as of last night.

Though it does not seem right that I should be so incredibly thankful and relieved when I've spent the entire day seeing just how much suffering this war has already caused.

The things I have done today—I still cannot entirely believe them.

We are still in Brussels, all of us—Kitty, Harriet, Mrs. Metcalfe and I. I am writing this in my room at the Forsters' house. It is evening—I have just heard the clock strike nine—and it is pouring sheets of rain outside, and the wind has an unearthly howl. The soldiers out in the field must be passing a horrible night. And they have to fight in the morning. Everyone says that the Duke of Wellington has taken up a position at Waterloo, and has every expectation of leading his troops into battle tomorrow.

I wish I could somehow send word to Edward. Or that he knew I was in Brussels. Or would that only make it worse for him, if he had to go into battle distracted by worrying about my being here?

All of Brussels has been in an uproar, all day long.

Men and women trying to beg, borrow, or steal horses to convey them to Antwerp; they say the roads leading out of the city are choked with traffic. I lost count of the number of times today I heard reports from hysterical townsfolk that the French were practically at the city gates. But I did discover that there is a limit to how afraid one can feel, and apparently I reached mine today. Because after a while, I noticed that I was scarcely bothering to pay attention to all the alarms and prophecies of destruction and despair.

I did see Ruth very early this morning—we met in the *Parc* completely by chance, too, which seems incredible in all the confusion and uproar.

She *is* travelling to Antwerp, with Lady Denby and her daughter. We had only time for a brief word. Even Ruth's usual composure was ruffled. She looked strained and pale. And she tried to persuade me to join them in Lady Denby's carriage. But I said that I would stay in Brussels.

I am glad now that I did. At least, I suppose in a way I am glad.

Because soon after I saw Ruth, the men wounded in yesterday's fighting at *Quatre Bras* started to pour into town.

At first Kitty, Mrs. Metcalfe, Harriet and I went out into the streets to see whether we could gain any reliable news. But after a bare few minutes, it was clear that the injured and dying were in need of any assistance we could give. There were so many of them. So, so many. And a bare handful of army surgeons to see to them all.

Mrs. Metcalfe looked at the scene before us: soldiers sprawled in the streets, huddled in the small shelter of doorways with blood-saturated, filthy rags pressed against their wounds. And then she turned to Harriet and said, "Go back to the house and tell that Madame Duvalle to give you every sheet and towel in the house. They can be ripped up for bandages for us to use out here."

Harriet looked completely sick. Sick and . . . lost. Since the regiments of the militia never are sent into battle, I suppose she was not at all prepared for what it would mean to be the wife of an officer in the regular army. "You mean you want to—to stay out here? I couldn't." She gulped, trying to swallow, and pressed her handkerchief over her mouth. "I can't—the smell—the blood—"

To my surprise, it was Kitty who interrupted her. She had been staring at a man—a boy, really, he looked horribly young—slumped against the side of a house on the far side of the street. His head was all wrapped up in bloodied bandages. "Oh, do shut up, Harriet, and just go and fetch the towels," Kitty said. "What if Colonel Forster is somewhere out here?"

Harriet's mouth opened and closed, and she turned a shade paler—her plump, pretty face was nearly green. But she did turn back to the house to fetch the household supply of spare linens.

Kitty herself was sick three times before we had gone the length of the street, bandaging wounds and giving men drinks of water from the flasks Mrs. Metcalfe herself had gone back to fetch. We all were. I felt bile rise in my throat every time I looked at a raw wound or leg shattered by a cannon ball.

Kitty and I kept going, though, working together when we could. And even Harriet stayed through the early afternoon, when Mrs. Metcalfe began to look too tired to carry on. I think she *would* have carried on, for all that. But Kitty and I insisted she ought to rest, at least for a little while. And Harriet—looking greatly relieved—agreed to escort her grandmother back to the house.

"Not that I blame Harriet." Kitty watched them go, stretching as though she were trying to ease an ache in her back. "I can't help but look at the men's faces. Every time I see a soldier with an officer's sash, I'm afraid it is—"

She broke off. But she didn't have to finish. I felt exactly the same. The suffering all around us was horrible—so horrible it was almost numbing.

And yet every time I saw a man in officer's uniform lying on the ground, my heart contracted at the thought that it might be Edward. And every time I saw that it wasn't he after all, I drew a breath of guilty relief.

"I know," I said to Kitty.

We each took a sip of water—lukewarm by that time—from the flasks we carried. And then I asked her, "How do you feel? Do you think you can keep going?"

Kitty pressed her eyes closed for a moment. But then she nodded and tried to smile as she pushed perspiration-soaked hair back into the knot at the nape of her neck. "I'm fine. Only I must look worse even than I had thought. Three of the last men I helped called me Mother."

And then we looked at each other, and I felt tears sting my eyes even as Kitty's eyes filled, too. Because so many of those too delirious with pain even to know their surroundings *were* calling for their mothers. Hardened veterans and raw young recruits alike.

In a book, I would have discovered a new-found passion for caring for wounded soldiers, or at least found I had unexpected nursing skills. But in reality, neither of those happened. I am glad we could help the wounded men, but I hated every moment of today—the blood-ied wounds and torn limbs; the copper-sweet stench of blood and sweat and filth.

Some of the men were too much hurt and too exhausted even to walk, and had to crawl. Some simply collapsed and died on the streets; several times today I crouched down to offer help to a soldier, only to realise that he was already gone.

I don't wonder Edward has nightmares, if he has ten years' worth of scenes like today to carry in his head.

And with all of them I felt so completely clumsy and inept, with no idea how even to begin to treat wounds of such severity, when the worst I had seen before today was a pricked finger or skinned knee.

There were a good many other ladies out, besides Kitty and me, all of them looking as sick as I felt. And by some strange quirk of fate, we were all the wounded men had.

I blinked hard and said to Kitty, "Don't make me cry, or I really *won't* be able to go on."

And Kitty said, "No." And then we both drew shaky breaths, and Kitty said, with another attempt at a smile, "I'll let you pick—do you want the right side of the street or the left?"

It's strange. I don't think I ever in a hundred years would have imagined living through a day like today. But if I had, and if I'd had to pick a companion for wading through all the blood and death, Kitty Bennet would have been the last person I would have chosen. But I was so grateful she was the one with me today.

It was just a short while later that we found Sergeant Kelly. Not that we knew who he was at first. I had crouched down beside yet another wounded soldier—a big, burly bear of a man lying on his side with his cheek resting in the muck of the gutter. And I was trying to brace myself for finding that he was yet another of those already dead and beyond aid. But when I took hold of his shoulder and rolled him face up, blue eyes flickered open, cleared, and fixed on my face.

"Can I help you?" I asked—just as I had all the other men.

The man cleared his throat and coughed, trying to speak, and I dribbled a little water between his lips. The man swallowed and coughed again and let out a sigh. "That's better, thank ye kindly, miss. Me throat was as dry as sand in the summer."

I won't even try to write the dialect properly—but his voice had a thick Irish brogue. And then he frowned, staring at my face harder as though trying to call up a memory. "Sure an' I know you, don't I? You'll be Miss Georgiana Darcy o' the Devonshire Darcys, isn't that right?"

I had fallen into a kind of numbed daze: moving from soldier to soldier, offering water or other assistance, and then moving on. But hearing my own name startled me out of the stupor and I stared at the man lying on the ground before me. He was an older man, forty or forty-five at a guess, with a bushy black beard and fierce black eyebrows and a pair of very deep-set blue eyes. His nose looked like it had been broken at least once.

"I'm sorry," I said. "I don't think . . . that is, have we met before?"

The man let out a wheezing chuckle that ended in a grunt of pain. "No, we've never met. I knew you from the miniature the Colonel carries with him. Must have been painted some years ago, I'd be guessing—but you've still the same look about you. Your eyes are the same."

I felt my breath go out in a rush and my vision shimmered for a moment at the edges. My voice sounded tinny and far away when I managed to ask, "Do you know Edward—Colonel Fitzwilliam? Have you . . . do you know where he is now?"

The wounded man had a bandage wrapped around his right arm that was completely saturated with bloodstains, some already dry, stiff and rusty, some sticky scarlet. But he raised himself up a little on his good elbow and looked at me, bushy brows creased in concern. "He's not killed, if that's what you be fearin', miss. He was right as rain last night—he's the one that dragged me off the battlefield before I could get trampled on."

I dug my fingernails hard into my palms and managed to drive the dizziness away. "Are you one of Colonel Fitzwilliam's regiment?" I asked him.

The man nodded. "Sergeant Patrick Kelly, at your service, miss. Been with him since he was a wet-behind-the-ears lad o' nineteen."

The last words cut off in another grunt as Sergeant Kelly gritted his teeth together against what must have been another jolt of pain. I recollected myself and said, "You've been wounded. Can I help you at all?"

Sergeant Kelly looked down at his bandaged right arm. "This? Nothing but a scratch, miss. Got it while we were trying to rally the bleedin' Belgians to stand and fight. Beggin' your pardon, miss. But the buggers took one look at those Frenchies, turned around and ran like their tails were on fire."

He had slumped back against the ground, though, and he didn't resist when I started to unwrap the bloodstained bandage from his arm.

I ought by that time to have got used to the sight of raw, bloodied wounds. And I suppose I had, at least to a degree, because I didn't faint or gasp or even turn dizzy again. But still, I had to clench my hands to keep from stumbling backwards at the sight, and if I had had anything to eat I think I would have been sick again.

The wound was a cut—a sabre cut, Sergeant Kelly said—running up his forearm and laying it open nearly to the bone. He had tied a rag very tightly around his upper arm to slow the bleeding. But even still the cut oozed blood. "I think—" I took a breath and was surprised to find that my voice sounded almost normal. "I think that ought to be stitched?"

Sergeant Kelly glanced with apparent unconcern down at his own wound and shrugged. "So it ought. Don't have me sewing kit, though. I had to drop me pack somewhere on the road back to Brussels. Couldn't carry it and haul me own carcass at the same time."

I nodded. "Can you stand, do you think? Walk, with my help? Here, take my hand," I added quickly, as the effort of rising made the sergeant sway unsteadily on his feet. Harriet had already agreed to take as many of the wounded as we could manage into the house. Most of the men on the streets were too weak to be moved—at least by us. But a few of the most gravely injured had already been carried back to the Forsters' by those of their fellow soldiers who could still stand. "If you can come with me," I told Sergeant Kelly, "We can get that wound seen to. It's not far."

I called across the street for Kitty to come and help us, and between the two of us we managed to get him back to the Forsters' house. Harriet was sitting in a corner of the drawing room, still looking pale as she ripped up sheets and towels for bandages. And Mrs. Metcalfe—looking completely recovered—was sitting in a big wing-backed brocade chair in the centre of the room. The scene looked like a cross between a hospital and a queen holding court; she had the wounded men who could still walk—I suppose there were eight or nine of them there, and more that she'd already treated going out the front door—form a line and then step up to her chair in turn.

Mrs. Metcalfe gave each man brandy and bandaged his wounds. And stitched some of them, too, when it was required. Part of me wanted to simply leave Sergeant Kelly to her. But she had her hands full. And besides, I was the one who had brought Sergeant Kelly there. It seemed like cowardice not to take care of him myself.

Kitty had taken fresh supplies of bandages and water and gone back out into the streets. So I told Sergeant Kelly to lie down on the carpet—all the space on the sofas and chairs was already taken—while I went to fetch a needle and thread.

Sergeant Kelly looked at me dubiously when I'd fetched the sewing supplies and sat down next to him. "Beggin' your pardon, miss," he said, "but I don't suppose you'll have ever done anything of this kind before?"

"Well, no," I said. "But I can do very good embroidery work. I promise you—the headmistress at my school gave me an absolutely glowing report."

"Embroidery, is it?" Sergeant Kelly tipped back his head and gave a shout of laughter at that, blue eyes crinkling at the corners.

I let out my breath and said, "Honestly, I have no idea how to stitch a wound. So it's up to you. I think that looks as though it ought to be attended to as soon as possible. But if you'd rather, I can try to fetch a surgeon. I'm not sure how quickly I can get one to come, that's all."

"A surgeon?" Sergeant Kelly shook his head. "No, they'll have enough to cope with just now, I'm thinkin'. No sense troubling them over the likes o' me. If you're game to try it, miss, you go ahead." And then he closed one eye in a wink. "Just don't be tryin' to add any fancy bits o' roses or such to your stitch-work, mind."

I probably hurt him terribly in stitching the wound closed—though he gave no sign of it and made no sound beyond a few quickly indrawn breaths. I felt my stomach lurch every time I had to pass the needle through his skin, and I was afraid the whole time that I'd make a mistake and somehow do more harm than good. But in the end I did manage to finish. The stitches looked slightly uneven and staggering—but the wound was closed.

I wrapped a clean bandage around his arm—and then went to fetch Sergeant Kelly something to eat and drink, because save for the few mouthfuls of water I had given him it appeared he'd had nothing at all since the previous day. He still looked tired when he'd finished the bread and cheese and apple I found for him. But he did seem restored, and he managed to sit up on his own. "Well, thank you kindly, miss. I suppose I'd best be taking myself off now."

"Wait." I put a hand on his arm. "Where will you go."

Sergeant Kelly shrugged. "Back to my billet, I suppose. Why do you ask, miss?"

"You could stay here," I said. " You ought to rest— and I'm sure we could find you room." I'm not sure what made me want so much for him to stay. Part of course was that he was a link, however small, to Edward—and I wanted to hear anything he could tell me of how Edward had been these last weeks, and how he had fared in the battle yesterday. But part I think was simply Sergeant Patrick Kelly himself. There was something reassuring about him: his broad, solid presence and humorous eyes. "We're on our own here," I went on. "Just four of us. Mrs. Forster"—I gestured towards Harriet—"and her husband have rented this house. But her husband is a colonel and has gone off to fight." I looked around the room at the other wounded men, lying on sofas and slumped in chairs. "Not that I imagine any of us cares for the proprieties at a time like this. But I think we'd feel safer, all of us, if you would agree to stay, at least for tonight."

I had been determined all day not to be a missish, fainting female—or give way to terror over all the what-ifs in our present situation. But on the other hand, it seemed to me that there was a definite line between bravery and stupidity. And four women, alone and undefended in a house in the wealthiest part of town, would make for an easy target for French soldiers. Or for the troops of our Prussian allies, for that matter; the Prussian soldiers are said to be even more rapacious than the French. Besides which, if any of the townsfolk tried to steal the Forsters' horses—I'd been watching such occurrences all day—I doubted any of us would be able to stop them.

Sergeant Kelly was frowning over what I had said. "Four of you on your own? No, that'll never do. Not but what I'm certain our lads will give old Boney's lot a grand beating tomorrow. But you ought to have someone here, just in case anything turns nasty." He nodded with sudden decision. "Right, I'll stay." His teeth flashed white in the midst of the dark beard. "Not but what I wouldn't stay for your own sake, Miss Darcy. But apart from that, I'm thinkin' the Colonel would make me wish

I'd had my arm cut off and both my legs as well if I let harm come to you."

Sunday 18 June 1815

They say the battle is to be fought at Waterloo, just as the Duke of Wellington said at the Duchess of Richmond's ball. Or maybe it has already begun. It is ten o'clock in the morning now. And I am sure it will be hours yet before we have any news.

Brussels this morning is quiet. So many have fled to Antwerp. Kitty and I went out earlier to the chemist's shop to buy more lint and bandages—only we didn't have to buy them, the shopkeepers are charging nothing.

We have been busy all morning with the wounded men who are staying here—the ones too gravely hurt to be moved. There are four of them: three younger soldiers who took shots to the body. And one—a dark-haired man a little older than the rest—in officer's uniform whose leg was crushed by a cannon shot. The field surgeons had to amputate before they sent him back here to Brussels in a waggon.

The first three are Captain Pringle, Sergeant Hawthorne, and Sergeant Smith. They're in terrible pain, I think. But they are so polite and grateful for any attention we give them. I don't know the fourth man's name—the officer who lost his leg. He has been delirious with fever ever since he arrived and has not been able to speak. Not coherently, at least. He mutters and tosses restlessly on the mattress we laid down for him on the dining room floor. I sat with him for a while early this morning, trying to get him to drink some broth that Madame Duvalle had made. I don't think he swallowed any. But I did bathe his face with water, which seemed to ease him a little. At least he stopped tossing and turning quite so much and seemed to fall into a more peaceful sleep.

If yesterday caring for the wounded men seemed a nightmare, I am grateful for it today. It helps to be kept busy—to feel as though I am doing something of use—instead of thinking of the battle that is to take place today. Barely ten miles south of here; I managed to find a map in Colonel Forster's study and looked up where Waterloo is.

Sergeant Kelly seems much better this morning. His arm is still bandaged, of course, but he says it scarcely pains him at all. And he has been helping with shifting the other wounded men so that we can bathe and tend them, so he must not be entirely lying.

Later . . .

I feel as though this day is never going to end. It is barely seven o'clock in the evening now—but already I feel as though it has lasted an eternity.

There was an alarm just a short while ago. A group of the Cumberland Hussars galloped through town shouting that all was lost and the French were on their heels. Not that that signifies. If I have learned one thing in the last two days, it is not to put too much credence in those sorts of alarms.

What is worse are the accounts from those who have seen the battle themselves. The first wounded are just beginning to trickle back. Sergeant Kelly went out into the town to see if he could gain any news. And when he came back he looked grave and said that by all accounts, the battle was the bloodiest any of the men he'd spoken to had ever seen. Impossible even to say who was alive and who had been killed in all the carnage and smoke.

He couldn't learn anything of Edward, nor yet of Captain Ayres or Colonel Forster.

I should get back to Kitty and Harriet. I don't think any of us wants to be alone tonight.

Monday 19 June 1815

The battle is won.

I can scarcely believe I am writing that. All the signs yesterday seemed to portent disaster and defeat. But it is true. Wellington and his armies have been victorious over Napoleon Bonaparte.

I should be relieved. I *am* relieved. Or I think I would be if I weren't tired enough to be in a kind of waking daze. We sat up nearly all through the night—Kitty, Mrs. Metcalfe, Harriet and I. All grouped together in Harriet's bedroom, so that we might not disturb the wounded men downstairs. We did finally persuade Mrs. Metcalfe and Harriet to lie down. And Kitty and I dozed a little, sitting in chairs beside the bed. And then this morning at around six o'clock we were woken with the news—our armies have defeated the French and put Napoleon's forces utterly to the rout.

It is good news—the best news we could have hoped for. And yet the cost of the victory already seems too much to bear.

Colonel Forster is dead.

Sergeant Kelly rode out at once to the field of battle to learn what he could. He came back this afternoon looking ten years older than when he had left here this morning. Older and in greater pain even than when I had found him lying in the street, every last trace of the usual humour in his face gone.

Kitty, Harriet, and I were all in the parlour, tending to the wounded. There is barely room to walk in the room now, the floor is so crowded with mattresses and feather beds that we stripped off the beds upstairs. We have taken in six more men, some wounded at *Quatre Bras*, some the first to return from the battle yesterday. And one of them—a red-haired man with a round, freckled face—has already died. Died before we could even learn his name.

When Sergeant Kelly came in, we all of us froze at the sight of his face. Harriet half rose, one hand going to her throat—as though she'd had some sort of premonition of what he was about to say.

Sergeant Kelly's blue eyes fixed on her, and his bearded face contorted with pity. But he got the news out in a single blunt sentence. "I'm sorry to tell you, ma'am. Your husband the Colonel was killed. Struck off his horse by a cannonball."

I'll never, ever forget the look on Harriet's face. It was as though some part of her had died, too. And then she just . . . crumpled. Folded up and fell to the ground, crying in great, gulping, wrenching sobs.

Mrs. Metcalfe came out of the kitchen—she has been helping Madame Duvalle there, since the servants are all gone—and between us we managed to carry Harriet upstairs and settle her into bed. Mrs. Metcalfe gave her a dose of the laudanum we have been giving the wounded men downstairs, and Harriet took it without even seeming to notice what it was.

That was mid-afternoon. It is evening, now, and she is still asleep. Which I suppose is kindness, to give her a short respite from facing the reality of Colonel Forster's death. I can't help thinking of what her waking will be like, though.

I am so sorry for her. And yet—

And yet I feel horribly guilty, too—because I seem barely to have space to grieve for her loss. Every part of me feels filled up, choked, suffocated with the fear that Sergeant Kelly is next going to fix me with that same look of pity, and say that Edward is dead, as well.

Tuesday 20 June 1815

I cannot believe it. I seem to be writing that over and over again. But it is true—these past days have been nothing I could ever have imagined or believed.

There is a chance Colonel Forster may still be alive.

This morning, a soldier—a sandy-haired man who gave his name as Lieutenant Jenkins—came to the house. He asked at first for Mrs. Forster. But Harriet was upstairs in bed. She wouldn't take any more of the laudanum last night—she said the wounded men need it more than she does. But she was awake nearly all the night through, lying in her bed and crying. Mrs. Metcalfe, Kitty, and I took it in turns to sit with her. And finally towards morning she did drift off to sleep.

I did not want to wake her, so I asked Lieutenant Jenkins whether he might give me whatever message he had for Harriet. I had to see him in the kitchen; the other downstairs rooms are all filled with wounded men.

Lieutenant Jenkins accepted my offer of tea and sat down with me at the big scarred kitchen table. And then he told me that he had been sent here by Colonel Forster, who greatly desired that his wife be reassured that he was alive, though gravely wounded.

At first I was so stunned I could only stare at him.

And then I asked him what he could mean by coming here with such a message—because we had heard yesterday that Colonel Forster had been struck by a cannonball and killed.

Lieutenant Jenkins' brow furrowed—and then cleared as he said, "Ah, that must be Colonel *Foster* you heard of, miss. Colonel William Foster of the Coldstream Guards. I did hear he had been killed that way."

It must have taken me nearly a full minute to find my voice. "And this man—this Colonel Forster you say is alive—you are sure it's the right man? The same Colonel Forster who has rented this house here?"

Lieutenant Jenkins shrugged. Now that the first shock of the news had passed, I had attention enough to notice that he looked exhausted—beyond exhausted, really. His eyes looked as though some part of him were still reliving the battle he had just fought. "That I can't say, miss, never having met the man before the battle was fought. We're still working to carry the wounded off the battlefield. There's hundreds of men still there, lying out in the open and dying of their wounds. I carried this man to one of the waggons. And he said his name was Colonel Forster and begged me to take a message back to Brussels for his wife. He didn't give me an address—he's wounded as I said, and too weak to talk much. But I asked all over the city and finally found that a Mrs. Forster lived in this house. So here I am."

I thought quickly. And then I asked, "He's wounded you said—wounded how? Do you think he will live?"

The lieutenant shrugged again. Which might have seemed callous, except that he ran his hand down his face as though trying to conceal the spasm of pain that clenched his jaw. "Even odds, I'd say. His arm looked like it would have to come off. The surgeons will probably have done it by now. If the shock doesn't kill him, he could survive."

"And where is he now?"

"Mont St. Jean. One of the farmhouses—a great many wounded have been carried there."

I nodded—and then stood up and held out my hand to Lieutenant Jenkins. "Thank you so much for coming. I will make arrangements to bring Colonel Forster here. And I will see that his wife gets the message."

And I will. But not until I know for certain that the man Lieutenant Jenkins brought word of really *is* Harriet's husband.

After Lieutenant Jenkins had gone, I went, not to Harriet's room, but out into the stable yard, where Sergeant Kelly was sitting on an upturned barrel and eating a quick meal of bread and bacon before going out again. He looked up when he saw me coming—and I saw his blue eyes had the same distant look as the lieutenant's, the same look Edward's eyes have after a nightmare.

I keep trying not to think of Edward. But it seems everything reminds me of him.

At least Sergeant Kelly's arm seems very much better.

I came to a stop before him and said, "I need you to take me to Mont St. Jean."

Sergeant Kelly's shaggy eyebrows shot up, and I said quickly, before he could protest, "There is a man there—it may be Colonel Forster. It seems there's reason to hope he is alive after all. But I can't tell Harriet. Not until we know for sure whether this man really is her husband. She is so lost in grief now, thinking him killed. If we raise her hopes, I don't see how she could bear it if the man turns out not to be Colonel Forster after all."

Sergeant Kelly's eyes widened slightly with shock. Then he frowned and nodded slowly, "Well, and if that's true it wouldn't be the first time names have got mixed or a false report's been taken for truth. But you can't be going to Mont St. Jean, Miss Darcy. That's right on the edge of the battlefield. It's no place for a lady just now. You stay here, let me go."

I shook my head. "That won't work. You have never met Colonel Forster. You won't be able to recognise whether this man really is he. And the man is wounded—very seriously so. He might not even be well enough to be moved. He might be dying, even."

"Well, and if he is dying, surely it's a kindness not to tell his wife about him at all? She already thinks him dead."

I shook my head again. "No. If it is Colonel Forster, Harriet needs to know. Even if he is dying. She might be able to see him one last time. And I know she would want that. Even if it was just for five minutes, she would want to see him, be with him at the end. I know I would feel the same, if—"

I found myself rubbing the emerald on Edward's ring again, and stopped myself before I could finish. But from the look on Sergeant Kelly's face, he knew what I had been about to say. The words felt like sharp-edged rocks in my throat, but I couldn't stop myself from asking, "If you had news of him—of Edward—you would tell me, wouldn't you? Even bad news. You wouldn't try to keep it from me, to spare me pain?"

"Of course I would." Sergeant Kelly's voice was gruff. "But I still say, Miss Darcy, that you oughtn't to go out there to the battlefield. You don't know what it's like. You—"

I cut him off. I had been stuffing everything—anger, grief, worry, terror—away, trying to lock it all up in a box somewhere just so that I could go on and keep getting through the hours of each day. But Sergeant Kelly's words made the lock on the box suddenly spring open and everything come flooding out. It felt like being torn and pulled by the furious gale of a thunderstorm.

"I don't know? I don't *know*?" I was almost shouting but I couldn't stop myself. I gestured to my gown—which used to be blue sprigged muslin and is now smeared with rusty brown bloodstains picked up from tending to the wounded. There has been no time to do laundry, especially without any of the servants to help. "I have spent all morning holding a man's hand while he died of the blood in his lungs. I have wrapped wounds with lint and had to look at broken bones poking through the skin. I sewed up the cut on *your* arm. So don't tell me that I don't know what the aftermath of a battle is like!"

I felt my eyes sting and my throat close off and start to ache fiercely. But I blinked the tears furiously away. Let myself start to cry, and I would only be proving the truth of what Sergeant Kelly said—that I was too weak, too soft to bear going to Mont St. Jean.

Sergeant Kelly looked at me a long moment. And then shocked me completely by giving a low chuckle. He still looked tired, careworn. But just for a moment, there was a gathering of humour about the edges of his eyes. "Right, then, Miss Darcy. I'll see to bridling the horses and getting the carriage ready. If this wounded man really is Colonel Forster and can bear the move, we'll be needing it to bring him back here."

My breath went out and I nodded. "Thank you."

"Don't thank me, Miss Darcy. You won't feel like it much when you've seen what there is to see out there, I promise you." Sergeant Kelly's voice was bleak. But then just the briefest twist of a smile flashed across his face again as he looked at me and shook his head. "No wonder Colonel Fitzwilliam's so caper-witted for you."

That was half an hour ago. And I have to leave. I have gathered up all the blankets and pillows we can spare and packed them in the carriage. And Sergeant Kelly has the horses ready. We are to leave at once for Mount St. Jean.

Harriet is still asleep. I am praying that if this man is not her husband, we can be back before she wakes up again, and she will never have to know we were gone at all.

Later . . .

We did take the carriage to Mont St. Jean. And it was—

If I am honest, Sergeant Kelly was entirely right. I did not know what seeing the ground where the battle was fought would be like. I thought myself prepared. But seeing the wounded in Brussels was only the palest rehearsal.

The ground is piled with the men killed in battle. Some have been buried in pits dug for mass graves. But there are so many of them that here and there a dead hand or the toe of a boot sticks up out of the soil. That's not the worst, though. The worst is that there are men still alive, lying on the field. There are many working to get the wounded up and carry them away. But they have to start with those whom they have some hope of saving. So the worst-wounded ones are simply left to die where they fell in the fighting.

I understand. I do. And I can't see any other way. But I can still hear the groans and cries of pain.

Just as we reached Mont St. Jean, I felt Sergeant Kelly press something into my hand and looked down to see a handkerchief. It was only then I realised I was crying.

Every single nerve in my body felt stretched and raw with the need to run out onto the battlefield myself, and look at the faces of every man until I knew whether Edward was among those there. It was the hardest thing I have ever done, staying in the carriage until we reached the farmhouse Lieutenant Jenkins had directed me to. But it was the barest chance I might really find Edward in all the chaos and slaughter. And I had an actual chance of doing both Harriet and her husband real good.

So we kept on. And it was worth the effort—because the man at Mont St. Jean really *was* Colonel Forster. Very ill and weak—he had indeed lost his left arm—but alive. And not so weak that he could not be moved. So together Sergeant Kelly and I loaded him into the carriage and padded him carefully with all the blankets and cushions I had brought. The roads are horrible—all rutted by the artillery waggons, and the jouncing of the carriage must have been agony to Colonel Forster, but he bore it all with scarcely even a groan. And then sometime before we got to Brussels, he slipped into unconsciousness from the pain. He was still unconscious when Sergeant Kelly carried him into the house.

I got to be the one to give Harriet the news when she woke up towards evening. And the look on her face when I told her almost wiped out the images of the field of battle that kept flashing across my mind's eye.

The surgeon came and left some leeches—and Harriet actually applied them herself to the stump of Colonel Forster's amputated arm.

But there is still no word of Edward.

BOOK II

Thursday 22 June 1815

I do not know where to begin. The clock has just struck midnight.

And I am writing this in the new diary Sergeant Kelly brought me today.

I can't remember his ever seeing me write in my old book. But this morning he came to me after breakfast and simply handed me a book—this book—and said he had picked it up yesterday when he went out to buy food and other supplies. Some of the shops in Brussels have started to re-open as the townsfolk trickle back in from Antwerp.

And I don't even know how to write down what I feel right now. Relief. Terror.

Neither of those seems even to come close.

Maybe the closest I can come is to say that some moments I feel as though I am drowning, and the next as though I am somehow disconnected from myself, watching from a long way off.

Edward is alive. He's *alive*.

I keep reaching my hand out to touch him, just to make sure he is real. Staring at his face and all the while feeling as though I am trying to breathe underwater, my heart is pounding so hard.

Sergeant Kelly came back to the house soon after I wrote that last entry in my old journal book—the one I scribbled on the flyleaf.

I was changing the bandages of our nameless officer—the man who has lost his leg. He is still nameless, though he has been in our care for days, since he hasn't yet been able to talk. We were all afraid—truthfully, more certain than afraid—that he was going to die. But today for the first time I am beginning to think he might recover after all. He is still horribly weak, and his face is so gaunt it looks like paraffin wax smeared over bone. But I think the fever is gone, and this morning he drank a little broth before he lapsed back into a stupefied sleep.

At any rate, I had just finished with him when Sergeant Kelly came in, looking sober and very grave. And a voice in my head screamed at me to run, to get away before he could give me whatever terrible news he had brought. As though postponing it even a few moments could make it any easier to bear.

But then Sergeant Kelly opened his mouth and said, "Don't look like that, Miss Darcy, I've brought him back to you. He's still alive. Just terribly hurt is all."

I don't remember the interval between those words and the moment when I stood beside the farm cart Sergeant Kelly had driven to the door and first caught sight of Edward's face.

Mrs. Metcalfe had come with me—I suppose Sergeant Kelly was afraid I might faint—and I was vaguely aware of her saying something else to me and holding my hand. But I still scarcely heard her. I was staring down at Edward, lying on a rough straw pallet on the floor of the cart.

He was unconscious, and so still I thought for a single heart-stopping moment that Sergeant Kelly had made a mistake and that he was dead after all. Then I saw the faint—very faint—rise and fall of his chest. And suddenly every detail seemed unnaturally clear and bright. So bright it hurt my eyes. The tattered and filthy remains of the army uniform he still wore. The lines of Edward's face, gaunt and greyish pale beneath smears of blood and dirt. The bloodied bandage wrapped around his head.

The bandage concealed what must have been a terrible blow to his head. I saw it for the first time when between us all, we had carried Edward into the house and upstairs. I said at once that he could have my room, and I would either move in with Kitty or sleep on the floor.

Sergeant Kelly hefted Edward as gently as he could manage onto the bed, and then went to fetch hot water. And Mrs. Metcalfe and I started to cut away the muddied rags of Edward's uniform and take stock of his injuries.

The head wound is his only serious hurt. For the rest he has a few cuts and bruises, but nothing of note. The head wound is bad enough, though. Not that I know much about such things, but Sergeant Kelly flinched visibly when he caught sight of it, and Mrs. Metcalfe opened her mouth as though to say something, looked at my face and then fell silent.

All through the time we were bathing Edward, cleaning the mud and dirt of the battlefield away and tending the minor cuts and scrapes, Edward did not move. His eyes didn't even flicker; his muscles didn't even twitch.

A surgeon came a short while ago—a Mr. Powell—but he said there was very little he could do. He left some leeches and said I might apply them at three-hour intervals. I asked whether he thought Edward could hear me, and Mr. Powell shook his head and said, briskly, "Oh, no, I shouldn't think so. The blow is a severe one, and days old. He's quite insensible, poor man."

And then he said that if Edward were still alive in the morning, he could try bleeding him; that might do some good. But he was far too busy to spare time on lost causes when the city was filled with men he could save.

All the breath seemed to have been stolen from my lungs. Which was probably fortunate, otherwise I might have starting shouting at Mr. Powell. But when the darkness at the edges of my vision cleared, the surgeon had already gone. Mrs. Metcalfe was standing next to me again, petting my hair lightly—I can just remember my mother doing the same when I was very small.

"Don't pay him any mind," she said. "Half the time these long-faced surgeons don't have the smallest idea what they are talking about."

I looked up at her. "Do you really think that? Do you really think Edward may yet recover?"

Mrs. Metcalfe looked away—but not before I had seen the flash of pity in her eyes. She touched my hair lightly again and said, "There, child. We none of us are given more in this life than we can bear."

I am sitting in a chair beside Edward's—my—bed, writing this now. Edward's face looks . . . remote in the flickering lamplight. Unreachable. He still has not stirred.

All the time he was missing, I kept promising myself and fate and God that if I could only have five minutes more with him, I would not complain of anything afterwards. But I lied. Whatever Mrs. Metcalfe says, I can't even think about Edward dying now.

Friday 23 June 1815

Colonel Forster is out of danger now: awake, sensible, and recovering well. He is able to sit up and feed himself one-handed. And Harriet helps him with everything else.

Which should be such a happy ending to it all, even with the loss of his arm. But it really does seem that fate has a cruel sense of humour at times. Because even Colonel Forster's recovery is marred by the news we got the very same day Sergeant Kelly and I brought the Colonel home. John Ayres is dead.

And there is no doubt about it, this time. We heard from another soldier in his regiment, a friend of Captain Ayres who had been with him at the end. Captain Ayres had given the other man a gold watch that had been his father's, and asked that it be brought to Kitty. It was his last request before he died.

Ever since, Kitty has gone about like someone sleep-walking. I have not seen her cry. Instead she changes bandages and writes letters for the wounded men and goes out to do the day's shopping with an absolutely expressionless face and a hard, bleak look in her eyes.

Edward's condition is unchanged.

Sunday 25 June 1815

It must be nearly dawn now. The sky outside the window is turning from midnight-blue to pearl-grey. Whatever Mr. Powell said, I have been talking to Edward—talking and talking and talking until my throat aches. Telling him about Elizabeth and baby James—because the last time Edward saw James he was just a tiny newborn. About our boat voyage to Ostend. Speaking to him of anything I can think of, and all the while holding his hand and hoping to feel some sort of a response, some sign he might be able to hear me after all.

But there has been none. And I have to rest at least for a little while. And since I don't want to fall asleep, I am resorting to writing in this book again.

Sergeant Kelly came into the room a little before one o'clock to see if there was any change. And he told me where he had found Edward—which I had not even thought to ask before.

It seems Edward was found unconscious on the battlefield, lying next to the dead body of his horse, which must have been shot out from under him. Edward was carried to a barn where others of the wounded were being cared for. But since he was unconscious and could not give his name, no one knew who he was. He lay there almost forgotten until Sergeant Kelly happened upon him in the course of his search yesterday.

Sergeant Kelly looked at Edward's face then, deathly pale against the pillows, and a shadow crossed his gaze. But then he clasped his hands behind his back and started to talk, telling me stories about Edward. Stories I had never even heard, because Edward so rarely speaks about his time on campaign. Sergeant Kelly spoke of his courage on the battlefield. The way he had rallied men who were on the verge of breaking ranks and running. And the story Edward himself told me about his having helped a baby into the world during the wintertime retreat in Spain—Sergeant Kelly told me more of the full story, which was that Edward himself had helped to carry the infant—tucked inside his coat for warmth—through the night. He had helped the parents right up until the regiment came under attack and he was called away to fight.

And then Sergeant Kelly caught sight of my ring—the *claddaugh* ring Edward gave me—and asked if I knew the story behind the design. I shook my head, and Sergeant Kelly said, "Well now, seein' as how I'm an Irishman myself, I can tell you. Two hundred years ago and more, there was a man—Richard Joyce, his name was—one of the Joyce clan, and a native of Galway. He loved a girl, but was too poor to marry her. So he set sail to work in the West Indies, meaning to marry his love when he'd made his fortune and returned. But his ship was captured by pirates on the voyage out. And as for Richard Joyce, he was sold as a slave to a Moorish goldsmith, who taught him the goldsmith's craft. And Joyce, longing for his love, made a ring as a symbol of his love for her—hands for friendship, a crown for loyalty, and a heart for love."

"Now it happened that Richard Joyce was set free. Maybe his master was tender-hearted and let him go, maybe the king demanded he be released, I can't say. But he got his freedom. And the goldsmith—the one who'd bought him for a slave—had such a respect for Richard Joyce that he offered Joyce his daughter and half his wealth if Joyce would be agreeing to stay. But Joyce, he said no, thank you kindly, but he was bound to get back to his home and the love he'd left behind. So he set sail, back to Galway. And his love—she'd been waiting for him, all these long years. Richard Joyce gave her the ring he'd made her, and they were married."

Sergeant Kelly stopped speaking. I raised my hand to brush at my cheek, and realised that I was crying without ever having noticed.

Sergeant Kelly dropped a large hand onto my shoulder and gave me a clumsy pat. "Colonel Fitzwilliam, he'll be fightin' to get back to you just the same way. So you just stay here and talk to him and remind him of why he's got to pull through."

"The surgeon said—" I started to say, but Sergeant Kelly interrupted.

"Bollocks to the surgeon. Beggin' your pardon, miss," Sergeant Kelly added quickly. "The Colonel, he's not one to make a song and dance of his feelings. But I saw the look on his face when he'd touch that miniature painting of you, and I heard his voice the few times I heard him speak your name. Whatever Mr. High-and-Mighty-Surgeon says, the Colonel knows you're here. You've just got to convince him to stay with you."

Sergeant Kelly spoke with such conviction—he made it sound so sure, so easy. Just before he left the room again, he stepped close to the bed and dropped a hand on Edward's arm and said, "Battle's over, sir. But don't you quit fightin' now."

Tuesday 27 June 1815

This is likely to be another completely disjointed diary entry—because I have been sitting here for the last quarter hour debating with myself whether I even want to write down what happened tonight. But I think I do. There is no one else I can tell.

George Wickham came to the house tonight.

I had been sitting beside Edward all day, holding his hand, talking to him, wiping his face and holding a moistened sponge to his lips, hoping to coax him into drinking a little. Madame Duvalle brought me supper on a tray, but I wasn't hungry enough to take more than a few bites. So I took the food downstairs with me for Mrs. Metcalfe to offer to the soldiers who are recovered enough to be able to eat. And then I went out into the stable yard, meaning to find Sergeant Kelly. Because I was so, so tired—and all but entirely out of hope that Edward might still wake up.

As soon as I stepped out the door, though, a hand clamped over my mouth and I was jerked backwards against a man's body; I could feel his breath, hot in my ear.

My heart seized—and then started to race because

the next moment the man hissed at me, "Don't scream, Georgiana." And I recognised George Wickham's voice. Though at first I could not believe my ears.

My pulse was pounding. But I forced myself to nod to show that I understood. And he released me, keeping hold of my wrist but slackening his grip so that I could turn around and face him.

It *was* George Wickham. Sergeant Kelly was nowhere to be seen. But he had left a lantern burning above the stables, and by its light I could see Wickham's face clearly. He looked even worse than he did a year ago, when he came to Pemberley trying to blackmail my brother and me. The boy he once was—the boy I grew up with on my father's estate—is entirely gone. So much so the two—boy and man—seem like two separate people in my memory. Wickham's blue eyes now are nearly lost in pockets of flesh, his once handsome features puffed and coarsened by lines of dissipation and drink.

Even still, I half expected to find he was just part of my imagination, some sign that sitting up night after night being terrified for Edward's life had started me hallucinating. The night back at Longbourn—when Elizabeth told me that Wickham was in Brussels, and warned me that I might see him here—seemed inexpressibly far away. I had not thought of him even once in all the days since we arrived.

The hand gripping my wrist painfully hard was real enough, though, and I pushed the wave of shock back and said, "What do you want here?"

Instantly, Wickham's hand was clamped over my mouth again. He hissed, "Quiet!" And I noticed what I hadn't before: that his eyes were darting nervously back and forth, and that there was a glitter of sweat on his forehead. "I don't want to be seen," he added in the same harsh undertone. "No one can know I've been here."

"Then why come here at all?" Now that I was looking at Wickham more closely, I could see the other signs of fear. The fingers wrapped around my wrist trembled slightly, and when one of the horses in the stables beyond us whickered softly, he started and his head snapped around towards the sound.

But at least the fear left him unwilling or unable to prevaricate or try to spin a lie. He moistened his lips and then said, "Money. I need enough money to get me out of the country. I thought you could give it to me."

I stared at him. And then the pieces assembled themselves in my mind. Wickham was wearing an army uniform—just like so many other young men in Brussels now. But where most of the other red coats you see on the streets are still stained and torn from the battle, Wickham's looked almost new. And he himself hadn't a single wound or mark on him that I could see. Not that that signified, necessarily. I know some men—not many, but some—were lucky enough to come through the battle at Waterloo completely unscathed. But coupled with the uniform, and his patent fear—

"You're a deserter." I heard the words come out of my mouth before I realised I had even decided to speak. I suppose I was simply too tired—and too much infuriated—to check myself. "You ran away from the battle. And now you need to get out of the country before you can be shot for a coward and traitor."

Wickham's face darkened with anger and his jaw clenched. And for a moment I felt another spasm of fear. I was alone with him in the darkened stable yard. And however fallen into ruin he is, he is still both larger and stronger than I am. He must have decided he would get further by trying to charm than to threaten, though. Because his lips stretched into something that tried to resemble a smile and he said, "Please, Georgiana. For old times' sake. We were always good friends. I heard you were in Brussels. But you've no idea how hard it is to get you alone. I've been waiting outside this house for two days now. I haven't even had anything to eat. I thought you were never going to come out." He exhaled a laugh that was even less convincing than the smile and said, "Anyone would think you were a prisoner in there."

That brought it all rushing in on me, harder and more suffocating than ever, of course. I had not left the house at all because I had been sitting day and night by Edward's bedside, watching him die by slow degrees. Die of the hurt he had got in the same battle George Wickham had run away from.

I jerked my hand out of Wickham's grasp—and managed to catch him off guard enough that he had to let me go.

"Get out of here." I spoke the words through clenched teeth.

The anger flashed across Wickham's face again, and his hand shot out, this time settling around my bare throat. "Careful, Georgiana. I could decide to ask less politely."

"And unless you get your hands off me, I could decide to scream. Someone from the house would come out here in seconds. Do you really want to risk anyone else seeing you? Or getting caught here by someone with authority in the army?"

Wickham's jaw clenched. But he did let his hand fall away. His eyes darted around the stable yard again and then he said, his voice half-sly, half-sullen, "There are still stories I could tell about you, you know."

I heard myself laugh. "What? That you tried to seduce me and failed?" And then I leaned forward until my eyes met his and spoke slowly. "The man I love is upstairs in this house, dying. And there is not a single thing I can do to help him. Do you really think you can frighten me?"

Whatever he saw in my eyes made Wickham take a stumbling step backwards. He raised a trembling hand and wiped the sweat from his face. That was when, quite suddenly, I felt a tiny thread of pity start to worm its way into my feelings for him. It was the last thing I had expected to feel. Everything I have written about George Wickham was true—it still is. And to end it all, he had deserted his duty during battle, turned tail and run.

But at that moment I did feel pity for him. How brave are most of us, really, in facing what we most fear? How brave am I? Just the thought of Edward dying makes me want either to scream or to curl up somewhere hidden enough that I can disappear.

"Wait here," I told Wickham. Back inside the kitchen, I found a few apples, a wedge of cheese and a meat pie, and knotted them together in a napkin. I half expected Wickham would have run off—but he was still standing in the stable yard, sweating and shaking, when I came back outside. I suppose he was hoping I might give him money after all. "Here." I put the food into his hands. "Take it and go."

I caught a glimmer of what looked very much like hatred in Wickham's eyes as his hands closed over the bundle. But he turned and walked away without speaking another word.

Just as Wickham left the stable yard, Sergeant Kelly

returned; they even passed each other at the gate. "Sorry, Miss Darcy, I just stepped around the corner to the public house to see if there's any news of old Boney."

Napoleon's armies were defeated at Waterloo, but Napoleon himself remains at large; the word in Brussels is that he has fled back towards Paris.

"Did you want something, miss? Or—" Sergeant Kelly went still as the thought struck him, sudden alarm tightening the edges of his mouth. "Or has something happened? Is there any change with the Colonel?"

I shook my head quickly. "No, nothing like that. I mean, he's no better. But he's not— Nothing has changed."

Sergeant Kelly let out a breath. "Well, thanks be to goodness for that, anyway." He rubbed a hand along his jaw and then added, as though as an afterthought, "Who was that man? The one I passed coming in here? He wasn't bothering you, was he?"

"The man?" I looked across the stable yard to the gate where George Wickham had gone out. "Just a beggar. I gave him some food. But I'm sure he won't be coming here again."

Later . . .

It is barely dawn. And I am so tired that an hour ago I would have said I couldn't stay awake even a few minutes longer. I am not sure I can now. But I want to write this down—I have to write this down, just so that once I do wake up I'll know that it really happened, that I didn't just dream it all.

After I finished my last diary entry, Edward was still lying exactly as he has lain since Sergeant Kelly brought him back: his face so still and greyish-pale that he might have been an effigy statue carved on a coffin. I touched his hand, and it was cold.

I don't remember very much from when my parents died. It is all such a confused blur of grief, and of course as a child I was not allowed to see them for more than a moment or two at a time. But I do have a knife-sharp memory from when I was six of being taken by my nurse into my mother's room, when she was ill for the last time. My mother was sleeping, and the nurse said we must not wake her, not even to see me, because my mother needed her rest. Which frightened me. So I tried to take hold of my mother's hand, and found her fingers chilly cold. And two days after that, she died.

I suppose that is why feeling the coldness of Edward's hand tonight made something tear inside my chest.

I have been determined all this time not to let myself cry. But tonight I couldn't stop myself. I wrapped my arms around Edward and rested my head against the curve of his shoulder. I still couldn't stop crying, and I could feel my tears soaking his shirt under my cheek.

Sergeant Kelly had said that Edward could hear me. So far I hadn't seen a single sign of that being true. But I waited a moment, feeling the slow, laborious rise and fall of Edward's breath, the thump of his heart. Then I drew in a ragged breath and shut my eyes and prepared to try one last time.

"You can't die, Edward." The house was silent all around us, and my whisper sounded tiny in the shadowy, lamp-lit room. "Do you hear me? When you went away almost the last thing you said to me was, *I swear I'll come back to you.* Do you remember? And I know"—I had to swallow before I could force the words past the tightness in my throat—"you always keep your promises. So I need you to come back to me now. Come back to me, Edward. I love you."

The rhythm of Edward's breathing changed; he gave a kind of ragged gasp. And I felt my heart slam hard against my ribs at the fear that he really was dying, or that in lying down with him I had hurt him somehow. But then his head moved restlessly against the pillow. His eyelids lifted for just a moment, and his lips seemed to shape an unintelligible, silent word.

I sat bolt upright, staring at him. And then I scrambled out of bed and reached for the water pitcher, and raised Edward's head enough that I could hold a cup to his lips. He drank it—he actually drank it. Though the effort seemed to exhaust him, for he sank back onto the pillow and at once was deeply unconscious again. But I had put my hand into his. And before he sank back into sleep, I felt a press of his fingers against mine. Just a brief, light pressure. But I felt it. I am sure of it.

Saturday 1 July 1815

It has been days since I last wrote anything in this book. Partly because I have scarcely had a free moment. But I think it is partly also because I have not wanted to.

Edward is alive—and getting stronger every day. Even Mr. Powell the surgeon proclaims him officially out of danger now.

But he is blind. His eyes are open and undamaged. And yet he can't see anything at all. Which is an occasional side effect of a blow to the head, according to Mr. Powell.

Mr. Powell said a great many other things, too, that when condensed meant that he has no real idea why Edward is blind and can do nothing at all to help.

But what he cannot say is whether Edward will ever recover his sight. His vision may clear. Or it may be gone forever.

For myself, I would not care if Edward lost both arms and both legs as well as the use of his eyes—just so long as he came back to me still alive. And the fact that he is still alive after he came so near to dying feels like a miracle, every moment of every day.

It's Edward I mind for.

Mrs. Metcalfe—meaning well, of course, and trying to comfort me—said, "Never fear, your young man will bear it—as we all bear what we have to in this world. As my granddaughter's husband bears the loss of his arm."

She *did* mean well. It is not her fault that right now, all those sorts of statements make me want to scream or smash something.

Sergeant Kelly has had to return to his regiment now that his arm is healed. He was grieved, of course, over Edward's condition. But he clasped my hand before he left and said, "The Colonel's alive. That's the main thing."

And when I asked what I ought to do for Edward, he considered and then said, "He'll need time. Don't push him. Just be there when he's ready to let you help him find his way."

Sergeant Kelly promised to write to me. Or rather, he promised that he would find someone to write for him, since he does not read or write himself. And I said that I would write him letters that he could find someone else to read. I miss him—more than I would have believed, considering how short our acquaintance was.

But he was so confident that I could help Edward. And I could desperately use that confidence right now.

The first time Edward woke—really woke enough

to speak and to be aware of his surroundings—was the afternoon after he had half-woken for that very first time. I had my back turned to the bed, straightening up the room. And Edward suddenly said, "Georgiana." The first word he had spoken since we carried him into the house.

My heart leapt and I whirled around and took Edward's hand. "I'm here. I'm right here."

And Edward's hand squeezed mine and he let out a breath and said, his voice raspy and hoarse with disuse, "You're really here? I thought . . . I thought I must have only dreamed you."

And then I felt his muscles tense and his head turned against the pillow. He said, voice tightening, "But I can't see you. Why can't I see? Everything's dark."

But ever since that first moment of panic, Edward has been so stoically accepting. He faces each day with a kind of battle-hardened calm, and he has not complained or been impatient or angry even once. He is able to sit up, now, and to stay awake for longer and longer periods. And he asks to hear everything I or the other soldiers can tell him about the outcome of the battle. He only remembers the beginning of the fighting, and nothing at all about how he was hurt.

He drinks the broth and the milk that the surgeon prescribed with apparent grim determination to regain his strength. But he never speaks of how he is feeling or whether his head aches—though I know from watching his face that it must.

And I know—I can feel it twisting inside me like blades all the time I am with him—how much he must hate being blind and helpless. Even if he never lets himself speak of it.

Save for that first moment, though, he has not asked

for me, either. He allows me to sit with him, and he will answer when I speak to him—perfectly calm, pleasant answers. And sometimes when he is sleeping, he will toss and turn restlessly, and only settle when I take his hand or touch his cheek.

But he never asks for me when I am not there.

Sunday 2 July 1815

Today I went downstairs for almost the first time in the last three days. I spent a short while this morning sitting with Edward. Helping him to eat his breakfast. Which I know he absolutely hates. Though the only sign of it is the play of muscle along his jaw when I have to put the spoon into his hand and guide it to what's on the plate.

Soon after he finished eating he told me he wanted to sleep awhile.

"Do you need me to—" I started to say, but Edward interrupted.

"No. I can at least manage to sleep all by myself." His voice was rough, clipped. But then he drew in a slow breath and groped for my hand. I moved it closer, and he took it, fingers closing around mine. "I'm sorry. I'm just . . . tired. I couldn't sleep last night."

The flash of anger had gone, and his lean face was set in a look of pain and sadness both. His dark eyes— blank and sightless, now—stared ahead without seeing anything at all.

My heart twisted up tightly and I said, "I could stay if you like. I don't have to say anything."

But Edward shook his head, his expression flattening and hardening once again. "No. I—I think I'm better off on my own for a little while."

I left him. I didn't—I still don't—know what else to do.

Downstairs, I found that nearly all the wounded men we had been caring for are gone. Those who are able to travel are being sent back to England. Harriet and Colonel Forster had gone out to walk in the *Parc*—Colonel Forster is well enough to go outdoors and take a little exercise now—and Mrs. Metcalfe was alone with the three injured men who are left.

She was spoon-feeding gruel to a fair-haired boy who was shot through the abdomen, but miraculously seems to be recovering from the wound. I asked whether I might do anything to help. And Mrs. Metcalfe slid the last spoonful into the boy's mouth, then got up and crossed the room to me. "I think we are coping tolerably well, thank you," she said. "How is your young man this morning?"

"Edward is . . . he's fine," I said.

Mrs. Metcalfe gave me a keen look. But thankfully she did not ask anything else. Instead she lowered her voice and said, "You could see if you can get a word out of our officer friend over there." She nodded to the corner, where the dark-haired officer was lying staring straight up at the ceiling. His face was unshaven, stubbled with several days' worth of beard. But someone—Mrs. Metcalfe, I suppose—had at least managed to get him into clean shirt and trousers. The empty right leg of the trousers was pinned just above the knee.

"He's not dying." Mrs. Metcalfe kept her voice to the same near-soundless murmur. "Not unless he manages to starve himself to death. He will barely touch a bite of food. And I have not managed to get him to say two words to me. Not even to tell me his name." Her gaze travelled to the nameless man and she shook her head.

"He has been like that ever since he woke up in his right mind enough to realise that his leg was gone. Just lies there, staring at the ceiling all day."

I felt dread curling in the pit of my stomach as I crossed the room. If I have no idea what to do for Edward, I felt still more inadequate to try to help this man. But anything was better than going back upstairs. Where Edward was either asleep, or would pretend to be as soon as I came into the room. So I knelt down by the nameless officer's mattress and said, "Good morning."

He did not answer or even turn to look at me, but instead stared straight up, his gaze almost as blank as Edward's. A part of me—the selfish, cowardly part—wanted to give up right then and there and leave him to himself and whatever dark thoughts were lurking behind his eyes. I am glad we have been able to care for as many wounded men as we have these last weeks. But just at that moment I was utterly sick of illness and sadness and the grim shadow of war and death.

I stayed where I was, though, and said, "Is there a name I can call you by?"

There was a long moment's silence when I thought that he was simply going to ignore that question, as well. But then his head turned on the pallet and his eyes, golden hazel-brown, glared into mine. "Why?" His voice sounded hoarse and creaking, but thick with a kind of contained fury all the same. "Do you want to read me a sermon like the priest who came in here did? Tell me I should bear my wounds like a Christian and give thanks to God for sparing my life, even at the cost of my leg?"

I held very still. At least he had spoken to me. That felt like a victory of a kind. "No," I said. "I was going to ask you whether you would like milk or sugar in your tea."

The man glared at me a moment more. But then a slow, unwilling smile started to twitch at the corners of his mouth—though I saw him try to fight it. Now that the gauntness and pallor of illness have gone, it is clear he's a very handsome man. His hair is very dark, and falls across his brow, and his features are lean and a little hawk-like. That was what he made me think of, lying there with his angry, hazel-gold eyes: a tethered hawk, furious at being restrained.

He was silent again. And then he said, "Neither. Thank you."

He looked away from me again, and I could feel that I was losing him. So I said, quickly, "Is there anyone you would like to write to? Anyone you want to contact to let them know that you are out of danger and alive? I can find you paper and pen—or write the letter for you, if you would like."

"No." His answer came so quickly it was spoken nearly on top of my last words.

"There must be someone—some family waiting for you back in England," I said. "Someone who will wish to know that you are safe."

The man's jaw hardened. "I told you—there's no one."

"Still." I am not sure what kept me from giving up and walking away. I think part of it was that he was on the verge of making me lose my temper. Which is not a very creditable reason, perhaps. But I am glad that I pressed on. "You ought to give me your name, at least," I said. "You're an officer. A captain by your uniform, isn't that right? You must have men—fellow soldiers—who will be asking all over the city for you, wanting to know what has become of you."

The man started to shake his head, but I stopped him, catching hold of his hand. "You're thinking right now that I know nothing about you—that I can't possibly know what you have faced or seen or what you're feeling now. And you are right. I don't. But I *do* know about the bonds men form while fighting a war. I know that fellow soldiers are willing to die for each other, if need be."

I was thinking of Sergeant Kelly and his search for Edward. And of the other soldiers I have seen—many of them gravely hurt themselves, but somehow summoning the strength to drag or carry their mortally injured fellows back to Brussels from the fields of battle at Waterloo.

I kept my hand on the nameless man's, holding his gaze. "Somewhere out there in the city are the men who were willing to die for *you* in battle. They must be searching for you, wondering whether they failed in their duty to you, since you've vanished without a trace. Your life is your own, and you can do with it as you chose from now on. But you can at least ease their minds."

Something—pain and anger both, I think—flickered at the back of the man's hazel-gold gaze. But then he let out his breath in apparent defeat and closed his eyes. "It's Tomalin," he said. His voice was quiet and suddenly more tired-sounding than angry. "Lord Giles Tomalin."

At the time, the name struck a vague chord of familiarity in my mind. But I was too much focused on the victory of having got him to tell it to me to sort out where I had heard it before. It was only when I went upstairs to my room that it struck me. Lord Giles Tomalin—that was the man who was once secretly involved with Ruth Granger, the man I met once when I was eight.

Of all the tens of thousands of men in the British army, I have somehow stumbled on the man Ruth once loved.

The question is—do I tell him that I have met him before? Do I tell him that I know about him and Ruth?

Monday 3 July, 1815

You would think that these last weeks would have completely cured me of any last lingering vestiges of romanticism. But apparently I have not yet been cured after all.

I lay awake last night, thinking about Giles Tomalin and Ruth. When I wasn't listening to Edward pacing up and down—but never coming to my door or asking for me—in the bedroom across the hall.

Now that Edward does not need care at night, I have taken over what used to be Harriet's dressing room for my own bedchamber.

I finally decided that I ought to tell Lord Tomalin the truth. It felt dishonest not to. And besides, I suppose—this is where the romantic illusions come in—that it seemed to me that there ought to be a *reason* that he'd been carried here, to the house where I was staying. A reason that Kitty and I had found that old letter of his.

So this morning I went downstairs and sat down beside his mattress in the sickroom and told him everything. I didn't say that I thought Ruth still loved him, of course—I might think it, but it is not for me to say when Ruth has never said it herself. But I did tell him about Ruth's illness and her recovery. And that she has never married anyone else.

Of how she is in Antwerp, even now.

I don't know what I was expecting. That Lord Tomalin would determinedly push his blankets back and say,
his eyes kindling with sudden fire, *Now I have a reason
to go on living*?

I suppose if I am completely truthful, I must have
been at least hoping for something like that.

What really happened was that his hawk's features
settled into an expression even more stony and angry
than before and he said, "She can congratulate herself
on a lucky escape. If she'd married me, she'd be saddled
with a cripple for a husband now."

Tuesday 4 July 1815

Ruth returned to Brussels from Antwerp today. Lady
Denby and her daughter are making a tour of the field
of battle. The battlefield at Waterloo is already famous;
visitors go by the waggon- and carriage-full to collect
whatever souvenirs they can find—swords, helmets,
Bibles or letters dropped from the pockets of soldiers.
The native residents of the village are apparently turning a brisk profit by charging admission to see the bed
where Wellington slept on the night before the battle,
the bloodstained bedding on which Lord Uxbridge's leg
was amputated.

But Ruth chose not to visit the site, and to call on me
instead.

She looks pale and tired—though I suppose we all do,
after these last weeks of strain. And she turned paler
still when I told her that Giles Tomalin was right there
in the house, just one room away from the sitting room
where we were speaking together.

I suppose I told her more bluntly than I intended.
But I was too tired to find a way of breaking the news

gently; I can't even remember the last night where I slept more than a few hours. And Mrs. Metcalfe told me this morning that she is increasingly worried for Lord Tomalin. He still barely eats or drinks anything, and only lies silently on his pallet all day.

I didn't quite tell Ruth all that. But I did say that he was taking the injuries he had got in battle very hard, and that perhaps she might be able to help him, somehow—because so far none of us had been able to reach him.

All the colour seemed to bleach out of Ruth's face, even to her lips, and her eyes went to the door of the front parlour, where I had told her Giles' pallet lay. But she shook her head. "No." Her throat contracted as she swallowed, but she tried to speak with her usual brisk calm. "What was between us is now just . . . just history, and ancient history at that. I am sorry to hear of his being wounded, of course. But I am sure it would do him no good at all if I were to see him."

I let it go. Because of course Lord Tomalin told me yesterday that he has no desire whatever to see Ruth, either. And there seemed a limit to how much I could reasonably meddle in their private affairs.

Ruth asked me, then, how Edward did.

"He's—" I began. But I hadn't the chance to say more, because Edward himself came into the room then.

He is much stronger, now, and able to come downstairs. In the last two days he has—doggedly and grimly—begun to memorise his way about the house. So many steps down the stairs, so many steps to the door of the sitting and dining rooms. He even sits and talks with the other wounded men, sometimes.

This morning he stood in the doorway, frowning a little. The hesitation in his steps, the way his head

turned from side to side as he tried to listen for clues to
what his eyes can no longer see—it all made me want to
run to him and put my arms about him. Except that I
knew he would gently but firmly put me aside.

"Georgiana?" he asked.

"Yes, I'm here." I did get up—but only to cross and
lightly take his hand in mine. "And Ruth is here, as well.
You remember Ruth Granger, from back at Pemberley?"

"Of course." Edward took Ruth's hand. She greeted
him—and said how very sorry she was to hear about his
eyes.

Edward smiled—or at least his mouth curved up-
wards—and he said, "I got out with my life, which is
more than many poor devils did. I can't complain."

Which sounds all right—as though Edward is accepting of his condition enough to please even Mrs. Metcalfe.

And yet . . . and yet it is all *wrong*.

Edward is not sullen or angry or withdrawn like
Giles Tomalin. In a way, I wish he were—because at least
I would know he was letting himself show something,
feel *some* natural emotion.

Ruth left soon after that. Her eyes strayed again to
the parlour door. But she did not mention Lord Tomalin's name, or even mention the possibility of seeing
him.

Wednesday 5 July 1815

Kitty came in a short while ago. I have barely spoken to
her these past days—I think she has spoken very little
to anyone since the news came about Captain Ayres.
But this morning just after Madame Duvalle had taken
away my breakfast tray, Kitty knocked on the door of

my room.

Her eyes have a bruised look, and her face is still bleak and hard. She took a single jerky step into the room and then said, "I'm leaving Brussels. I wanted to let you know."

"You're . . . leaving?" The abrupt announcement caught me completely by surprise. It sounds strange, but I have not even considered the question of leaving this city. I suppose I have not been able to look ahead that far.

Kitty gave a short nod. "Yes. Some friends of Harriet's are travelling back to England. A brother and sister—Mr. and Miss Edgerton. They leave at the end of the week. And they've said I may accompany them."

"At the end of the week," I said. And then I rubbed my eyes. "I'm sorry, I am usually capable of doing more than simply repeating back what someone else has said." I swallowed and then said, "I can understand your wanting to get away from here. But all the same, I . . . I wish you would stay."

I suppose I have not written very much about Kitty—about what it was like before we learned Captain Ayres had been killed, I mean. But all through those days of the battle, all during the times we were caring for the wounded, Kitty and I were together, trying to make jests of our fears and make each other smile. She was so good with the injured soldiers, too—as good as she was at caring for her nephews.

This morning, though, her mouth twisted and a flash of feeling broke the icy composure of her face. "I suppose you think I ought to stay here? Keep changing bandages and picking maggots out of wounds? Being as nice and sweet and giving as you?"

"I'm not—" I started to say.

"No, *I'm* not." Kitty cut me off. "I'm not nice or sweet or good, remember? I'm the girl who kisses scoundrels in the middle of Christmas parties and breaks off engagements to decent if boring men. And I am leaving Brussels. The day after tomorrow."

Her voice had flattened and hardened. But her eyes looked wounded, raw with pain. I touched her arm. "Kitty," I started. But she jerked her hand away.

"Stop! Don't touch me—don't say anything to me. Don't you understand that I *hate* you right now?"

"You hate me?"

"Yes!" Kitty's hands were balled into fists at her sides. "Edward came back to you. And John never will!"

The words seemed to ignite something hot and sour as acid in my chest.

Last night, I heard Edward walking the floor again. And I did try going to his room—I couldn't stop myself. I have not been pushing him—just as Sergeant Kelly advised. But last night I said, "Edward, you know it would be . . . it would be only natural for you to be angry, grieved at the loss of your sight."

Edward's face went as blank and stony as a marble statues and he said, with an edge of weariness in his tone, "I'm fine. I just couldn't sleep, that's all."

I think the worst—almost the worst—of these last days is how *careful* I always feel I have to be with Edward. As though I am treading on eggshells, afraid every moment that I am going to say the wrong thing, something that will upset him or drive him even further away. But after a moment's hesitation, I said, "I could stay. I could read something to you, if you'd—"

"For God's sake, just go!" Edward spoke with sudden violence. But the next moment, all anger, all emotion whatever was gone from his tone. Though his muscles were still rigid with tension. "I'm sorry. But just . . . I would rather be by myself for now. Please."

I left. I did not know what else to do. But somehow Kitty's words—however sorry I truly am for her—cracked the tight hold I had been keeping on my control. "That is true, I didn't lose Edward in the battle," I flashed back. "Instead I get to sit by, helpless, while he slips further and further away from me by slow degrees every day!"

And then I stopped, snatched my bonnet off the dressing table and yanked it on.

Kitty blinked at me in surprise. "Where are you going?"

"To see if I cannot accomplish at least *some* good today."

I found the address Ruth had given me of the place Lady Denby had taken in town. It was just a few streets away from the Forsters' house. And Ruth was in, supervising the packing of her employer's things for their return to England in another week's time.

She was wrapping some fine-stemmed crystal glasses in tissue paper when I burst in and seized her by the arm. "You are coming with me," I informed her.

Ruth stared at me. "Georgiana, what on earth—"

I did not stop, though. "You are coming back to the Forsters' house with me. And you are going to see Lord Tomalin, if I have to drag you into his presence."

Ruth started to protest, but I talked over her. "If I can spend day after day, beating my head against the brick wall of trying to reach Edward, you can at least make one small attempt to reach Giles Tomalin—before he manages to will himself into an early grave."

Ruth shook her head, her face blanching. "He must have a wife by now—or some woman, at least, waiting for him to come home to her."

"There is no one. I asked, when he was first conscious. He said there is no one at all in his life whom he even wishes to write to."

Ruth began, "But Georgiana, he won't want—"

I stopped her, though, looking directly into her eyes. "Ruth, can you honestly tell me that if you go back to England without seeing Lord Tomalin, you won't regret it? That you won't spend the rest of your life wondering what would have happened if only you had?"

Ruth was silent a moment, looking at me, her lips pressed into a tight line. But then she let out her breath and gave a quick, shaky nod of assent.

Ruth was silent all the time we were walking back to the Forsters' house, her eyes fixed straight ahead and her hands clasped and twisting themselves together in front of her. She looked as we approached the door to the parlour more as though she were being taken to face a firing squad than a wounded young man. And when we first came through the door, I thought I was going to regret ever having meddled at all.

All our other wounded soldiers have gone, now. The parlour was empty save for Giles Tomalin, lying on his pallet on the floor, his arms clasped behind his head, his eyes focused dully on the ceiling. He was at least dressed and shaved. At Mrs. Metcalfe and the surgeon's combined insistence, he has been forced into bathing and getting up to practice propelling himself twice about the room on crutches every day. But his face bore more than ever the smouldering, tethered-hawk look, and when he saw me come in with Ruth, he started convulsively upright, his expression darkening into fury.

"Get her out of here! I don't need her damned pity-visit."

Ruth had gone very still at the sight of him, her face turning ivory-pale once again. But at that she stiffened. "You think I came here out of *pity*?" Two bright spots of colour appeared in her cheeks and her fingers clenched. "Very well then. If the sight of me is so repugnant to you, I'll go."

She turned and started blindly for the door. But not before I had seen her lips tremble and her eyes flood with angry tears.

Giles must have seen it, too, because he swore under his breath and heaved himself up off the pallet, reaching for his crutches. "Ruth, wait—"

Ruth didn't stop or turn, and Giles swore again as he propelled himself on his crutches after her. "Dammit, Ruth, will you stop a moment? I can't keep up with you this way."

Ruth did turn, then. Her jaw was clenched, fighting the tears that still brimmed in her eyes. "Well?"

Giles drew in his breath; his chest was heaving with the effort of movement made after so many weeks of illness. When he spoke, his voice was quiet, gentler. "I am sorry. I'm a swine. But not yet such a pig that I want to make you cry."

Ruth's mouth trembled, and her stiff shoulders sagged as she shook her head. "I would not blame you if you did—after what I did to you, eight years ago."

Giles' lips twisted in a brief, wry smile. "Yes, well. I ought to have ridden straight back to Derbyshire the instant I got your letter and shaken some sense into you. I would have—had I not been such a stiff-necked, proud young idiot." He stopped and then lowered his voice, looking at Ruth very intently. "I have regretted not trying to see you again every day for the last eight years."

Ruth looked at him. And then the tears in her eyes brimmed over, spilling down her cheeks as she said, unsteadily, "I have, too."

I backed out of the room, then, leaving them alone—though I don't think either of them so much as noticed I was there. I was sitting in the morning room—staring at a blank page that *ought* to turn into a long-overdue letter to Elizabeth and Fitzwilliam—when Ruth came in.

Her face was still tear-stained, but she was smiling and her eyes shone. I always thought that an exaggerated figure of speech—but Ruth's whole face seemed to fairly glow with happiness.

"I am going to resign my position with Lady Denby," she said. "But then I will be back directly. And we are going to be married. At once. As soon as we can find a clergyman or priest here in Brussels to do it." And then she laughed—a younger, freer laugh than I had ever heard from her. "I suppose that is shockingly sudden. But we've neither of us any family to object. Giles' parents are dead, now, and of course there is no one for me, either. And we neither of us want to waste any more time than we already have."

I hugged her, and gave her my most sincere congratulations. And Ruth showed me the ring Giles had given her—his signet ring, emblazoned with his family crest. "He said he would get me another—one that is the proper size for my finger—as soon as may be," she said. "But that he wanted something concrete to mark this, otherwise he might start to imagine that today had all been a dream." Ruth sobered a little, then, as she turned the ring round and round between her fingers. "I know he still has a long journey of recovery ahead of him. And that it won't always be as . . . as easy as it was today. But—"

"But you will be together," I finished for her. "That is all that really matters."

I am so very happy for Ruth—for her and Giles both. And I will be thoroughly sick of myself if I sit here weeping over my own diary like the heroine of a gothic melodrama. It's just that I cannot help hoping—praying, with every part of me—that Ruth and Giles' happiness is a sign. A sign that I may yet somehow manage to reach Edward behind the walls he has put up between himself and the world.

Thursday 6 July 1815

It hardly felt at first like an answer to prayer when I heard Edward cry out in the middle of the night tonight. I knew it was a nightmare. He had them last year, too— before he even had to go back to war. And I know he has had them in these last two weeks since the battle. But every time I ask him about it or go to his room, he either denies dreaming at all or pretends to be asleep until I leave him again.

I had almost given up on even trying to get him to speak to me of the dreams.

Tonight, though—I suppose it was seeing Ruth and Giles together that made me get out of my own bed and go to Edward's door at the sound of his ragged, wordless cry. I did not knock—that would only have given Edward the chance to send me away—just turned the doorknob and went in.

Madame Duvalle must have left a small lamp burning when she had brought Edward his supper tray, so that I could see the room clearly: Edward's coat, lying atop the wooden clothes press. The collection of medicine bottles on the bedside table from when he had been ill. And Edward, lying on the bed. He still wore breeches and a wrinkled shirt, open at the neck. His skin was drenched with sweat, and his chest heaved as though he had been running.

"Ed—" I bit my lip before I could finish saying his name. Because he plainly was not aware of me; I wasn't even sure whether he was yet awake or still lost in the nightmare. His eyes were open, but he hadn't even turned his head or reacted at the noise of my opening the door.

So instead I crossed to the bed, moving as quietly as I could. I hesitated—then sat down on the edge of the bed and lightly touched Edward's cheek. "Edward." I said his name again, but in a barely audible murmur. Still, the response was immediate: one of his hands flew up to seize my wrist and he sat bolt upright with a wrenching gasp.

"Edward, it's all right." I sat very still. "You were dreaming, that's all."

Edward was still breathing hard. But he shook his head as though trying to physically break free of whatever dream had gripped him, then rubbed his eyes. "Georgiana. What—"

"I heard you call out. So I came in."

I started to gently loosen Edward's grip on my wrist. And Edward started and swore, letting go his hold on me so quickly I nearly lost my balance and fell off the bed. His blind eyes looked past me, of course unseeing— but his face was stony hard. "Please tell me I didn't hurt you."

"This?" My wrist was reddened where his fingers had gripped, but nothing more. "It's nothing, Edward. You won't even be able to see it in the morning."

The next second I could have bitten my tongue out for my choice of words, because Edward gave a harsh, humourless sound that was almost a laugh and said, "*I* won't be able to see it. That's entirely true."

His shirt was nearly plastered to his skin, and when he moved I could see the pull of the muscles in his arms and shoulders. The jagged line of the scar on his shoulder, mark of the wound he took at Toulouse last spring.

"Edward, I didn't mean—" I stopped, unsure of what I could find to say. I suppose it was cowardly in a way, but I was still afraid of saying something that would only make matters worse. So instead I asked, "Do you . . . would it help to tell me what you were dreaming about?"

I thought at first Edward was going to refuse to speak to me again, or to say only that he didn't remember and that I ought to go back to my room. But then a change—a kind of ruthless determination—seemed to come over his face, and he said, "War. Battle. I still don't remember much about the fighting at Waterloo. But that doesn't mean I haven't plenty of other material for my mind to obligingly dredge up in nightmares. Tonight it was the time I lost two of my ensigns on the same day. They were right beside me, both of them—standing close together, just before we charged. And a French cannonball struck the spot where they were standing. Afterward, you could barely sort out the pieces of them—what belonged to which man."

None of the tension had gone out of Edward's frame as he spoke. If anything, his muscles looked more rigid than ever, his lean face grimmer still as he spoke in a flat, determined tone.

And I realised abruptly that his telling me did not mean that he was finally ready to confide in me or come out from behind his walls. Rather the reverse. He was telling me these horrors in an effort to drive me away.

He said in the same tone, "I always wondered why I wasn't killed that day. Now I think it would have been better if I had been."

"Edward, you don't mean that!"

"Don't I?" Edward gave another harsh laugh. At least the stony control had finally started to crack; his voice was no longer flat but angry and taut as wire. "Are you telling me that you still want to marry me? A blind man whom you'll have to lead about by the hand—and who can't get through a single night without falling down a rabbit's hole of memories of blood and gore?"

I did not let myself hesitate. Sergeant Kelly had told me not to push Edward, to be patient, wait and give him time. But if Kitty yesterday had managed to crack some measure of control inside me, Edward's words, the look on his face, had just smashed it entirely.

I was furious, afraid, uncertain—all the emotions churning together in what felt like a thunderstorm under my ribcage. But I leaned forward and kissed Edward, fitting my mouth against his.

It helped, I think, that he wasn't able to see me and anticipate what I was about to do. I felt his breath go out in a rush of surprise and he tried to pull away. But I wrapped my arms around his neck and wouldn't let go—and after a moment he surrendered to the kiss with a half-groan and kissed me back hungrily, his hands sliding up to tangle in my hair.

When he finally did break away, he was breathing hard. I could feel his heart pounding through the thin fabric of his shirt. But he shook his head as though trying to clear it and said, "Georgiana, you don't—you can't—"

I was still angry, I suppose—too angry to try to go carefully or guard what I said. "I can't *what*?" I demanded. "Love you? Yes I can! And *you*, Edward, certainly can't tell me what I can and cannot do."

Edward's jaw dropped open slightly, but I went on, "What if our places were changed? What if it were me that were blind right now? Would you still want to marry me?"

Edward blinked, a furrow appearing between his brows. "Of course, but—"

"But what? But I couldn't possibly love you as much as you love me?"

Edward shook his head. "It's not—"

"It's not the same thing?" I finished for him. "Yes, it is—it's exactly the same! I want to marry *you*, Edward. Not some romanticised, idealised version of Edward Fitzwilliam. I want to marry you exactly as you are now—whether or not your sight ever comes back. Whether or not you ever get over dreaming about your time at war. You are still you—blind or no. And I still love you, and I always will."

He looked as though he were about to argue. But I leaned forward and touched my lips lightly to his neck, then his jaw. I felt him shiver slightly at the touch, and I said, more quietly, "Do you know what I thought when I came in here tonight? The very first thing that came into my mind?"

Wordlessly, Edward shook his head. I shifted again so that I could look up into his face, trailing my fingertips across the lean, hard angle of his temple and cheekbone. "I thought that if only we were already married, I could be in bed with you when you had a nightmare, not all the way across the hall."

I kissed him again, softly, lingeringly.

"Georgiana, I—" Edward's breathing had gone ragged. "I think you're vastly overrating my capacity for self-restraint."

"Good." I caught his hand and held it when he moved to pull away, off the bed. "Because I don't want you to keep shutting me out. And I don't want to wait until we're back in England to marry you. Ruth and Lord Tomalin are going to be married here in Brussels as soon as they can. I think we should be married here, too."

Edward's breath went out, and he said, "All right."

"After all, I'm sure my brother would not—" and then I stopped, abruptly realising what Edward had just said. "Did you just say *all right*?"

Edward laughed at the astonishment in my voice. I hadn't heard him laugh in so long—not since the battle. The sound made my heart seem to turn over.

"I told you you were overestimating my powers of self-control," he said. Our fingers were still interlaced, and he turned my hand and kissed my palm. "Yes, I'll marry you. Tomorrow, if you like." He laughed unevenly again. "Anything to save me from finding you in my bedroom at one o'clock in the morning—and having to remember that I'm supposed to be a gentleman."

I laughed, too. And then I looked up at him and said, "Edward, are you . . . are you really sure?"

"Am I sure?" Edward pulled me towards him and into his arms, burying his face against the crook of my neck. His voice was soft with regret as he whispered, "God, I wish . . . I wish that I could see your face again." But before I could answer he exhaled an unsteady breath and said, "Georgiana, I know I have a long way to go before I'm all right—I don't know that I ever will be entirely all right, or able to talk about any of this easily. All I can promise you is that I will try—I *will* try. But am I sure that I want to marry you?" I felt his chest shake as he gave another half-laugh. "God, you have no idea how sure I am."

Saturday 8 July 1815

I am going to write it all down exactly as it happened. I will never believe that it really *did* happen otherwise.

Edward and I spoke this evening to the elderly clergyman of the *Église protestante du Musée de Bruxelles* —the only Protestant church in Brussels, as it happens, since the country is almost exclusively of the Roman Catholic faith.

Not that I would have cared especially—if a village witch could legally marry Edward and me, I would kiss her on both cheeks and let her perform the ceremony with my sincere thanks. But a Catholic priest would refuse to marry us on the grounds that we are neither of us Catholic. So it is just as well that we found Father Jean-Pierre Charlier. Who is very nearsighted, very kind—and has consented to marry us by special license in two days' time.

Two days. That seems incredible, even now. Though it shouldn't—not after tonight.

Edward and I were coming home from the church. Night was beginning to fall; the air was smudged with purple shadows, and the shopkeepers were closing their shutters and locking their shops.

It was the furthest Edward has been from the Forsters' house since Sergeant Kelly carried him inside two weeks ago, and we walked slowly, my hand in his to guide him around the other pedestrians or over any broken or muddied patches of the streets.

I was afraid that might bother him, bring home the reality of his condition more sharply still. But Edward only asked me quietly to describe to him as much as I could of what I saw.

It was hard not to edit my account. The streets are still so full of all the reminders of the battle. Broken supply waggons. Wounded and recovering soldiers— pale and drawn-looking, many missing legs or arms and hobbling on crutches or canes. One poor man had lost both his legs and was dragging himself along on a kind of wheeled cart.

But if Edward could accept having to ask me to be his eyes, the least I could do was serve as honest ones. So I told him everything.

We were passing through a narrow, cobbled lane when it happened—so fast I hadn't even time to scream. A man came looming up at us out of the shadows of one of the doorways, launched himself at Edward and knocked him to the ground.

I heard Edward's head strike the pavement—I think I did scream, then. But the next moment I froze, my whole body turning cold as the light from a shop lantern fell across the attacker's face. It was George Wickham.

I do not know, still, what he intended. Mischief, certainly. Perhaps robbery, likely coupled with revenge— for my having refused to give him the money he wanted to flee from town. I cannot believe, whatever George Wickham's faults, that he intended anything more sinister. Though he did have a knife. I saw the blade flash in the glow of the lamplight.

Edward, though, reacted instantly, even as he lay sprawled on the pavement. Wickham had fallen almost on top of him, and Edward executed some kind of a lightning-quick scissor manoeuvre that sent Wickham flying over his head and landing with a crash on the cobblestones. I heard Wickham groan as he thrashed on the dirty cobbles, trying to rise.

Edward was already on his feet, though, hauling Wickham up, as well. I don't know how he managed, without being able to see—I suppose by touch and sound.

Edward grabbed Wickham by his collar, drew back and delivered a blow to Wickham's jaw that sent him reeling again.

The rest of the fight was a blur. I think Wickham might have managed to land one or two glancing blows. But he was off balance from Edward's punches, unsteady—and they were grappling at such close quarters that Edward hadn't really any need of being able to see. The end result was that Wickham turned tail and ran off, limping and swearing.

"Was that—" Edward began, when the sound of his footsteps died away.

"George Wickham." I was still so stunned that my voice sounded far off and tinny in my own ears.

"I thought so." Edward wiped blood from his lip. "I recognised his voice."

I nodded. "He came a few days ago—to ask for money. He—"

But Edward was not listening. A slow grin was spreading over his face as he turned to me. "I can still do it!" He laughed—a free, easy laugh—and wiped his mouth again with the back of his hand. "Georgiana, did you see that? It didn't matter about my eyes—I could still fight him!"

I stared at him. And then, when I could trust my voice enough to speak, I said, enunciating each word, "Edward Fitzwilliam. I've spent the last two days telling you how much I always have loved you and always will. We have a license to be married in another two days' time. But what *really* makes you feel a whole man again is the fact that you can still punch another man in the jaw?"

Edward laughed again, and I glared at him—which was a wasted effort of course, given that he couldn't see the look—and said, "I will never, ever understand men."

Edward was still grinning. "Yes, well. Just so long as you love—" and then he broke off, his whole body going taut and still as he suddenly gripped my hand.

"Georgiana." His voice was husky and all at once tense as his muscles. "Georgiana, is there a light just there?" He gestured to the lighted shop lantern that hung above the sign for the bakery shop on our right. "A hanging lamp of some kind?"

I nodded shakily. "Yes—that's right, there is."

"I can see it!" Edward's hand shook as his fingers tightened around mine. "Just a kind of yellow glow— but I can see it!"

And that was just the first. Edward and I sat up together through the night—we neither of us could have slept—in the downstairs parlour of the Forsters' home. And slowly, steadily, his vision cleared. Cleared enough that by the time the first pale-grey light of dawn was filtering through the windows, Edward could read the words of the newspaper that Colonel Forster had left lying beside his chair.

Mr. Powell came and gave it as his opinion that the blow to the head Edward took in battle caused a swelling of the brain—and that the second blow, the one he took when Wickham knocked him down tonight, somehow relieved the pressure and cured his sight.

Life is so strange—my own private miracle, and I owe it to George Wickham. Or maybe that is fitting, somehow, in the grander scheme of things.

When Mr. Powell had gone and Edward and I were

alone again, Edward drew me close, framing my face with his hands and gazing down at me with a look in his dark eyes that made my bones feel weak and my head light. I laughed, a little unsteadily, and said, "Be careful. Mr. Powell warned you against straining your eyes for a few weeks' time. You'll wear them out entirely if you keep looking at me so."

Edward only shook his head. His voice had gone husky again. "It would be worth it, at that," he said. He swallowed. "You've been my guiding light—my Northern Star all through out these last weeks. I would never have come through them—would never have recovered at all, I don't believe, if it had not been for you. And now, to be able to actually see you again—" I realised that his eyes were wet as he continued to gaze at me. "I love you," he said. "More than you can ever possibly know."

I stood on tiptoe so that I could kiss him, then. And after a long, long while, I drew back just enough that I could murmur against his lips, "Oh, but I do know. Because I love you the same."

Epilogue

Letter from Georgiana to Elizabeth Darcy:

Tuesday 11 July 1815

Dearest Elizabeth,

Kitty should be with you in no more than a fortnight's time. She left Brussels yesterday, and will sail from Ostend on the 13th.

I have been debating whether I ought to write this to you or not. But you are her sister. And Kitty will be staying with you at Pemberley. I think you ought to know.

I wrote you, of course, of Captain Ayres' death in the battle at Waterloo. But I was entirely wrong about the manner of Kitty's grief over his death.

She came to my room the night before last, to say good-bye. But even after we had said our farewells, she did not go at once, but sat down on the edge of my bed and was silent for a long moment, curling and uncurling one of the ribbons on her dressing gown. When she finally looked up at me, I saw that she was crying—the first tears I have seen her shed since the news came about Captain Ayres having been killed.

"You know," she said, "I knew—even all the time John was being so kind to me in Ostend, all the time we were together on the night before the battle. I knew that we were still completely unsuited to each other in disposition, in our temperaments. That however shabbily I had treated him, I had been right to call off the engagement. Because marrying me would still make his life a misery. We'd nothing in common, really. But—"

Kitty's voice wavered and she dashed impatiently at her eyes before going on, the words coming in a dull rush, as though some inner dam had broken. "But John asked me that night we saw him at the Duchess of Richmond's ball . . . he asked me whether there was not yet a chance of matters being righted between us. Of us becoming betrothed again. And I didn't have the heart to tell him no—not when he was just hours away from marching off to war. So I said that of course there was a chance." Kitty's voice broke and she swallowed hard. "As if it wasn't bad enough that I betrayed John by flirting with Lord Carmichael—I also let him go to his death believing a lie."

I said, "You gave him a last night of happiness—of hope for the future. You surely can't blame yourself for that."

But Kitty shook her head. "But he knows now." Her hand clenched on something, and I saw that it was the gold watch Captain Ayres had sent to her with his last breath. "He must. He's in Heaven now. Which means that he knows that the girl he thought he was in love with—the girl he thought of as he lay dying—was vain and silly and selfish and utterly unworthy of his regard—"

I stopped her. "If he does know anything, it's that you have a truly kind, generous heart. And that you esteemed him enough to wish him happy."

Kitty wiped her eyes again and thanked me in a dull, exhausted voice. She still looked white and strained when she hugged me and left my room to finish her packing.

But she will find her way in time, I know she will.

Why am I so sure?

For one, she has you waiting to help her—the best sister anyone could wish. And for another—

For another, I believe everything happy in the world is possible just now.

Edward and I were married yesterday morning. The church—the Église protestante—is a beautiful place, all airy, high ceilings, decorated with white plaster-work and tall Corinthian columns. It was once the chapel of the Palace of Charles de Lorraine. Mrs. Metcalfe and Harriet were my only attendants, and Sergeant Kelly—I wrote to you of him, didn't I?—had special leave from his regiment to serve as one of our witnesses. The entire ceremony was in French, since Pastor Charlier speaks barely a word of English. But I—shamefully—am not sure I heard more than one word in ten in any case. All I could think of as we spoke our vows was that Edward was looking at me—truly _seeing_ me again, his whole heart in his dark eyes.

After the wedding breakfast—organised by Mrs. Metcalfe—we drove straight out of town, all the way to the village of Malines. Already the countryside is so different from what it was a few weeks ago. Or rather, it seems to have returned already to a land untouched by the horrors *of war: abundant cornfields and verdant meadows, and the people all still rejoicing in Napoleon's downfall. That is the only reminder of the battle—the puppet-shows and ballad singers one hears, all detailing the defeat of the infamous Bonaparte.*

Edward and I found the tiny but charming inn at Malines and engaged a room—that was where we spent our wedding night last night.

And that is why any and all things seem possible to me right now, even unto miracles.

Give my love to my brother, and kiss baby James for me— I am longing to see how much he must have grown since I have been away.

And now you, my dearest friend and sister, have the signal honour of receiving the letter on which I first sign my name:

With all my love,

Georgiana Fitzwilliam

THE END

DEAR READERS—

Thank you for reading *Pemberley to Waterloo*. Please read on for a preview of *Kitty Bennet's Diary*, Volume 3 in the PRIDE AND PREJUDICE CHRONICLES. Kitty's diary picks up where Georgiana's leaves off.

If you have enjoyed this book and would like to see more like it, please consider reviewing and/or tagging it on your favorite sites and telling your literary friends about it. Plans for future projects will be based in part on reader feedback and the success of previous projects. It would give me great joy to write what you want to read. If you have found errors or would like to comment privately, I would be grateful for an email at ae@AnnaElliottBooks.com. Thank you again.

Please visit
www.AnnaElliottBooks.com
for a current list of Anna Elliott titles.

Preview of

KITTY BENNET'S DIARY

Wednesday 20 December 1815

I am going to find my sister Mary a husband. I have decided: I will see Mary wedded to a nice, eligible, and if possible handsome young man within the next year if it kills me.

Which to be honest, and given Mary's past history, seems entirely probable.

It is strange. I would never in a hundred years have thought Mary cared one way or the other about attracting male admirers, much less a husband. I didn't think she cared very much for anything—except proving how very much cleverer and more accomplished she is than anyone else.

But tonight, after we had returned from Lady Dorwich's ball and gone to bed, I woke in the middle of the night to hear Mary crying.

Since we are staying with my Aunt and Uncle Gardiner in their London home, we are obliged to share a room.

I sat up—certain I must be dreaming, because I can't recall ever having heard Mary cry since she was six years old and I was five, and she fell off the pianoforte bench and cut her head on the coal scuttle.

But she was. She was huddled under the blankets, sobbing softly into her pillow.

I lay quiet, uncertain of what to do. It's not as though Mary and I have ever been especially close, despite the nearness of our ages. If I am being completely honest, sharing a room with her these last weeks has occasionally made me contemplate—well, not actual fratricide. Or whatever the equivalent for sisters is; Latin has never exactly been my strong point.

But I have felt that if I have to spend one more day listening to Mary making weird gargling sounds in her throat first thing at dawn every morning—she read somewhere or other that it strengthens a weak singing voice—I would be tempted to catch several dozen live toads and put them in her bed.

Except that there are no live toads to be had in London in January.

But the whole point of my sharing a room with Mary is that it's a kind of penance. And the unpleasant truth that I've recently discovered about doing penances is that they are practically never the kind of acts that come easily. So I pushed back the covers and got up—despite the cold floorboards and the fact that my feet were bare—and sat down on the edge of Mary's bed.

"Mary? Is something wrong?" I asked.

Mary didn't answer, she only lay absolutely still, the covers pulled over her head. And after a second's pause, she let out the most unconvincing snore I have ever heard—half snort, half suppressed sob.

"Oh, for heaven sakes, Mary, I know you're not asleep," I said. "You wouldn't fool baby Susanna." Baby Susanna being our youngest Gardiner cousin. "You may as well sit up and tell me what the trouble is."

Mary lay without moving a second more—and then she suddenly sat up in an explosion of blankets and sheets and sat glowering at me from under the ruffles of the old-fashioned night cap she always wears.

Mary is only twenty, a year older than I am, but even

at night she dresses as though she is practising for the role of elderly maiden aunt.

Mary's eyes were red and puffy-looking, but she lifted her chin. "If you must know, I'm crying because not one single gentleman asked me to dance tonight."

I was taken aback. I have never thought that Mary cared for dancing before. Usually at any entertainment we attend, she does nothing but clutch her sheet music to her chest and hover by the pianoforte. Poised to be the first to jump at the keyboard as soon as any ladies are invited to perform a song.

"I thought you said that in your opinion, dancing was a frivolity suited only to small and meagre minds?" I said.

Which sounds as though I were being spiteful. But I have also discovered that it's extremely wearing to force myself to be sweet all the time.

And it is also quite true that Mary said exactly that; she really does talk that way. Constantly.

Mary sniffed and looked balefully at me. "And so it is. But it would have been nice to at least be *asked*," she said. She wiped her nose on the sleeve of her nightdress. "I talked to one young man for at least a quarter of an hour during supper. Mr. Porter. He was eating a very large helping of the roast duck, and I told him that modern medical opinion holds that a diet of too many rich meats can lead to gout in later age. I even outlined for him what a scientific paper I read recently gave as a recipe for a healthful diet—brown bread . . . raw onions . . . a great many carrots. But he *still* did not ask me to dance afterwards."

"Imagine that," I said.

Mary wiped her nose again and glared at me. "I knew you wouldn't understand, Kitty. *You* had men asking you for dances all night long. And you didn't accept one of them."

That is also true. It's very ironic, really. Since I have sworn off men entirely, I am besieged by invitations at every ball or assembly we attend. Tonight I started telling overly persistent gentlemen that I have a mother in the madhouse, a father in the penitentiary, and feel myself coming down with a touch of bubonic plague. And they only thought I was being charmingly witty; I was still refusing invitations to dance throughout the entire evening.

Apparently the secret to attracting male attention is to cultivate an air of unattainability. If only I had known that a year ago.

Mary doesn't know the full story of why I have sworn off men and dancing. So I suppose her glare was in some way justified. But it didn't last long. Her face crumpled after a moment, and she started to cry again.

"I'm never going to have anyone fall in love with me." She spoke between sobs. "No one will ever write poetry about me. Or try to kiss me. I'll never get married. I'll never have a house and a husband and babies of my own."

I stared at her. Thinking about how it is perfectly possible not to know your own sister at all. I admit the thought of anyone writing poetry about Mary strains even my imagination. Actually, it strains my imagination even more to picture Mary *accepting* a poem written in her honour, without being tempted to write up an answering critique of the meter and rhyme.

And Mary as a mother? The mind—or at least *my* mind—boggles.

Though I will admit that Mary is very good with baby Susanna. In Susanna's company, she forgets to be serious-minded and full of conceit with her own clever-ness. She will even make ridiculous faces to get Susanna to utter one of her fat, delicious baby chuckles. But I had never imagined before tonight that Mary might want a family of her own.

But she is, after all, my sister. And, really, why shouldn't she have a husband and children if she wants them?

Besides, since there is no purpose in attending all the balls and parties of the London Season for myself, I might as well dedicate my energies to seeing that Mary takes some benefit from it all.

Mary fell asleep soon after that last outburst. But I've been lying awake, formulating plans and going over lists of possible young men in my mind—and determining that getting Mary wedded will be my good deed for the New Year.

Do present good deeds make up for past wrong ones? It would be nice to be able to believe it. But I can't imagine that life works that way.

Tuesday 2 January 1815

There are five of us Bennet sisters—which fact always makes strangers sigh and make comments about our poor mother, burdened with the task of getting five daughters married off, without even the benefit of decent dowries for us.

But while we were growing up, it always seemed to me that each of us had our assigned roles in the family. Jane was the oldest, and the most beautiful. Then came Elizabeth—Lizzy—who was always the most charming and witty. And then Mary.

Whom I suppose I can't entirely blame for turning

herself into such an appalling blue-stocking, because she spent her entire childhood hearing what a shame it was that she was not as pretty as her older sisters. It's no wonder, really, that she started trying to distinguish herself as the most bookish and intelligent one of us.

I am next in age after Mary, and then Lydia is two years after me, the youngest of us all. Lydia was always the most spirited and vivacious of us. Which left me the only one of us without any distinguishing characteristic. I couldn't be the prettiest or the wittiest or the cleverest or even the most bouncing and lively. Which makes me . . . what? The boring sister? The one without any special talents—except possibly the ability to make terrible choices with her life?

This is turning into a very whining and self-pitying post—and another of my recent discoveries is that there is no fun whatsoever in feeling sorry for yourself when all you keep coming back to is that everything from start to finish has been entirely your own fault.

Besides, what I really meant to do when I started out writing was to set down how Mary and I came to be the only two out of the five of us who are unmarried, still.

Jane and Elizabeth married extremely well. Much to my mother's delight. Jane is married to Mr. Charles Bingley. Who is not only handsome and rich, but also agreeable and kind—and madly in love with Jane, even though they have been married now for nearly three years and have one daughter, Amelia, and another baby expected quite soon.

Lizzy married Mr. Fitzwilliam Darcy. Who is even richer than Charles. And who always struck me as very proud and disagreeable. But Lizzy seems to actually love him. And he loves her, too. I have stayed with them at Pemberley, Mr. Darcy's estate, and I've seen the way he looks at Lizzy. Mr. Darcy—he may be my brother-in-law, but I still cannot bring myself to call him Fitzwilliam—may be stiff and proud, but he would walk to the ends of the Earth just to see Lizzy smile.

And Lydia—

Lydia was always the closest to me, all the time we were growing up. I suppose mostly because she was the nearest to me in age. Lizzy and Jane were always perfectly nice to me. But I was so much younger that I was always a baby to them, and they had their own secrets and games that I was never a part of.

No one could possibly make a special confidante of Mary. Which left me and Lydia to play together when we were small and then be confidantes when we grew up.

Even though Lydia was the younger, she was always the leader. I wanted to be just like her. Fearless and bold, with scads of admirers to flirt with.

That Kitty Bennet seems so distant from me now. Thinking about myself then is like looking through the telescope the wrong way round. But it's quite true. Even when Lydia created a scandal by running away with George Wickham, I admired her. At least she had *done* something, instead of simply sitting on the sidelines of all the assemblies and balls like the rest of us, waiting for some gentleman to overlook our lack of fortune and save us from becoming old maids.

It is only in the last year that I have seen exactly where all Lydia's vivaciousness has got her: married to a man who is a lout and a drunkard—and a coward, as well. They have to live in France, because Wickham deserted from the army at the Battle of Waterloo, and now can't come home. The only time Lydia writes to any of us is to ask for money and to complain that

French society is so very dull and stultifying compared to home. Which really means that she and Wickham haven't enough funds for her to cut any kind of a figure in the social scene.

At any rate, that is how Mary and I came to be the last sisters left at home. Our mother has more or less given up on seeing Mary wedded. But even after everything that has happened in the last twelvemonth, Mother has made it her especial mission to see me betrothed. To whom, she is not particular; her criteria for potential sons-in-law seem to be first a sizeable income, and second a beating heart.

That is why I was so happy to accept our Aunt Gardiner's invitation for me and Mary to spend the winter in London. Lizzy invited me, too. But I cannot possibly face her again. And Aunt Gardiner is such a calm, restful person to be around. She never fusses or worries. Besides, though she is very kind, she is too busy with the children to be overly occupied with Mary or me.

And beyond the one time Mary informed me that it was better to have loved and lost than never to have loved at all—and I emptied the entire contents of a teapot over her for it—Mary leaves me alone.

In my defence, at least the tea was (mostly) gone cold.

Wednesday 3 January 1815

Today marks the first day of putting my plan into effect: I dragged Mary out to the shops to buy her some new clothes. I was expecting it to be a battle royale, preferable only when compared to a visit to the dentist. But it actually went much better than I would have thought.

And it got me out of the house when Mrs. Ayres made

her weekly effort to see me.

I will have to see her eventually, I know. But so far I haven't managed to force myself to be at home when Mrs. Ayres calls at the house. There are penances and then there are penances. And I still feel as though I would rather hurl myself under the wheels of a runaway carriage than see her— because even I can't seriously contemplate a bare-faced lie to a woman whose son has just died at Waterloo.

If I see Mrs. Ayres, I will have to tell her the truth about me and John. The truth he apparently never told anyone, even his own mother.

It is honestly not for myself that I would mind. I *would* tell Mrs. Ayres the truth about John's and my engagement—and expose myself for a brainless, heartless flirt. If it weren't for the fact that I'm afraid it would tarnish her memories of John, to know he was once in love with me. And she and John surely deserve better.

So I took Mary shopping instead.

Mary has plenty of money—she has spent practically nothing of the allowance our father gave us, or the Christmas gifts from Lizzy and Jane. Until today, all she had bought were a few books. So I was able to bring her to the shop in Conduit Street of Madame LeFarge, the very fashionable modiste who makes all of my sister Jane's dresses.

Mary balked a bit at the prices—well, at the whole process, really. But I asked her did she want to spend the rest of her time in London a confirmed wallflower, or did she wish to occasionally have a dance? And she actually submitted to Madame LeFarge's measuring and clucking and draping her with various silks and gauzes and muslins.

Madame LeFarge was at least very enthusiastic. I

think she saw Mary as a unique professional challenge. If she could manage to make Mary beautiful, she could succeed with anyone.

Though Mary is not so ill-favoured, really. Especially not now that her skin has cleared and her figure is no longer all awkward angles. She might even be pretty if she learned to arrange her hair properly, instead of simply scraping it straight back from her face. And if she left off wearing her spectacles.

She doesn't even actually need the spectacles—they are only plain glass, set in silver frames that she bought because she thinks they make her look more intelligent.

At any rate, if left to herself, Mary would have chosen the plainest, dullest materials Madame LeFarge had. But Madame and I joined forces and overruled her, and in the end actually persuaded her into some pretty things. A rose satin that is to be made up with an overdress of cream-coloured spider-gauze and trimmed with pearl rosettes. And an evening gown of pale blue crepe, ruffled at the sleeves and hem, that Madame Le-Farge promised me faithfully she would have ready for the dinner party my Aunt Gardiner is giving in two days' time.

That gives me two days to coach Mary in proper etiquette and persuade her not on any account to bring up the subjects of gout, brown bread, or raw carrots to any of the young men she meets.

I will write down in this journal whether I am successful or no. And whether Mary and I both survive my efforts.

Though I have some hopes. After we had finished at Madame LeFarge's, I made Mary come with me to Gunter's to eat ice cream. And she only mentioned once that the pastries and ices were shockingly over-priced and not at all healthful, and that she was afraid some of the other customers—she was staring at a pair of very elegantly dressed women with obviously rouged cheeks and varnished fingernails who were eating ices at the table next to ours—might possibly be *less than respectable*.

Thursday 4 January 1816

As it happens, I only need a single word to sum up the dinner party tonight: disastrous.

The evening began well enough. Madame LeFarge did manage to finish the blue crepe gown for Mary. It was delivered this afternoon. And it is lovely—Madame added rows of pointed lace to the sleeves and collar line, and caught up the overskirt with rosettes of deeper blue satin.

I forced Mary into it. And managed to persuade her to stop tugging at the neckline. Which was really not so very low-cut. Though certainly more revealing than the high-necked dresses Mary usually wears.

And then I sat Mary down in the chair in front of my dressing table—our room has two, one for each of us—and made her allow me to arrange her hair.

Mary's hair is quite pretty, really: glossy dark brown, with a natural curl. It's just that she invariably wears it dragged straight back from her face and pinned in a knot at the nape of her neck that makes her look more like a prim, priggish governess than any actual governess possibly could.

Tonight I gathered her hair into a lose knot on top of her head. And then took my sewing scissors and—ignoring Mary's squeaks of protest—ruthlessly snipped and clipped so that a few loose, curling tendrils framed her face.

The difference in her appearance was amazing. I took out a pot of rouge—I have it, still, though I've not opened it in months—and added just a light tough of colour to Mary's lips and cheeks. And she looked lovely, she really did.

I turned her to look in the mirror, and she caught her breath, her eyes going wide. And then she reached for her spectacles, which she had left on the edge of my night table.

"Don't even think it!" I slapped her hand away. "Do you want to undo all my efforts?"

"But—" Mary cast a longing look at the glasses.

I cut her off. "I don't care how much more intelligent you think they make you look, you are not wearing them tonight."

Mary looked up at me—then down at the floor. "It's not that. It's just . . . I started wearing them when my face had so very many blemishes," she muttered. "They seemed—it felt as though I could hide behind them, a little. And now I feel . . . naked, without them."

I was taken aback. Because as a rule, Mary never admits to uncertainty or self-consciousness—or to anything, really, but absolute certainty of her own wisdom and opinions.

But then she added, "And they *do* make me look more intelligent."

Which sounded much more like the sister Mary I know.

"Gentlemen don't want a woman who looks intelligent, they want a girl who looks like a charming and agreeable companion," I said.

Another flicker of uncertainty crossed Mary's face. "I . . . is that not like lying, then? Pretending to something

I am not, just for the sake of attracting what must surely be fickle male attention, if it is based on such untruths? As the poet Mr. Cowper says—"

I sighed. Because I haven't really anything to say to that. It is certainly not as though my own record in that regard has been so outstanding.

But I still interrupted before Mary could start unleashing quotations from poetry. "Let's just start with getting some agreeable gentleman to ask you to dance," I said. "We can worry later about your baring your souls to one another, all right?"

I looked at the clock, then. And realised that I had barely a quarter of an hour until Aunt Gardiner's guests were due to arrive. Which meant that I had approximately ten minutes to dress myself.

I rummaged in the wardrobe and yanked on the first dress that I found—my ivory silk with silver embroidered acorns. And then I sat down at the dressing table to fix my own hair.

I had been playing knights and dragons all afternoon with Thomas and Jack—they are Aunt and Uncle Gardiner's two boys—followed by doll's tea-party with Anna and Charlotte, who are Thomas and Jack's older sisters. And I had spent a good deal of the time holding baby Susanna on my shoulder, as well. So that when I looked in the mirror, I discovered that I still had a smear of green paint on my neck from the dragon's costume—the headdress the boys and I made together hadn't quite dried when I put it on. And that at some point during the tea party, baby Susanna had managed to deposit a sticky smear of what looked like grape jelly in my hair.

There wasn't time for me to do more than hastily scrub the green paint off, though, with the cold wash water in the basin. I pulled my hair back into a tight knot that rivalled the severity of Mary's usual hairstyles, and then covered the jelly with a silver lace bandeau.

After all, it was not as though it mattered especially what I looked like. And I am sure Mary could quote me some verse of the Bible or something that has something or other to say about the dangers of vanity over one's looks.

"All right," I said to Mary. "Let us go down. And for heaven sakes, don't forget what I told you. Do not quote poetry, do not criticise any of the gentlemen's apparent vices. And above all, smile from time to time."

Mary looked as though she were preparing to argue— probably thinking up some other quotation about gout and the evils of drink. But I never gave her the chance, only took her by the arm and marched her downstairs, to where the guests Aunt Gardiner had invited were beginning to arrive.

The dinner itself was also perfectly fine. I was seated next to a Mr. Frank Bertram, who talked mostly about—

Actually, I have no idea what he talked about. Horses, possibly? Or boating? My entire attention was occupied with trying to overhear what Mary was saying to her dinner companion. And wishing that I were seated near enough to her to stamp on her foot if she broke any of my rules and started lecturing or sermonising.

She seemed to do all right, though. She was seated next to Rhys Callahan, who is a clerk in Uncle Gardiner's employ. He is somewhere about twenty three or four, and on the compact side—only a head or so taller than I am— but square built and sturdy-looking. His colouring is Welsh—black hair and dark eyes—and though he is not strictly speaking handsome, he is a pleasant young man.

Well, to be strictly accurate, I suppose I should say

that he *appears* to be a pleasant young man. He is so excessively shy that I have never actually managed to get him to say a word to me, though he is often at the house to discuss business with my uncle, and frequently stays to dine.

He appeared all through dinner to be listening to whatever Mary was saying. And his eyes did not even appear to have glazed over with boredom, nor did I see him yawn. Though perhaps he was only grateful to have been blessed with a dinner companion who did not require him to talk.

After dinner ended, and the gentlemen had joined us in the drawing room, Aunt Gardiner proposed that we have some dancing. I could see Mary poised to offer to play. But I stepped in before she could get the words out, and volunteered to accompany the dancing myself. I don't play nearly so well as Mary. Not even so well as Lizzy, really. But I can manage a few reels and a "Sir Roger de Coverley."

The only drawback to that arrangement was that, though I had prevented Mary from playing, I could not both accompany the dancing and find a way to force Mary to actually dance. Or rather, force one of the gentlemen to ask her; she stood at the side of the space Aunt Gardiner had cleared for dancing. Moving her shoulders awkwardly in time to the music and looking hopeful. But not one of the young men there approached her.

Then at last Rhys Callahan came to stand beside her. But not to ask her to dance. They only resumed their dinnertime conversation.

I could only hear part of what they said, but they seemed to be discussing the new gas lights that are being put up around London. It sounded stultifyingly boring to me. But I actually heard Mr. Callahan utter a sentence or two, so he cannot have been entirely uninterested. And—perhaps it was the new dress and hairstyle—but Mary looked quite bright and interested, too. She even smiled.

Then Aunt Gardiner approached the pair of them—and I actually had some hopes, because she was intent on seeing Mary and Mr. Callahan dance.

The other drawback of my sitting at the piano was that I was *still* not immune from invitations to dance myself. At least five of the gentlemen present approached my bench and either offered to turn pages for me or said how hard it was that I could not dance, and surely my aunt or my sister could take a turn?

I kept having to break off playing to decline. I really am not especially skilled at the instrument, and attempting to talk and play at the same time usually leads to disaster.

At any rate it was during one of these lulls—I was refusing Mr. Bertram, my companion from dinner—that Aunt Gardiner approached Mary and Mr. Callahan. So I was able to hear the whole of the exchange.

Aunt Gardiner said, "Come, Rhys—Mary. I must have you dance. The two of you are the only couple here who have yet to take a turn on the floor."

Rhys Callahan's face flushed beet-red to the roots of his hair, and he started to shake his head and stammer some sort of refusal. Something about Mr. Gardiner requiring that he look over some accounts before tomorrow.

Mary, watching him and listening, looked mortified. Because after all, it is not especially pleasant to have the young man whom you have been speaking with for the past half hour look as though he would much prefer to run a mile in tight shoes than ask you to dance.

Aunt Gardiner saw Mary's face, too. She is very perceptive, as well as kind. She turned to Mr. Callahan and said, "Nonsense, Rhys. You work far too hard, as my husband is well aware. He would not wish for you to cut short your enjoyment of the evening for a mere accounts book. I am sure whatever business it is can very well wait."

There was no way Mr. Callahan could refuse without crossing the line into outright rudeness. Still blushing furiously, he offered Mary his hand and bowed. And Mary took it and moved with him onto the dance floor.

That was when disaster struck. I could kick myself for not thinking of it. But in all my coaching Mary these last two days in how to attract a gentleman's invitation to dance, it never occurred to me to question whether she *can* actually dance.

She cannot. At least, she cannot dance well. I remember her having dance lessons when we were young, with all the rest of us. And I can't recall that she was so especially unskilled then. But I suppose it has been years since she had the opportunity to practice. And I am not sure that she has ever danced in company with a young man.

Not that it was her fault entirely. Once he was on the dance floor, I could understand Mr. Callahan's reluctance. He is, quite possibly, the worst dancer I have ever seen. He tripped and stumbled and stepped on the other dancers' feet—and could not to save his own life keep to the beat of the music.

I could only see them out of the corner of my eye, since I was playing. But the combination of him and Mary together was like something from a *Punch and Judy* show. They reeled around, crashing into the other couples in the line. And then Mr. Callahan stepped on the hem of Mary's gown as she turned to move away from him during the *allemande.*

There was a rending sound of tearing fabric. And Mary lost her balance and was yanked backwards off her feet, her arms flailing wildly. She landed flat on her back in the centre of the dance floor.

There was a moment of absolute silence when the entire room seemed to stare at her, collectively uncertain of what to do or say. And then Mary scrambled ungracefully up and bolted from the room, her hands covering her face.

I got up from the piano and ran after her. Mr. Callahan was standing where Mary had left him, looking acutely horrified and miserable, as well. But I was much less concerned with him than with Mary. It was entirely my fault that she had attempted dancing tonight at all.

I should have expected her to run upstairs to our room. But I suppose she was not thinking clearly and simply chose the nearest bolt-hole. Which happened to be the downstairs cloakroom at the foot of the stairs.

As I came out of the drawing room and into the hall, I saw the door bang behind her, and heard the key turn in the lock.

"Mary?" I knocked on the door. But there was no response. Nothing but the sound of a muffled sob from inside. I felt truly dreadful, then. That's twice in three days that Mary-the-Complacent has been reduced to tears.

"Mary, please come out." I knocked again. "Everyone knows it was just an accident. No one will laugh at you. Besides, it was my fault. I ought to have made sure that you weren't a complete disaster on the dance floor before I sent you out there tonight."

In hindsight, it was not the most tactful way I could have phrased it. I didn't mean to say it—I was just feeling both guilty and irritated at the same time, and it simply slipped out.

Renewed sobs sounded from behind the locked cloak-room door. But Mary didn't answer or show any signs of being willing to come out.

I tried several more times. Without any better results. And then finally I gave up, leaning against the panel, uncertain of what to do. Clearly I was making no headway with trying to apologise or reason with Mary. And yet I didn't feel, either, as though I could simply go and rejoin the party and leave my sister weeping in a cloakroom.

I was debating whether to try knocking again, when I felt a touch on my elbow and turned to find a young man standing beside me. A very handsome young man— really, one of the most handsome men I have ever seen, with wheat-blond hair combed very straight back from his brow, a lean, chiselled face and eyes of a deep, piercing shade of blue.

He cleared his throat. "Miss Bennett, I wonder if you would—"

However handsome he was, at sight of him my temper abruptly snapped. I had been refusing offers from young men like him all night—and for weeks before this. Scores and scores of handsome young men incapable of getting it through their thick skulls the definition of the words 'no thank you.' And now this young man had followed me out here to pester me while I was already feeling wretched about Mary.

I cut him off. "No. I would *not* care to dance. I would *not* care to have you turn pages for me at the piano. I would not like to step outside with you to see

the moonrise." I looked him up and down. "As you are
no doubt already aware, sir, you have very pretty blue
eyes. But go and turn your lovelorn attentions on some
other girl than me, because there is no invitation you
could issue, no request you could make that could lead
me to say yes. Do you understand?"

The man took a step backwards at the vehemence of
my tone. And then he said, one eyebrow raised, "Not
even if I requested you to convey my regrets to your
Aunt that I must leave at once? I am called away to
attend a parishioner, who is gravely ill."

He held up a scrap of folded paper in one hand—
the message, presumably. And I noticed what I had
overlooked before: that above his black evening jacket,
he wore the white collar of a clergyman.

His mouth quirked up at one corner. "Though I am,
of course, deeply sensible of the compliment about my
eyes."

It was, I suppose, proof of whatever that quotation
is about the mills of God and divine justice and all that
sort of thing. It was my fault that Mary had been so
mortified. And now the celestial mills had obligingly
provided me with an opportunity to feel toe-curlingly
embarrassed, as well.

There was a silence during which I silently prayed—
of course without result—that God would be obliging
enough to let me sink down through the floor and van-
ish from sight.

And then finally the man cleared his throat and said,
"I don't believe we have been formally introduced. My
name is Lancelot Dalton."

I heard myself say, "Good heavens, *Lancelot*? Surely
not."

Mr. Dalton's eyebrows lifted again. And I felt my

toes re-curling themselves.

You would think, wouldn't you, that I would by now have managed to govern the habit of speaking without pause for thought. It just seemed too much, that a man could look quite so much like the illustration of the prince in a book of fairy tales—and have a name like Lancelot, besides.

Mr. Dalton said, gravely, "My mother had an unfortunate fondness for the old medieval romances. At least I never had a brother for her to name Gallahad. Though I do have a sister called Gwenevere."

I looked at him, uncertain of whether he was serious or joking. And then I recollected myself enough to offer him my hand and say, "And I am Kitty—Catherine Bennett."

Mr. Dalton took my hand and said that it was a pleasure to meet me. Which proves that even clergymen must occasionally tell lies.

And then he said, "If you wouldn't mind conveying my message to your aunt? My parishioner was in dire straights when I left this evening to come here. And I'm afraid this message means that she must have taken a turn for the worse. I left your aunt's address so that I might be summoned if there was any change."

I said that of course I would give Aunt Gardiner his regrets, and he thanked me, bowed, and left. Luckily before I could manage to insult him again.

I looked at the cloakroom door, but Mary was silent. No more muffled sobs. If I knew her, she was probably pressed with her ear to the keyhole, delighting in every embarrassing detail of my exchange with Mr. Dalton. Though I decided that after the debacle of her dancing, I needn't begrudge her that much, and went to find my aunt.

Aunt Gardiner made a soft sound of distress when I delivered Mr. Dalton's message. "Oh, I am sorry. But not surprised that Lance should have gone to whoever it is who is ill. He is the most conscientious and selfless young man I have ever met."

"Of course he is," I muttered.

Aunt Gardiner looked faintly surprised by my tone. But she said, "Yes, indeed. It is such a shame, really. Lance is the son of my dearest school friend, Harriet Winters. But she and her husband Mr. Dalton—Lance's father—died when Lance was just sixteen, and Lance and his sister were left almost penniless. Lance has taken holy orders. But he has neither money nor connections to find a position as vicar of a parish of his own. He has been doing charity work in the East End while he looks for a benefice somewhere. I suppose it must be one of his charity cases who needed him tonight."

Really, it only needed that. The man whom I accused of being a lovelorn swain is actually a clergyman who is not only a paragon of every virtue, but is also selflessly dedicating his life to ministering to the London poor.

When I consider what Mr. Dalton must think of me—

Actually, I don't know why I should still care what Mr. Dalton thinks of me. It's not as though I am ever likely to see him again. Certainly not if I consult my own wishes in the matter.

Thank you for previewing *Kitty Bennet's Diary*.

For a current list of Anna Elliott titles, please visit www.AnnaElliottBooks.com.

REGENCY TITLES
FROM ANNA ELLIOTT

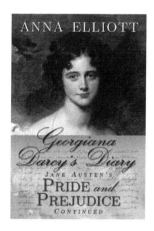

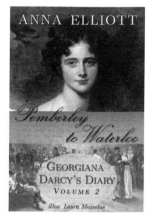

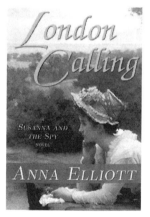

www.AnnaElliottBooks.com

Made in the USA
Middletown, DE
14 February 2015